Post-Romantic Consciousness

Post-Romantic Consciousness

Dickens to Plath

John Beer
Emeritus Professor of English Literature
University of Cambridge
and Fellow of Peterhouse

First published 2003 by
PALGRAVE MACMILLAN
Houndmills, Basingstoke, Hampshire RG21 6XS and
175 Fifth Avenue, New York, N. Y. 10010
Companies and representatives throughout the world

PALGRAVE MACMILLAN is the global academic imprint of the Palgrave Macmillan division of St. Martin's Press, LLC and of Palgrave Macmillan Ltd. Macmillan® is a registered trademark in the United States, United Kingdom and other countries. Palgrave is a registered trademark in the European Union and other countries.

ISBN 1–4039–0518–5 hardback

This book is printed on paper suitable for recycling and made from fully managed and sustained forest sources.

A catalogue record for this book is available from the British Library.

Library of Congress Cataloging-in-Publication Data

Beer, John B.
   Post-Romantic consciousness: Dickens to Plath / John Beer.
      p. cm
   Includes bibliographical references and index.
   ISBN 1–4039–0518–5
      1. English literature–20th century–History and criticism. 2. Consciousness in literature. 3. Dickens, Charles, 1812–1870–Knowledge–Psychology. 4. Plath, Sylvia–Knowledge–Psychology. 5. Subconsciousness in literature. 6. Psychology in literature. I. Title.

PR478.C65B44 2003
820.9'353–dc21

                                                        2002044814

10   9   8   7   6   5   4   3   2   1
12   11   10   09   08   07   06   05   04   03

Printed and bound in Great Britain by
Antony Rowe Ltd, Chippenham and Eastbourne

For Gillian, again

Contents

Abbreviations

Place of publication is London unless otherwise indicated.

APrW	Matthew Arnold, *Complete Prose Works*, ed. R.H. Super (11 vols., Ann Arbor, MI, 1960–77)
APW	Matthew Arnold, *Complete Poems*, ed. Kenneth Allott; 2nd edn., ed. Miriam Allott (1979)
BE	*The Poetry and Prose of William Blake*, ed. D.V. Erdman and H. Bloom (New York, 1965)
BK	Blake, *Complete Writings, with Variant Readings*, ed. G. Keynes, 1957; reprinted with additions and corrections in the Oxford Standard Authors series (Oxford, 1966)
CBL	Coleridge, *Biographia Literaria* [1817]; ed. James Engell and Walter Jackson Bate, *CC*, 7 (2 vols., 1983)
CN	Coleridge, *Notebooks*, ed. Kathleen Coburn (5 vols., Princeton, NJ and London, 1959–2002)
DCED	J. Cuming Walters, *The Complete Edwin Drood* (1912).
DLN	*The Letters of Charles Dickens*, ed. Walter Dexter (Nonesuch edn., 3 vols., 1938)
DLO	*The Letters of Charles Dickens*, ed. Madeline House, Graham Storey, Kathleen Tillotson et al. (Oxford, 1965–2002)
DOED	Dickens, *The Mystery of Edwin Drood*, ed. Margaret Cardwell: The Clarendon Dickens (Oxford, 1972)
HBL	Ted Hughes, *Birthday Letters* (1998)
HNP	Ted Hughes, *New Selected Poems 1957–1994* (1995)
HSGCB	Ted Hughes, *Shakespeare and the Goddess of Complete Being* (1992)
HWP	Ted Hughes, *Winter Pollen: Occasional Prose*, ed. William Scammell (1994)
LL	D.H. Lawrence, *Letters*, ed. J.T. Boulton et al. (6 vols., Cambridge, 1979–)
L Phoenix	*Phoenix: The Posthumous Papers of D.H. Lawrence*, ed. E.D. McDonald (1936)
L Phoenix II	*Phoenix II: Uncollected, Unpublished and Other Prose Works by D.H. Lawrence*, ed. Warren Roberts and Harry T. Moore (1968)

L Record	'E.T.' [Jessie Chambers], *D.H. Lawrence: A Personal Record* (1935)
MP	John Milton, *The Complete Poems*, ed. B.A. Wright and G. Campbell (1980)
PJ	*The Journals of Sylvia Plath 1950–1962*, ed. Karen V. Kukil (2000)
PBJ	Sylvia Plath, *The Bell Jar* (1963)
PJP	Sylvia Plath, *Johnny Panic and the Bible of Dreams, and Other Prose Writings* (1977)
PP	Sylvia Plath, *Collected Poems* (1981)
SPR	*Proceedings of the Society for Psychical Research* (1882–)
VWD	*The Diary of Virginia Woolf*, ed. Anne Olivier Bell (5 vols., 1977–84)
VWE	*The Essays of Virginia Woolf*, ed. Andrew McNellie (1986–)
VWL	*The Letters of Virginia Woolf*, ed. Nigel Nicolson (6 vols., 1975–80)
WL (1821–53)	*The Letters of William and Dorothy Wordsworth, The Later Years, 1821–1853*, ed. E. de Selincourt; 2nd edn. revd, A.G. Hill (4 vols., Oxford 1978–88)

Preface

In my first volume I discussed a preoccupation to be traced in some English Romantic writers involving the divergence between rational consciousness as it had come to be commonly conceived in the West and a sense of what constitutes the true 'Being' of humanity. I also examined the sense among some of the most characteristic writers in the Romantic period that rational consciousness might need to be subsumed into a larger sense, in which the human might be linked to the divine.

About the middle of the nineteenth century it became increasingly difficult for thinkers to accept this kind of conspectus, as encouraged by Coleridge, Wordsworth and their successors, yet the underlying question raised by a disparity between the worlds created by conscious rational organization and that believed to be inherent in the human unconscious continued to be recognized. From now on, the question of Being became more personally focused, with writers recognizing contradictions within their own experience that could be solved only by reconciling their conscious view of the world with a universe ratified by their own unconscious.

My approach to these questions in the present volume begins in twofold fashion: intensive discussion of a single individual in whom this problem can be seen to be half unknowingly embodied is followed by extensive consideration of an enterprise set up to deal with it in a scientific manner: the setting up of the Society for Psychical Research. In the case of my single individual, Charles Dickens, conflict between a consciously affectionate and benevolent view of the world was increasingly at odds with his unconscious attraction to the criminal and violent, The interest that Coleridge had shown in the alternative modes of consciousness suggested by the phenomena of animal magnetism became a crucial element in his view of the world also, but he still apparently found it difficult to recognize this element of self-contradiction. The resulting internal struggle was, I argue, central to the steadily increasing turmoil of his later fiction and partly responsible for his failure to complete his last novel, *The Mystery of Edwin Drood*.

A similar sense of contradiction at the heart of human experience resulted in the early activities of the Society, where it was hoped that rigorous investigation not only of the hypnotic powers that had fascinated both Coleridge and Dickens but abnormal psychical experiences of all kinds, might complement awareness of the conscious self and lead to further insight into the nature of what it was to be human. In the thinking of F.W.H. Myers, the main focus was upon the question of human immortality; his contemporaries, however, found their strong stimulus in the full range of his thought and that of his friend Edmund Gurney. Myers's postulation of a 'subliminal self' in all human beings suggested another solution to the problem of the relationship between consciousness and Being which William James, in particular, would find extremely profitable. By that time, however, the problem of 'Being' was becoming a widely discussed topic elsewhere. In a further chapter I take some account of the differing versions developed not only by James, but by European thinkers such as Heidegger, Sartre and Havel.

In spite of this wider twentieth-century currency, the early Romantic writers, and notably Coleridge, had given a psychological direction to thinking about the issue that would not easily be lost: Virginia Woolf, in particular, with her 'moments of Being', and Lawrence, with his insistence on the existence of another level of consciousness in which human beings found their true selves, and his tracing of this by way of vital energy and human response to it, both revealed a continuity with this subterranean English tradition. In turn, Sylvia Plath and Ted Hughes – themselves devotees of Woolf and Lawrence, respectively – would offer in their personal and artistic lives a vivid demonstration of the dialectic involved: Plath displaying the potentialities of a Being that identified itself most readily in motion, even while she exhibited the problems besetting a highly developed consciousness, while Hughes insisted on the importance of the firm, physically rooted identity that was his own version of Being – and which became increasingly his poetic subject as well. In the choice of title for his late study, *Shakespeare and the Goddess of Complete Being,* Hughes was acknowledging the importance for him of a question that will be seen to have haunted, in their differing ways, all the authors dealt with in these studies.

The material in one or two chapters of this book has appeared previously: some pages on D.H. Lawrence first formed part of an essay contributed to *The Spirit of D.H. Lawrence,* edited by Gāmini Salgādo and G.K. Das, while an earlier version of my work on Dickens was contributed to *Dickens Studies Annual,* XIII. I trust that such uses will make good sense when seen against the background of my larger discussion. In the same way, I am glad to have the opportunity of quoting from various recent writers, who are still in copyright. I am assured that the use of these brief quotations, taken up into my larger critical discussion, amounts in every case to 'fair dealing'. I am also grateful to Professor Philip Collins and Elaine Feinstein, respectively, for having read and offered valuable comments on earlier versions of my chapters on Dickens and Ted Hughes and Sylvia Plath. Finally, I am again grateful to the Master and Fellows of Trinity College, Cambridge, and to the Houghton Library, Harvard, for permission to reproduce or quote from items in their Myers collections and to the Museum Oskar Reinhart am Stadtgarten Winterthur for permission to use the picture by Caspar David Friedrich, 'Chalk Cliffs on Rugen 1818/9', as my dust-jacket illustration.

1
Questioning Consciousness

In my previous volume I began by citing Antonio Damasio's arguments against the Cartesian '*I think, therefore I am*' and the alternative formulation that he offered:

> for us now, as we come into the world and develop, we still begin with being, and only later do we think. We are, and then we think, and we think only inasmuch as we are, since thinking is indeed caused by the structures and operations of being.[1]

It is not only scientists who have preoccupied themselves with this question. A point hardly recognized in Damasio's book is that while scientists have made their way towards such a questioning of René Descartes' affirmation, the vulnerability of his position has not escaped the attention of philosophers themselves. It was the twentieth century, after all, that saw the rise of 'existentialism', even if this was seen as peculiarly contemporary in its concern. The philosophers who wrote under its sign did not claim many predecessors apart from Søren Kierkegaard, who saw himself as swimming against the tide of fashion, adopting a position that was essentially anti-Romantic and, in particular, presenting an answer to G.W.F. Hegel. The questions involved in existentialist thought were, as might be expected, notably important in France, where the strong influence of Descartes called for equally powerful counter-arguments, but it also had a significant effect in Europe at large. In England the interest has been more limited. In one of her postwar essays, Iris Murdoch remarked on the fact that the kind of Anglo-Saxon philosophy most fashionable at that time never discussed terms such as 'being' and 'consciousness', even though these questions were at the time being debated urgently by their French contemporaries.[2]

The achievements of twentieth-century existentialists may be left for later discussion; however; we need comment here only on the degree to which all such debates have continued to be dominated by a philosophy emphasizing the power of rational thought.

The issue is relevant to further modern concerns, such as the question whether it would be possible to devise a computer that could completely replicate the mind of a human being. This is a matter much discussed, and indeed it is to be supposed that at present a record number of people are working on the problem. If the Cartesian formulation is taken literally, it follows that the computer's ability to mime thought would establish its existence as a human substitute. Damasio would presumably argue that the omission of feeling from the formula not only marks the essential gap in Descartes' view, but indicates the central deficiency in any attempt to make a computer which totally reproduces human behaviour. And it seems that such an objection would be supported by some researchers, who would contend that in order to mimic humanity in a satisfactory manner it would not be sufficient to devise a sufficiently subtle network of electronic circuitry; one would also need a biochemical basis. For reasons that have already been adumbrated, however, it can be argued that any simple distinction between reason and emotion neglects the subtlety of the issues involved. Apart from what are normally thought of as emotional factors, there are elements in mental activity itself that cannot easily be replicated artificially. A computer may be programmed to perform acts of recognition – indeed some of its most useful and complex functions can involve just that – but programming it to *initiate* recognition is a more difficult task; it seems clear that some other element is involved. And this lack can be generalized to cover much creative activity in the mind. In problem-solving, computers can make massive contributions, producing a solution with unbelievable speed by investigating thousands of possibilities until an answer that fits the question exactly is found. The human experience of going to sleep and waking up with the answer to a problem unsolved the previous evening may perhaps involve a similar process, continued far into the night, but the possibility remains that sleep involves, rather, the enhancement of unconscious processes that have little to do with multiplex searching. This certainly seems a better account of other creative activities, as in the arts, where the appearance of the best form for a painting, music or a literary work may involve at some point or points the intervention of a 'shaping spirit' which takes over, resembling chemical process in its power to create at every point simultaneously an instantaneous effect of transformation.

In my previous volume I presented a historical dimension to the question by arguing that this sense of a precedent to rational consciousness was something that had been contended for also by various Romantic thinkers, beginning with William Blake, and had been affirmed with particular emphasis by those writing under the sign of Samuel Taylor Coleridge. At the same time, I pointed out, such writers had usually been aware of a metaphysical implication, their conception of Being needing prominently to be related to their idea of the Supreme Being, so that in some sense or other, ranging all the way from Coleridge's Anglicanism to Percy Bysshe Shelley's atheism, the idea of Being had for them a religious (or equally strongly, anti-religious) overtone.

Half a century later, the existence of this apparent consensus was to affect some of the reactions to the publication of *The Origin of Species*. It has increasingly come to be recognized that for many the shock produced by this was not due to a supposed sudden emergence of the idea of evolution. In various forms, that had been at work for a long time. Charles Darwin's grandfather Erasmus Darwin had, in fact, set out such a conception, which had interested some contemporaries through its relationship to contemporary ideas of development, The difference that Charles made was not to introduce the idea as such, but to argue that it did not take the form that was commonly supposed. Whereas the concept of development had not necessarily been unwelcome, suggesting to some Christians a means by which a benevolent creator might have unfolded his purposes, the principle of the survival of the fittest, as authorized by Darwin, seemed to allow little room for such an all-encompassing benevolence.

While the growing acceptance of such modes of thought made it increasingly difficult for thinkers to accept the kind of conspectus that had been encouraged by Coleridge and Wordsworth, they continued to recognize the underlying question raised by a disparity between a world created by conscious rational organization and one which might be less amenable to mental analysis. From now on, the question of Being, which had tended to be studied in a context acknowledging the role of religion, became more personally focused, with writers recognizing contradictions within their own experience that could be solved only by reconciling their conscious view of the world with a universe ratified by their own unconscious. An exemplary figure here is Charles Dickens, in whom the conflict between a consciously affectionate and benevolent view of the world was increasingly at odds with unconscious processes fascinated by the criminal and the violent, and who (perhaps recognizing this element of self-contradiction) took up the interest in alternative modes of consciousness suggested by the phenomena of animal magnetism that had previously been explored by, among others, Coleridge and Shelley. This internal struggle may be seen as central to the steadily increasing turmoil of his later fiction and – arguably – responsible for his failure to complete his last novel.

As the discussion in the present volume proceeds, a similar sense of contradiction at the heart of human experience will be traced in the early activities of the Society for Psychical Research, where it was hoped that scientific investigation not only of the hypnotic powers that had fascinated Coleridge and Dickens but abnormal psychical experiences of all kinds might lead, as a complement to the activities of the conscious mind, to further insight into the nature of what it was to be human. In the thinking of F.W.H. Myers, the main focus was upon the question of human immortality; his contemporaries, however, found their strongest stimulus from him in the full range of thought both of himself and of his friend Edmund Gurney. Myers' postulation of a 'subliminal self' in human beings suggested another solution to the problem of the relationship between consciousness and Being which William James, in particular, would find extremely profitable. By now, however, the problem of 'Being' had become a widely discussed topic elsewhere: it will be necessary to consider the differing versions found not only in James but in European thinkers such as Martin Heidegger, Jean-Paul Sartre and Václav Havel.

It is not only philosophers who have preoccupied themselves with the question, moreover. It has emerged as an issue in recent work on the divided self, and its manifestation in literature: Karl Miller's *Doubles*, for example, and Jeremy Hawthorn's work on multiple personality.[3] Hawthorn takes his theme from modern case-histories involving patients who exhibited more than one personality, such as Miss Beauchamp, the classic case reported by Morton Prince,[4] or the Eve White and Eve Black of *The Three Faces of Eve*;[5] he shows how similar phenomena can be found in certain texts, from Fyodor Dostoyevsky's *The Double* onwards, and examines well-known novels such as Charlotte Brontë's *Villette* and Josef Conrad's *The Secret Sharer*. His argument is primarily undertaken from a point of view extending from the private to the public, however: he is particularly concerned with instances where a character develops parallel personalities to cope with the demands of public and private life. A classic example, in his view, is that of Wemmick, in *Great Expectations*, with his 'the office is one thing, private life another'.

When the device of multiple personality is adopted by novelists, it is often to present just this sort of tension. Hawthorn has particularly shrewd discussions of the tension in modern society resulting from the need for human beings to balance self-interest – particularly in their public and commercial dealings – against their need to achieve or maintain a sense of solidarity with others, a tension which, he believes, often manifests itself in the development of dual personalities within the same individuals as a means of ministering to their opposing needs:

> if an individual is brought up, and has to survive, in an environment constituted by contradictory systems of value, then he or she will become internally divided unless the external contradictions are clearly recognized.[6]

This is evidently true in many cases, and Hawthorn has little difficulty in showing its validity in cases ranging from *She Stoops to Conquer*, where Marlow expresses the different behaviour required of a man trapped by the double standards of behaviour towards women produced by the presuppositions of his society, to the young Captain in Conrad's *The Secret Sharer*, whose dealings with the mysterious Leggatt bring out his own current social anxieties. It should be observed, however, that since individual novelists may well be wishing to bring out the relationship between the private and public concerns of a particular character by way of such a division, their employment of the device in a work of fiction cannot necessarily be universalized as if it were the key to all divided human behaviour.

For the present study, in any case, a different point is to be presented. Multiple personality in the fictions just described is necessarily based on a division between cognate forms of consciousness, as if of separate people. The reason that this cannot accurately represent the division between consciousness and Being is that the latter can never be so separately represented. Being can never be totally and exclusively conscious, even if, for any particular individual, it can only be known, or mediated, by way of a consciousness – which may, indeed, be making its paradoxical appearance at a subconscious level, as in dreams. For this reason we are concerned with something different from what is presented in, say, *The Strange Case of Dr. Jekyll and Mr. Hyde*, where it is not the case that the characters represent different forms of the conscious and the unconscious (even if that is sometimes half hinted at) but rather alternating states of full consciousness – a phenomenon which often seems to be true also of clinical, as opposed to literary, cases of multiple personality. (Karl Miller points out that dualities of the clinical kind are to be traced as far back as Mesmer, in whom he finds sources for what he terms 'dipsychism' and 'poly-psychism'. He does not remark, however, the part played by the very different factors just mentioned.)

Hawthorn recognizes that in cases of multiple personality we are dealing with a phenomenon that has been recognized only recently, maintaining that to provide a full account the whole discussion we should need to return to previous ages. He draws particularly on the work of the Soviet writer A.S. Luria, whose *Cognitive Development* traced the emergence of the subliminal self to a problem in the acquisition of what he calls the 'higher mental activities'.[7] Luria compared the mental states of a group of illiterate peasants and one of 'farm activists', noting the remarkable development of ability in self-analysis between the two, and thus encouraging Hawthorn's conclusion that the latter depends on the growth of literacy. This would help explain the belatedness of its appearance. So long as the majority of mankind was living in simplicity of character, it might be held, there was much less need to recognize such different components of human consciousness.

Hawthorn also follows Luria in maintaining that 'self-awareness' is 'a product of socio-historical development' – a plausible view provided that one accepts the reverse as well: that socio-historical development has its own dependency on the growth of self-consciousness in the population. His final conclusion that only by establishing a society that is undivided, in a world that is undivided, can there emerge human individuals free from hypocrisy and duplicity',[8] admirable as it may be in sentiment, seems to fall short of recognizing that in the development of self-consciousness 'duplicity', at least, is necessarily involved. So true is this that it played a part in one of the best-known formulations of recent times, the so-called 'Dissociation of Sensibility', making its first appearance in T.S. Eliot's proposition that 'in the seventeenth century a dissociation of sensibility set in, from which we have never recovered; and this dissociation ... was aggravated by the two most powerful poets of the century, Milton and Dryden'.[9] He never, apparently, repeated the terms of his formulation or even fully reasserted it, being indeed somewhat embarrassed by the currency which they gained. Twenty-five years later, he produced a modified version:

> the general affirmation represented by the phrase 'dissociation of sensibility' ... retains some validity; but I now incline to agree with

Dr Tillyard that to lay the burden on the shoulders of Milton and Dryden was a mistake. If such a dissociation did take place, I suspect that the causes are too complex and too profound to justify our accounting for the change in terms of literary criticism.[10]

Eliot remained fairly sure, in other words, that his distinction had been significant, yet had come to suppose that it was of a kind that could not be accounted for in terms of poetic history alone. A similar point has been made by John Needham, discussing both Eliot and Richards. He draws attention to the essay on A.C. Swinburne in which Eliot sets up an antithesis between him and John Dryden, declaring that Swinburne's words are 'all suggestions and no denotation; if they suggest nothing, it is because they suggest too much. Dryden's words, on the other hand, are precise, they state immensely, but their suggestiveness is often nothing'.[11]

Although the mention of Dryden alongside Milton in the original assigning of responsibility for the 'dissociation of sensibility' idea justifies considering this passage, it may be noted that Eliot is here talking not about feeling but about suggestiveness – which may or may not be the same. Where Eliot's original assertion is undoubtedly to the point is in his identification of John Donne and similar poets as managing to fuse thought and feeling in their writing. It might have been more accurate, however, to assert that during a certain period there had existed an *association* of sensibility in the writings of particular poets, of whom Donne and his school were outstanding examples. He would not have been likely to argue either for or against the proposition that Donne lacked feeling. (His statement that Dryden lacked suggestiveness ranges wider; it is also one that veers towards the affective, taking account of the effect on the reader rather than the nature of what is being expressed. This is fully in line with his general position, which is always concerned with objective elements in art rather than subjective.)

In general the term 'dissociation of sensibility' is open to the objection concerning Damasio's theories raised in my previous volume. It suggests that there are two positive and equivalent forces at work in human beings which, by being separated, cause a damaging split. Whatever the truth of such a position in terms of reason and emotion, the argument to be pursued here is that if the results of such a dissociation have indeed been at work in Western culture for many years now, it has been accompanied by a more important one, better regarded as a dissociation between *levels* of consciousness. The failure to take full account of the fact that more than one kind, ranging from the fully alert analysing consciousness to unconscious states in which important mental actions can still take place, may be effective in the same person acts as a block to recognition of this further dissociation, which in one sense is a matter of everyday experience, in another one too subtle to be easily appreciated or defined.

Rather than focusing on the existence of alternating personalities that are, in the end, like one another in the way that Jekyll and Hyde may, and do, simply substitute for one another, an important legacy of Romantic work has been to indicate a difference between states of conscious ratiocination (of a kind that might be replicated by a computer) and states of what I have found it convenient to term Being (which cannot). These are commonly revealed in subconscious activity; they may even be on occasion unavailable to verbal consciousnesses of any kind, calling for other means if they are to find representation.

In earlier work I also pointed out that when writers in any way forsake allegiance to conventional society they may also turn their backs on conventional means of expression and so find themselves on the wider sea of Being, where they lack familiar points of organization. In that case their energies are likely to move in one of two directions: to that which directly favours the immediate, the 'occasion', the *kairos,* and that which leans back to the 'eternal', the *aionic.* Drawing on the work of Kermode and, more directly, Panofsky, I summarized the way in which these two conceptions have played their part in traditional iconography:

> These two great figures, which Panowsky ascribes to the classical world, indicate an attitude to Time in which the quantitative perception of Chronos (and consequent melancholia at the inevitability of impermanence) plays a strictly subordinate part. 'Kairos' (or Opportunity') is normally represented as a young man with wings at shoulders and heels, and scales – originally balanced on the edge of a shaving-knife, and later on one or two wheels; he has a forelock which can be seized. 'Aion' has two forms: connected with Mithra, he may appear as a grim winged figure with lion's head and lion's claws, tightly enveloped by a huge snake and carrying a key in either hand; alternatively, however, he appears as the Orphic divinity commonly known as Phanes, a beautiful winged youth, surrounded by a zodiac, equipped with various attributes of cosmic power, and (likewise) encircled by the coils of a snake.[12]

Among the English Romantic writers, I have further argued, Wordsworth (particularly in *The Prelude*) has shown himself most notably aware of these issues, his 'spots of time' recording occasions when unusual exertions of energy in some form achieved an immediacy of occasion which was followed by an experience of aionic trance:

> ... and oftentimes
> When we had given our bodies to the wind,
> And all the shadowy banks on either side
> Came sweeping through the darkness, spinning still
> The rapid line of motion, then at once
> Have I, reclining back upon my heels,
> Stopped short; yet still the solitary cliffs
> Wheeled by me – even as if the earth had rolled
> With visible motion her diurnal round![13]

While Wordsworth had thus been showing how the aspirations to *kairos* and *aion* could be given intertwining poetic form, Shelley and Byron, I have maintained, exhibited what each of the same urges could achieve when taken to an extreme: Byron the young figure of *Kairos* stretching towards an adequate Occasion (which he eventually found by reaching beyond poetry and joining the war for Greek freedom) and Shelley, under the sign of the Snake, looking for an all-encircling cosmic vision that might leave him beaconing 'from the abode where the Eternal are'.

In the phase to which we now turn, writers turned away from such metaphysical versions of Being and the iconography that might figure them to an art which would reflect back the divisions in and beyond their own consciousness. In the case of Dickens, for example, just such a subtle division is increasingly discernible during his career. For reasons similar to those just indicated it could never be brought straightforwardly into his consciousness but must be traced as emerging rather from the fuller activity of the novelist's dramatizing mind.

2
Dickens's Unfinished Fiction

Cultural changes in the middle of the nineteenth century were reflected in a shift of argument that gave increasing importance to experiences of the individual. No longer would discussions concerning the nature of 'Being' be carried out in the terms belonging to an earlier period, where young men such as the early Apostles were attracted to seek solidarity within their own group while hoping to serve the larger community as enlightened members of a given profession, even if this promised the advantage of relating them both to their fellow human beings and, possibly, to a moral framework authorized by the divine.[1] With Darwinian assumptions increasingly setting animal life at the centre of attention the focus of Being itself shifted from concern with the divine to preoccupation with the physical and mental condition of single human beings, and the conflicts that might arise within them. The focus on consciousness (and its relation to Being), which is the overall theme here, was accordingly transposed from the public sphere to the private – where Thomas De Quincey had already been a pioneer in locating it.

Charles Dickens, whose public popularity, it will be argued, masked personal conflicts relevant to this shift of theme, offered a relevant case. Educated well outside the mainstream of academic life that had produced figures such as the Cambridge Apostles, he had at first sight little to do with the issues that concerned them. The social issues prominent in his writing could not ultimately be separated from theirs, however, as he discovered – both on a wider scale and within his own experience – discrepancies between the expectations of his contemporaries and pressures generated by his own unconscious impulses. Most notably, there was an implicit conflict between the lore of human affection that was cultivated by his middle-class audience as a reconciling factor to help resolve human conflicts, and instinctive impulses – including those to violence that fascinated many readers. For much of his career the tension between them could be kept in place simply by dramatization, sometimes with separate characters representing the different kinds of force involved. One result was the frequently remarked difference between the sentimental effects produced by characters notable for their affectionate nature and the attractiveness of those behaving instinctively – even if that behaviour might be villainous.

Gradually, the problem became one less of dramatization than of personal involvement, as Dickens came to realize the degree to which he himself empathized with his own more instinctive characters. There was, in other words, a growing conflict between his consciousness as a novelist and what might be termed his own artistic Being, in all its mysterious creativity. The tension between the two increased steadily, so that it was never more manifest than in the mysteries left behind at the time of his sudden death in 1870. First and foremost, of course, as his readers recognized sorrowfully, was the missing completion of his last novel, *The Mystery of Edwin Drood,* which had reached no further than its twenty-third chapter – enough to present many complications of plot, but without showing how any of them would be resolved. Predictably, enthusiasts were soon at work to make good the omission: sequels and projected conclusions abounded. In subsequent years particular attention was naturally paid not only to Dickens's surviving notes and drafts for the novel, but to the accounts of his plans offered by friends, including his biographer, John Forster, according to whom Dickens's first idea for his new story, communicated in 1869, had been as follows:

> Two people, boy and girl, or very young, going apart from one another, pledged to be married after many years – at the end of the book. The interest to arise out of the tracing of their separate ways, and the impossibility of telling what will be done with that impending fate.

That was in mid-July. On 6 August he wrote to say,

> I laid aside the fancy I told you of, and have a very curious and new idea for my new story. Not a communicable idea (or the interest of the book would be gone), but a very strong one, but difficult to work.

Forster's reminiscences concerning the novel's gestation continued with a long account of the plot and a sketch of Dickens's plan for the dénouement which has since given rise to many attempts at reconstructing a plausible ending.

> The story, I learnt immediately afterward, was to be that of the murder of a nephew by his uncle; the originality of which was to consist in the review of the murderer's career by himself at the close, when its temptations were to be dwelt upon as if, not he the culprit, but some other man, were the tempted. The last chapters were to be written in the condemned cell, to which his wickedness, all elaborately elicited from him as if told of another, had brought him. Discovery by the murderer of the utter needlessness of the murder for its object, was to follow hard upon the commission of the deed; but all discovery of the murderer was to be baffled till towards the close, when, by means of a gold ring which had resisted the corrosive effects of the lime into which he had thrown the body, not only the person who murdered was to be identified but the locality of the crime and the man who committed it. So much was told to me before any of the book was written; and it will be recollected that the ring, taken by Drood to be given to his betrothed only if their engagement went on, was brought away with him from their last interview. Rosa was to marry Tartar, and Crisparkle the sister of Landless, who was himself, I think, to have perished in assisting Tartar finally to unmask and seize the murderer.[2]

Forster's account is plausible in terms of the story as it remains, nor has it proved altogether difficult for investigators to predict how some of the later events might have turned out, using some of the illustrations already in existence. It seems that there would have been an unmasking scene in the cathedral crypt, with the prospect that Helena Landless would have appeared there, disguised as the young Edwin in such a manner that an involuntary expression of his own guilt would have been wrested from Jasper when he came upon her. It is also likely that there would have been an exciting climax at the top of the cathedral tower, in the course of which her brother Neville would have died, while Tartar (already revealed as possessing an extraordinary agility) would have been able to use his climbing skill to advantage.[3]

The matter is not quite as simple as Forster suggests, however, since we now know that the plan he gives first, involving a betrothal and separation, was not a recent idea but had been planned (in precisely the same terms) in a notebook entry of nine years before – from which, indeed, Forster probably culled it.[4] There is obviously some relationship between that story and *Edwin Drood* as published: Dickens had not in that sense 'laid it aside' – but the longer time scale leaves room for more development between the original germ and its final form than Forster's account would suggest.[5*] The very straightforward suggestions in the text of Jasper's villainy have also raised questions among later critics, who have noticed that if it is read without any further complexity, it is difficult to see where the 'mystery' lies. They have therefore questioned the validity of Forster's main contention. Was Edwin Drood really dead, and if so, did John Jasper murder him? Yet the overwhelming testimony of those who knew Dickens best agreed with Forster's statement that he was indeed dead and that he was murdered by his uncle. Charles Collins, first illustrator of the novel, claimed to have been told by Dickens that Edwin was murdered by Jasper;[6] Luke Fildes the second was told that the scarf which Jasper was described as wearing was to have been used by him to strangle Edwin;[7] Charles Dickens Junior recalled a last walk with his father near Gad's Hill, during which he asked him, 'Of course, Edwin was murdered?'

> Whereupon he turned upon me with an expression of astonishment at my having asked such an unnecessary question, and said: 'Of course; what else do you suppose?'[8]

Guilt is frequently indicated in Jasper's behaviour. He is represented as working continually through calculation and plot. Even his surname, always the form used in describing him, corresponds to that of a conventional villain in stage melodrama:[9*] it would surely be an impercipient reader who did not pick up a directing overtone from that, as from his appearance in the opium-den and even the first description of his fellow cathedral-dignitaries as 'rooks'.

This evidence, taken together, is impressive; but it has left some readers dissatisfied. They have suggested that Dickens was misleading his friends and in fact planning a surprise dénouement in which it would be revealed that Jasper's personality was more complex. The boldest attempt to discuss the novel in these terms was Felix Aylmer's in *The Drood Case*. Reading the novel in the early years of this century and acting on the premise that in the average detective story the criminal is unlikely to be the person who is suspected throughout, he came to the conclusion that Jasper was in fact innocent, and amassed over the years in support of his hypothesis an extraordinary amount of evidence. The chief strand in his argument was provided by the various associations with Egypt in the novel, suggesting to him the possibility that Drood was in fact at risk through a blood-feud that had involved his parents and those of Rosa Bud many years before. Jasper he supposed to be party to this secret and to the fact that Edwin could be shielded from vengeance only so long as he remained betrothed to Rosa. Jasper's role was that of guardian, therefore, and his constant agitation for Drood's safety well founded. There is much that is ingenious and fascinating in such a theory. It seems strange, for instance, that Dickens should not only have given to a villain a name commonly assigned to the villain in melodrama, but then have pointed up the fact still further by referring to him, throughout, as 'Mr. Jasper'. Would it not have been more natural to give him that name but to use it as sparingly as possible – leaving it merely as a buried hint?[10]*

At this point, moreover, it becomes relevant to recall that Jasper is not only the stock name for a villain, but also that of a precious stone. In the New Testament it has an outstanding significance. The figure seen sitting on the throne in Revelation 'was to look upon like a jasper and a sardine stone'; the light of the new Jerusalem 'was like unto a stone most precious, even like a jasper stone, clear as crystal'; the wall 'was of jasper: and the city was pure gold, like unto clear glass'.[11] One of the most haunting visions of the Old Testament is that contained in the prophecy to the King of Tyre who was 'full of wisdom, and perfect in beauty'. 'Thou wast perfect in thy ways from the day that thou wast created, till iniquity was found in thee,' says the prophet, who in describing his beauty mentions the jasper among the many precious stones that had been his covering.[12] Ten chapters before there occur the words 'When the wicked man turneth away from his wickedness ... he shall save his soul alive,'[13] which, by way of their appearance as the opening words for the services of Morning and Evening Prayer, provide a key irony in the opening chapter of Dickens's novel; throughout his conception of Jasper, in other words, Dickens may have been considering an ironic turn by which a man whose behaviour is increasingly a stereotype of villainy could also have been seen as an ideal man fallen.[14]*

In spite of such considerations, it is hard to return to the novel and read Jasper's behaviour as that of masked and misunderstood innocence. The later descriptions of him are so firmly weighted in many places, indeed, that any readers who found him being presented as innocent at the end could justifiably complain to have been wilfully misled. The most notable example is the scene between Jasper and Rosa by the sundial in chapter 19, where Aylmer finds his greatest difficulty in maintaining Jasper's innocence, as against the descriptions of his threatening behaviour and hypocrisy. His defence here is to argue that Jasper is indulging in deliberate burlesque in order to draw Rosa on and see what she suspects about him.[15] One can only reply that if this were so he would still be guilty of wanton cruelty in view of the effect of his behaviour: she is left in a state of collapse. This could not be regarded as the behaviour of a man fundamentally innocent and noble.

Although Aylmer's theories as a whole may seem exaggerated, however, one of his initial points is telling. In discussing the very earliest chapters he draws attention to the look of Jasper when he turns his eye on Edwin Drood: 'Once for all, a look of intentness and intensity – a look of hungry, exacting, watchful, and yet devoted affection – is always, now and ever afterwards, on the Jasper face whenever the Jasper face is addressed in this direction. And whenever it is so addressed, it is never, on this occasion or any other, dividedly addressed; it is always concentrated.'[16]

Aylmer shows in detail how Dickens's corrections to this passage went to sharpen and emphasize the point – the 'once for all' and 'whenever' (for 'when') being added to the original draft – and argues that Dickens would not have done this if he were planning to reveal Jasper later as the murderer. How, he asks, could he have murdered Edwin with a look of such 'affection' on his face? In the remainder of the scene, also, we may notice how, as he talks to his nephew of his sense of imprisonment in Cloisterham, he speaks with an honesty hardly to be expected from one who was primarily a calculating villain.

This is at first sight a strong point, and indeed leads one on to question whether Dickens might in some way have been losing his grip, a point aired among the wide range of critical reactions to his achievement. To those who read Dickens for his characterizations and descriptions, his last, unfinished novel showed, if anything, an intensification of his powers. The old ability to create atmosphere and to conjure into existence characters who live in small fictional worlds of their own was as evident as ever, but suffused now with an additional imaginative power deriving from reminiscences of the Rochester of his youth.[17*] One thinks of Lord Byron's return to Newstead in the closing stanzas of *Don Juan*, of D.H. Lawrence's accounts of Nottinghamshire in his late essays and fiction. (*Under Milk Wood*, with its revelation of unexpected under-consciousnesses in the local inhabitants, is even more relevant.) Dickens's daughter Kate said that her father's brain was 'more than usually clear and bright' during its writing; a view which her brother later corroborated.[18] Those who read Dickens primarily for his narrative, on the other hand, were less satisfied. Wilkie Collins, for whom construction meant much, described the work privately as 'Dickens's last laboured effort, the melancholy work of a worn-out brain'.[19*] Few readers would go so far, but if Collins's view answers indeed to a perfunctoriness in the plotting, a better parallel might be with Virginia Woolf's late novel *Between the Acts*, where any slackening of attention to the pace of presentation is accompanied by evidences of an increasing intensity in the thinking of the author herself.

In any case, it should be noted, Dickens had always been ready to subordinate plot and suspense to other considerations. In October 1859 he wrote to Collins himself, who had criticized the construction of *A Tale of Two Cities* and suggested an alternative method.

I do not positively say that the point you put might not have been done in your manner; but I have a very strong conviction that it would have been overdone in that manner – too elaborately trapped, baited and prepared – in the main anticipated, and its interest wasted.

He then continued with a revealing passage about his aims and methods:

I think the business of art is to lay all that ground carefully, not with the care that conceals itself – to show, by a backward light, what everything has been working to – but only to *suggest*, until the fulfilment comes. These are the ways of Providence, of which ways all art is but a little imitation.[20]

Dickens's assertion hints at his favoured method: not that of the 'backward light' beloved by contemporary storytellers, but of continual suggestions leading to a point of fulfilment.[21*] And it is notable that he equates the artist here with Providence herself, thus suggesting a direct relation to what is experienced in everyday life.

It should also be observed that the *originality* he posited for the novel had to do not with the plot but with a particular idea: the review by the murderer at the end in which the temptations to villainy would be treated as if happening to another man, not to himself. The idea was to involve, in other words, some version of double consciousness in the perpetrator of the deed, a consideration which may be seen as not irrelevant to changes in the author's own consciousness at the time, since he was being drawn increasingly into the world of subterfuge. His relationship with the actress Ellen Ternan, whom he had first met a few years before, was still, apparently, in an idealized state. As far as can be learned from the evidence that survives, it was just after that that its nature changed. In the summer of 1858 he made public statements about his marital state which included the assertion that he knew Ellen to be 'as innocent and pure, and as good as my own dear daughters'. The following summer, by contrast, he was complaining about his poor state of health, and Claire Tomalin's inference that he was suffering from sexual deprivation[22] is persuasive: it was presumably soon after that he decided the relationship must be consummated physically – at whatever cost to Ellen's 'innocence' and 'purity'. But this, of course, changed the relationship itself. Both he and Ellen were forced to recognize that in terms of his public statements, they were now living a lie. What was worse, she could have no social existence at his side, a fact which, whatever her feelings towards him, must have been disturbing.[23*] She was a sufficiently spirited woman to make her feelings plain, at least sporadically. Her later private confession that she had come to feel remorse during his lifetime and that her remorse had made them both miserable, coupled with her remark that she now 'loathed the very thought of this intimacy',[24] may refer more specifically to this new phase. Dickens, meanwhile, found that the relationship inevitably involved him in the intricate ways of secrecy and guilt. He was, after all, organizing a disappearance very like the one that would feature as the core of his last novel and probably enjoyed the plotting that resulted – the adoption of false names, the coded messages – though he must constantly also have feared an unmasking of his double life and the publicity that would bring (never more, no doubt, than in the moment when he found himself involved in the train crash near Sydenham while travelling with her).[25*] He who had been the supreme exposer of Pecksniff now found himself trapped unexpectedly in hypocrisies of his own, and so riven at the very core of his being.

Knowledge of this change in Dickens's personal circumstances, and the double life that resulted, has prompted some critics to work from a slightly different angle and ask themselves whether the 'very strong' idea of the novel of which Dickens spoke might not have involved effects connected with his interest in phenomena such as hypnotism and opium. From an early stage, attention was drawn to a statement about the existence of different kinds of consciousness in the same individual. Introducing Miss Twinkleton, principal of the academy attended by Rosa Bud, he writes,

As in some cases of drunkenness and in others of animal magnetism, there are two states of consciousness that never clash, but each of which pursues its separate course as though it were continuous instead of broken (thus, if I hide my watch when I am drunk, I must be drunk again before I remember where), so Miss Twinkleton has two distinct and separate phases of being.[26]

By day Miss Twinkleton is a staid schoolmistress, at night a more romantic woman who discusses the scandal of the town and remembers her own past in glowing lights. In her, clearly, the phenomenon appears in a mild and innocuous form. But might it not be the case that what is presented so lightly here was also to be shown working more insidiously in the consciousness of the novel's 'villain'? Those who explore this possibility point to the recent use of a similar device in Wilkie Collins's novel, *The Moonstone*,[27]* where the plot hinged upon the fact that a good man had stolen a jewel quite unconsciously, while under the influence of opium administered for medicinal reasons. The sequence of events is reconstituted, in the hope that when a further dose of opium is administered he will repeat the actions and reveal the hiding place of the jewel. The plot does not provide an altogether satisfactory parallel at this point, since in the event the hero's innocence is more or less established, and he fails to indicate the place where the jewel is hidden. The novelty of the device might well have attracted Dickens, however, as he considered ideas for his plot, prompting him perhaps to explore further as a central theme the idea of 'two states of consciousness'.

Edmund Wilson has given the most striking account of the novel in such terms.[28] Drawing upon the theme of discovery through recreation of the original circumstances, he also pointed to two essays which, both appearing shortly before his own study, had thrown new light on the plot. In the one, attention was drawn to various indications that John Jasper was practising techniques of animal magnetism; in the other, it was pointed out that many of the circumstances of the crime resembled those under which Thug devotees practised their murders.[29] Wilson believed that this apparatus was intended to present a man of double consciousness, 'a respectable and cultivated Christian gentleman living in the same soul and body with a worshipper of the goddess Kali', with the aim of thus exploring 'the deep entanglement and conflict of the bad and good in one man'. His final analysis draws on the hypocritical existence into which Dickens, through his relationship with Ellen Ternan, had himself been drawn.

In this last moment, the old hierarchy of England does enjoy a sort of triumph over the weary and debilitated Dickens, because it has made him accept its ruling that he is a creature irretrievably tainted; and the mercantile middle-class England has had its triumph, too. For the Victorian hypocrite has developed – from Pecksniff, through Murdstone, through Headstone, to his final transformation in Jasper – into an insoluble moral problem which is identified with Dickens's own.[30]

Did such self-division show itself in any other respect? Certain shifts of method and tone in this text which suggest that Dickens was not so much at ease as in previous novels may be noted. There is, for example, a curious and untypical lack of evenness in his practice of naming. In most of the names that Dickens invents throughout his fiction there is a memorable note of idiosyncrasy, together with hints of the grotesque. Typical examples occur in *Drood* – Grewgious, Durdles. Nicknames too are found, as with the Princess Puffer. But there are other names that do not have this 'Dickensian' stamp, intended it seems as moral signposts for the reader, good instances being Rosa Bud, who seems specifically designed to remind discerning readers of the innocence of Little Nell ('such a fresh, blooming, modest little bud', as Quilp saw her[31]) or Crisparkle, whose name, recalling words such as 'crisp' and 'sparkle', evokes (by way of snow imagery) qualities of attractive crystalline clarity and purity. (Other names occupy an intermediate place: that of Mr Honeythunder, the philanthropist, carries a strong charge of caricature while that of Mr Sapsea the auctioneer has an equally notably neutral quality.)

Such signs of fissure in text and texture make it worth inquiring further into the question, though it is difficult to accept that Jasper was operating so purely as Wilson suggests in terms of two distinct consciousnesses. When he makes his nocturnal expedition with Durdles to explore the Cathedral, for example,[32] he makes sure that Durdles is so well plied with liquor (probably drugged) as to fall asleep for some time while he is left to his own devices. There is no hint that he himself is affected in any way; indeed, when he drinks from the bottle, we are specifically told that he takes care to rinse his mouth only and then spit it out again.

More recently, Charles Forsyte has proposed a more sophisticated theory, accepting the idea of another consciousness in Jasper, but connecting it with his use of opium. His murderous behaviour was not intended to be a direct effect, however, his use of it simply helping to give expression to what was already at work. He points out that whereas the first fits, which suggest the turning of Jasper's mind into its criminal phase, take place under opium, later ones do not. On this reading, the role of the opium-scene in the opening chapter is rather like that on the heath in *Macbeth*.[33*] As with the witches, opium helps to bring out an evil that is already there in the mind.

Forsyte goes on to maintain that Jasper's states of consciousness *alternate* between an innocent one which knows nothing of the other and a murderous one in which he knows both elements of himself, this being the 'curious idea' which Dickens had in mind.[34] Such a scheme would fall in with the projected scene, mentioned earlier, in which the murderer's career would be reviewed by himself, 'as if, not he the culprit, but some other man, were the tempted'.

Forsyte's own version does not measure fully to its specification, however, since he assumes that in the murderous state of mind Jasper still knows his whole consciousness while in his innocent phase he is ignorant of the other side, whereas Dickens's surviving text fails to follow out all the implications of such a principle. When Jasper visits the watchmaker, for example, and makes it clear that he knows every item of Drood's jewellery,[35] this seems to come out of a longer process of cold-blooded calculation, far from a state of hidden consciousness that comes on only at certain times. In *Dr. Jekyll and Mr. Hyde*, Robert Louis Stevenson was to solve the problem of alternating states of consciousness effortlessly, if simplistically, by his device of a transforming drug. By not resorting to such a mechanical trick, Dickens makes it more difficult for his hero to be plausibly seen as moving between different states.

The failure, despite their insights, to provide fully convincing explanations at the conscious level leads one to ask whether the question of hypnotic powers may not have been still more deeply implicated, particularly since Dickens was even more fascinated than had been his Romantic predecessors. In the late 1820s, Richard Chenevix, a disciple of Mesmer, began producing a series of articles on the subject, which attracted widespread attention and opposition. John Elliotson, senior physician and a professor at the University of London was (unlike many) impressed by the results of the experiments, but reserved judgement owing to the pressure of his own concerns. It was not until 1837 that he was able to perform experiments of his own, undertaken eventually at University College Hospital. The demonstrations were attended by numbers of his colleagues and friends, including Dickens, and were followed by a general public scandal, with allegations by others of quackery and sexual impropriety.[36] Later, Elliotson resigned his professorship and left the academic medical profession.

Much had been made of the moral issues involved. A doctor who could thus claim control over a patient, it was argued, could easily indulge in manipulation without him – or, even worse, her – being aware. In the end, however, the development which led to the matter being largely dropped in England was not these scandalous possibilities but the introduction in 1847 of ether, a physical drug that brought with it uncontroversial control; after this the use of animal magnetism as a means of anaesthesia, which had been argued to be one of its great benefits, was largely abandoned in favour of a method which automatically avoided some of the dangers feared by its opponents.

The effect of the Elliotson controversy in mid-Victorian England was mainly that the opposition and his withdrawal held back for the foreseeable future opportunities of incorporating hypnotism into medical practice. Other possible implications, however, dwelt on above, remained intact for those who wished to explore them. It might still be contended that the act of magnetizing actually initiated the subject into a greater reality, beyond the reach of normal sense-perception. Just as the phenomena of gravity and magnetization in the physical world could not be directly accounted for by physics, so animal magnetism might reveal more about the mental world. As has also been noted, some sceptical scientists believed that in the magnetized state metaphysical truths might be revealed, even though they did not expect such truths necessarily to square with Christianity.

As has been increasingly recognized over the years, Dickens's interest in Elliotson's work remained a lifelong preoccupation. The demonstration that more than one level of consciousness could exist in the psyche was after all being given to a man who himself lived constantly so: divided socially, for example, between the respectability and moral values of the class which provided the bulk of his readership, and by which he wished to be recognized, and the world of theatre, which held sway over his imaginative consciousness from childhood. His novels provided a bridge across the gulf between that theatre and the respectable society that traditionally refused to include it. The phenomenon of hypnotism, with its strong theatrical element, suggested, even if loosely, a manner in which such divided values might be understood, calling on a different kind of interest in it from some examined earlier. Whereas Coleridge and his followers among the Apostles had been interested in discovering from consciousness an awareness of being that might throw light on ultimate (and divine) truths of Being, Dickens's interest corresponded rather to that other side of Coleridge which was fascinated by dramatic illusion and spoke of such phenomena as the 'willing suspension of disbelief'. It also raised a deeper question – not altogether dissimilar. What was the status of the self that was awakened in hypnotism? Was it in some way more *essential* than the conscious, everyday self? If so, and if it was possible to reach that self in a fictional performance, might it not be possible for that underlying self to be altered – in a way that the conscious self would have resisted?

For the most part reactions to knowledge of Dickens's interest have taken little account of such matters; instead, in the tradition of those who condemned Elliotson, there has been a tendency to ask what light a knowledge of this interest of his might throw on the behaviour of some of his more sinister characters, as in *Oliver Twist* or *Our Mutual Friend*. More recently, however, further illumination has been cast by Fred Kaplan's book, which makes prominent the degree to which Dickens saw the use of animal magnetism as a benevolent power – and practised it himself, at times, to good effect. This study brings out the significance of the case in which Dickens used his powers most fully, that of Madame de la Rue,[37] which he was still brooding over at the very time of writing *Edwin Drood*. A letter of 24 November 1869 provides a succinct account of the powers in himself which he had discovered:

I think the enclosed letter will interest you, as showing how very admirably the story of Green Tea was told. It is from the lady I mentioned to you in a note, who has, for thirty or forty years been the subject of far more horrible spectral illusions than have ever, with my knowledge, been placed on record.

She is an English lady, married to a foreigner of good position, and long resident in an old Italian city – its name you will see on the letter – Genoa. I became an intimate friend of her husband's when I was living in Genoa five and twenty years ago, and, seeing that she suffered most frightfully from tic (I knew of her having no other disorder, at the time), I confided to her husband that I had found myself to possess some rather exceptional power of animal magnetism (of which I had tested the efficacy in nervous disorders), and that I would gladly try her. She never developed any of the ordinarily-related phenomena, but after a month began to sleep at night – which she had not done for years, and to change, amazingly to her own mother, in appearance. She then disclosed to me that she was, and had long been, pursued by myriads of bloody phantoms of the most frightful aspect, and that, after becoming paler, they had all *veiled their faces*. From that time, wheresoever I travelled in Italy, she and her husband travelled with me, and every day I magnetized her; sometimes under olive trees, sometimes in vineyards, sometimes in the travelling carriage, sometimes at wayside inns during the mid-day halt. Her husband called me up to her, one night at Rome, when she was rolled into an apparently impossible ball, by tic in the brain, and I only knew where her head was by following her long hair to its source. Such a fit had always held her before at least 30 hours, and it was so alarming to see that I had hardly any belief in myself with reference to it. But in half an hour she was peacefully and naturally asleep, and next morning was quite well.

When I left Italy that time, the spectres had departed. They returned by degrees as time went on, and have ever since been as bad as ever. She has tried other magnetism, however, and has derived partial relief. When I went back to Genoa for a few days, a dozen years ago, I asked her should I magnetize her again? She replied that she *felt* the relief would be immediate; but that the agony of leaving it off so soon, would be so great, that she would rather suffer on.[38]

As one reflects on this case, a sense of its importance for Dickens grows in the mind. It was not that he had then been dealing with the phenomenon of hypnotism for the first time; as mentioned above, he had been deeply interested in it over a long period.[39] What is striking in this instance is the *extent* of his involvement. To be in such close and continual contact with another person and to see how someone quite normal to outward view might turn out to be haunted by the most extraordinary spectres, cannot but have affected Dickens's view of human nature deeply. The apparent effects of such phenomena became more prominent in his work meanwhile. Kaplan has shown that there are many touches in *Oliver Twist* that can be associated with his awareness of hypnotic powers,[40] but there, we note, the powers work directly and in line with the settled tendencies of the characters concerned. What is new after the experience with Madame de la Rue is a growing sense that things are not what they seem in human nature, that a person who presents one facet of his or her personality to the public may all unwillingly be harbouring other forces beneath – and this fact may have no necessary connection with conscious villainy, or with normal moral valuations. It is hardly accidental, equally, that the long relationship with her was the occasion of the growing alienation from his wife, Catherine. Dickens found it difficult to forgive her for her suspicions of impropriety in the affair, and demanded that she apologize to the de la Rues.[41] But the importance of the matter seems to have stretched much further, involving growing awareness of levels of communication between individuals which made those of his own married life seem superficial. From this time forward, certainly, Dickens became more divided in his nature, keeping up a surface play of high spirits while also increasingly aware at some deeper level of mysteries that could lie buried.

The question of opium is also important, particularly in view of the novel's opening scene. Apart from the possible link between the drug and various Oriental elements in the story at the level of plot,[42] and conceivable connections with the records left by Coleridge and De Quincey, we know that Dickens himself took the drug on medicinal grounds during his last years. He had frequent recourse to it on the American tour of 1867–68, for instance, and in a letter of 1870, written in the very midst of composing *Edwin Drood*, reported,

> Last night I got a good night's rest under the influence of Laudanum but it hangs about me very heavily today.[43]

In *Drood* opium is treated ambivalently. Its darker implications are firmly established at the outset by the setting of the first chapter, with all that that suggests of human degradation, but its general role seems less totally sinister. Angus Wilson sees the old crone who keeps the opium den, the 'Princess Puffer', as appearing 'on the side of Evil' in the novel,[44] yet it is not clear that the alignment is so firm. However grotesque the guise, she often appears there as an ancient nurse. And her exact moral role is equally uncertain: her appearance in Cloisterham at the end of the fragment may seem 'as malignant as the Evil One', but her role may also be seen as that of an avenging fury, intent on unmasking him and his perverted activities. To this extent, at least, her comment on the drug – 'it's like a human creetur so far, that you always hear what can be said against it, but seldom what can be said in its praise'[45] – would seem to carry some endorsement from the author; indeed, the common medicinal use of opium in the nineteenth century made a sense of its ambivalence almost inevitable. This would help to explain a point which puzzles Angus Wilson:[46] the fact that the old lady smoking opium appears at the bottom of the cover for the monthly parts under the various scenes which reflect the 'innocent' themes of the novel, indicated by a motif of leaves and flowers, while on the other side, reflecting the more sinister elements and ornamented by leaves and thorns, is another opium smoker, this time with the features of a Chinaman. Here her comments may again be to the point:

Well there's land customers, and there's water customers. I'm a mother to both. Different from Jack Chinaman t'other side the court. He ain't a father to neither. It ain't in him. And he ain't got the true secret of mixing, though he charges as much as me that has ...[47]

The ambiguity of opium had been treated also a little by Coleridge and more prominently by De Quincey, who indicates some of the qualities revealed in the subliminal self. The spectrum opened up between stasis and energy towards the end of 'The English Mail-Coach' has previously been mentioned.[48] Dickens could also use such effects lightly, and to comic effect, as in the case of the two waiters in chapter eleven: the 'flying waiter', who is in a constant rush of activity to repair the deficiencies of the service, and the 'immoveable waiter' who stands examining his work and criticizing him for omissions which are often his own, while emphasizing his own superiority by doing nothing. Dickens himself draws a light social moral, but as Forsyte points out, the waiters also act out double elements, which subsist in every human consciousness.[49*]

These elements can exist in a less comic mode. The static is, after all, the final resolution of the mechanical, and so has links with forms of activity that sometimes preyed on Dickens's imagination as nightmare. One need think only of Coketown, and its mechanical centre, where 'the piston of the steam-engine worked monotonously up and down, like the head of an elephant in melancholy madness'.[50] This in a chapter entitled 'The Key-note'. Cloisterham, also, suffers in its own way from the blight of the mechanical. One commentator has drawn attention to Dickens's criticism of the ways in which the service was performed at Canterbury during a visit in the summer of 1869, the officiating clergymen going through their duties in a 'mechanical and slipshod fashion'.[51*] In the very first chapter of *Drood* note is taken of the tardy arrival of the choristers to join the habitual procession in their 'sullied white robes', while Jasper's music brings him, we later learn, into 'mechanical harmony' with others, so that they exist together 'in the nicest mechanical relation and unison'.[52]

Jasper himself is not satisfied by that condition. Instead of yielding in compliance to the mechanical order around him, he revolts against it. The driving force which impels him is – as, paradoxically, with Dickens's noblest characters – a driving force of the heart. It is in fact the misdirection of this force – and the subsequent need for relief in the opium den – that can be said to be responsible for the evil in the novel. Jasper puts the point explicitly when he says of the bored monk whom he imagines preceding him long before,

> 'He could take for relief (and did take) to carving demons out of the stalls and seats and desks. What shall I do? Must I take to carving them out of my heart?'[53]*

This is a crucial speech in the novel, for it marks the point at which Jasper is forced to choose between two paths. In one sense it is a choice between death and life: elements that are always present in Cloisterham itself. Rochester had been the scene of some of Dickens's sunniest early scenes and there is something particularly sombre, therefore, about making this the scene for a story of murder. It is unusual, however, for the writer's early vision to be reversed completely, and in fact A.E. Dyson points out that in the case of Dickens the change of mood is not so total as one might at first think. There was always an element of sombreness in Rochester; it was there that Mr. Pickwick met the dismal man; David Copperfield passed through it in distress on his way to Dover; in *Great Expectations*, also, it was the scene of Pip's sadness as he sensed that Estella was lost.[54]*

Dyson also emphasizes the presence of the cathedral in this novel: from the very first paragraph to the last chapter, it is more richly described than any single character. Its Gothic architecture also has a double significance. Dickens had lived through a period during which it had come to be exalted as the major style of Western Europe, and its use revived for many buildings which were not ecclesiastical. Yet the 'Gothic' which Dickens knew in his childhood had been rather that of the Gothic novel, full of sinister implications – an aspect of Rochester that strikes with equal force if attention is turned to the presence in its precincts of tombs and monuments, or to the pervasive gloomy lights and dark hollows. Nevertheless it is not allowed to dominate the finished part, where the city is seen quite differently in the last scene:

> A brilliant morning shines on the old city. Its antiquities and ruins are surpassingly beautiful, with the lusty ivy gleaming in the sun,

and the rich trees waving in the balmy air. Changes of glorious light from moving boughs, songs of birds, scents from gardens, woods, and fields – or, rather, from the one great garden of the whole cultivated island in its yielding time – penetrate into the Cathedral, subdue its earthy odour, and preach the Resurrection and the Life. The cold stone tombs of centuries ago grow warm; and flecks of brightness dart into the sternest marble corners of the building, fluttering there like wings.[55]

The outward scene contrasts with that inside the cathedral, which gradually narrows down to the sight of the opium-woman, 'As ugly and withered as one of the fantastic carvings on the under brackets of the stall seats, as malignant as the Evil One.' Whatever her potentialities elsewhere as dark nurse, her part here cannot be seen exactly as beneficent. She is seen, moreover, against glimpses of the indifferent clergy and recalcitrant choir – signs in the cathedral of an inward and spiritual degeneration that Dickens located in the Anglican Church of his time.

The counterpart of this decay is provided by Crisparkle. From the moment when we see him taking his early morning exercise ('his radiant features teemed with innocence') he displays an outgoing love which expresses itself in such amiable behaviour as supporting his old mother's good conceit of her failing eyesight by pretending that he himself cannot read without spectacles. One vision of love is being set against another – and one can surmise how in the end Crisparkle's love would be shown to be as central to the moral order as is the sun which he enjoys in the natural world, while Jasper's would correspond rather to the shadows that constantly engulf his own room.[56]

Crisparkle, also, has a layered consciousness, though here one may disagree with Forsyte's symbolic reading of his closet.[57] This, he points out, has a dual organization, intimated by the shutters, which always hide one part of it. When the shutters are down, they reveal jams and pickles in the upper half; when up, oranges, biscuits and cake – with sweet wine and cordials in a leaden vault at the bottom. Despite the overtones of the last words, it is hard to see this closet as a simulacrum of the sinister under-powers in Cloisterham. The keynote is given rather by the closet's air 'of having been for ages hummed through by the Cathedral bell and organ, until those venerable bees had made sublimated honey of everything in store'. The relation to Jasper is one of contrast, showing the possibility of a duplicity which is simply self-reinforcingly beneficent. Crisparkle embodies everything that is good in the cathedral, including the sounds of its bell and music; the more one explored his depths the more one would discover repeated, in successive layers of distillation, versions of qualities that were already immediately evident on the surface.[58*]

The element needed to establish the centrality of such values, however, was no doubt to have been furnished by Helena Landless, intended, according to Forster's account, to be Crisparkle's wife at the end. She has something more than innocence: a basic vitality, shared with her brother, which is the only force in the novel likely to match Jasper's and which is shown partly as animal energy – including 'an indefinable kind of pause coming and going on their whole expression, both of face and form, which might be equally likened to the pause before a crouch, or a bound'. At the same time, there is 'a certain air upon them of hunter and huntress; yet withal a certain air of being the objects of the chase, rather than the followers',[59] they are vulnerable as well as dangerous, with a subliminal power that is suggested further by their claim to be able to communicate telepathically.[60]

Helena's central moral position in the novel is evident, both from the fact that throughout, her behaviour is never criticized, and from the explicit terms of Crisparkle's judgement when he talks to the pair and urges her to help her brother. Helena asks,

'What is my influence, or my weak wisdom, compared with yours?' 'You have the wisdom of Love,' returned the minor Canon, 'and it was the highest wisdom ever known upon this earth, remember.'[61]

Dickens touches lightly here on a theme dwelt on also in his more serious writings: his belief that religious wisdom consists in learning to guide oneself 'by the teaching of the New Testament in its broad spirit, and to put no faith in any man's narrow construction of its letter here or there'; that 'half the misery and hypocrisy of the Christian world arises ... from a stubborn determination to refuse the New Testament as sufficient guide in itself, and to force the Old Testament into alliance with it.'[62] Crisparkle would have found himself quite at home among the Cambridge Apostles, as well as others, whose affirmations displayed no awareness of contradictions in their Being. All this relates primarily to everyday consciousness, however, and to the contrast between death and vitality that is presented by the outward appearance of Cloisterham in its natural setting. Seen as aspects of the subliminal self, on the other hand, they transpose into the relationship between the mechanical boredom of

John Jasper and the urge that drives him towards the destruction, rather than the sustaining, of life.

'Love', the value that Crisparkle commends in Helena, was much in Dickens's mind during the late summer of 1869, as we may see from another story which he was publishing at that time in *All the Year Round* and which made a deep impression upon him. As has sometimes been pointed out, the very same letter in which he wrote to Forster about his 'new idea' for the novel, which was to become *Edwin Drood*, contained a reference to this story, which bore the title 'An Experience':

> I have a very remarkable story for you to read ... A thing never to melt into other stories in the mind, but always to keep itself apart.[63]

The story concerns a young hospital doctor who is visited by a woman and her child, who is lame. A new operation has recently been devised for this, and the doctor persuades both the woman and his colleagues to allow it to be performed by the surgeon concerned, despite the woman's threat that if the child dies, she will curse the person responsible. The operation takes place and is successful, but soon afterwards the child dies unexpectedly.

The doctor, who has been overworked, suffers a breakdown, from which he comes round to find himself being nursed tenderly back to health by the woman, with whom he finds that he is falling in love. Eventually, he proposes marriage; she accepts, but at the last moment tells him she cannot proceed, revealing that she had planned the whole nursing episode as a means of destroying him emotionally and so fulfilling her threat, but now finds herself incapable of administering the *coup de grâce*.

The deep impression made on Dickens by the story was already evident in his letter of acceptance to the author, Emily Jolly:

> It will always stand apart in my mind from any other story I ever read.[64]

The idiosyncratic use of the word 'apart' in both accounts is worth noting, particularly in view of Dickens's characterization of Jasper: 'Impassive, moody, solitary, resolute, concentrated on one idea ... he lived apart from human life'. It will be encountered again.

Three days before his letter to Forster, Dickens sent his daughter Mamie the second and concluding part of the tale to read and offered a prize of six pairs of gloves to whomsoever will tell me what idea in the second part is mine.... You are all to assume that I found it in the main as you read it, with one exception. If I had written it, I should have made the woman love the man at last.... But I didn't write it. So, finding that it wanted something, I put that something in. What was it?[65]

What it was that Dickens inserted remains matter for debate. To extricate the contributions of one writer from the work of another is always more difficult than one might imagine, and nothing in the second section has been shown to be indisputably Dickensian. There is, however, another element in the statement, introduced more casually and easily overlooked in our eagerness to answer Dickens's riddle. 'If I had written it, I should have made the woman love the man at last.' This suggests that the story had prompted some reflection upon his own tendencies in plot construction. It was not, after all, the case that he had an overwhelming propensity for happy endings: he had originally planned an unhappy ending to *Great Expectations* and only produced the one we have in response to others' persuasion. But in *this* story, at least, he felt that his own inclination would have been to end the relationship in love.

In Victorian terms the relationship depicted by Emily Jolly is unusually complex. The woman's behaviour towards the man is, apart from her final relenting, fiendish: she deliberately sets herself to woo his love with the express intention of destroying him. Yet for some readers, her behaviour could be partly explained by the death of her child. The grief occasioned is seen as possessing an absolute power, in terms of which her unrelenting purpose may be, if not condoned, at least understood. That that purpose should eventually have been thwarted by actual love, set in motion in the man's mind and, unintentionally, in her own, is in tune with the spirit of her age. But the point that evidently struck Dickens was that Emily Jolly made that encounter between absolute love and absolute destructive intent result, not in the transformation of the intent into reconciliation and consummation of their growing love, but in a simple nullity. 'I could have married you for hate,' says the woman,

'but for such love as has arisen in my soul for you – if indeed it is love, or anything but compassion and kindness towards the poor wretch I have helped back to life – never!'[66]

What is suggested is the emergence in her of a curious simulacrum of love, created by her own acts of affection and tenderness towards him, and powered by her own demonic intent. Despite its force, it is other than the kind of love that might have made marriage possible: the darkness of her grief is too deeply rooted to give way before this new inspirited artifice; yet the power, at least, is there.

Emily Jolly's story, which Dickens is thus known to have been pondering at the time when he was planning his new novel, may have played some part in its evolution, less as a detailed model than for its link between driving love and a driving destructive intent. And at this point it is important to recognize the restlessness that had risen in him when he was writing *Bleak House* in 1852 and which had persistently dogged him ever since.[67*] Increasingly, he recognized that he was indeed a driven man, describing this tendency with some eloquence in a letter he wrote to his wife when she was put out by the extent of his ministrations to Madame de la Rue:

> You know my life and character, and what has had its part in making them successful; and the more you see of me, the better you may perhaps understand that the intense pursuit of any idea that takes complete possession of me, is one of the qualities that makes me different – sometimes for good, sometimes I dare say for evil – from other men.[68]

An early crisis in this tendency towards cultivation of the extreme had come a few years later with his production of *The Frozen Deep*, a dramatic production into which he threw himself with all his resources.[69] It was a climactic experience in another sense, of course, since it was by his resulting association with the Ternan family that he came to know the young Ellen. Yet the indications are that his love for her was by no means the most important aspect of the affair for him at the time; rather that it grew naturally out of the more complex situation involved. Dickens was at this time in an unusual state of mind, and *The Frozen Deep* helped to provide an escape from the miseries of his domestic life. The excitement of the performances, during which he 'electrified' his audiences, was succeeded by a state of low spirits from which he roused himself to go on a walking tour with Wilkie Collins. Collins commented at this time on his extremism: 'A man who can do nothing by halves appears to me to be a fearful man.' Dickens confirmed the impression:

> I have now no relief but in action. I am incapable of rest. I am quite confident I should rust, break, and die, if I spared myself. Much better to die, doing ...[70]

There is a further perspective to the *Frozen Deep* affair. The importance of the production for Dickens was not simply that in acting the part of the 'villain' Richard Wardour he was able to forget himself temporarily but that he gained from it in a more intense form the pleasure he normally derived from writing:

> In that perpetual struggle after an expression of the truth ... the interest of such a character to me is that it enables me, as it were, to write a *book in company* instead of in my own solitary room, and to feel its effect coming freshly back upon me from the reader.... I could blow off my superfluous fierceness in nothing so curious to me.[71]

The creative and co-operative effect was matched by other intensities. Maria Ternan wept actual tears over him as he lay on the stage, and the total effect of the last scene was something to be recalled long afterwards:

> All last summer I had a transitory satisfaction in rending the very heart out of my body by doing that Richard Wardour part. It was a good thing to have a couple of thousand people all rigid and frozen together in the palm of one's hand – as at Manchester – and to see the hardened Carpenters at the sides crying and trembling at it night after night.[72]

The whole experience may be seen as a turning point, initiating the extraordinary urge that led him to endanger his health continually by the effort he threw into his later public readings.

In a previous study[73] the description by De Quincey of the aeonic state he entered into under opium was explored: an essay such as 'The English Mail-Coach' showed him, in that timeless state, failing completely, whatever his volition, to take the right action when facing the impending disaster to the little carriage. It was also pointed out that if one were looking in De Quincey for any example of the *kairos* of totally effective and fitting action one would be driven to look elsewhere, to his consideration of the perfect killing: a point inherent in his essay 'On Murder considered as one of the Fine Arts'.

If De Quincey was the prime memorialist of *aeon*, Dickens, the active, was pre-eminently the artist of *kairos*. When Jasper returns to the opium-den, he dwells on the unsatisfactoriness of his attempts to re-enact what is there in his mind. His insistence that he has re-evoked it 'hundreds of thousands of times ... millions and billions of times' is like De Quincey's re-enactments of the Mail-Coach episode: 'A thousand times ... have I seen thee... a thousand times... seen thee',[74] the expansions to infinity reflecting the expansions in his experiences of opium-trance, while he also reflects his predecessor in his dismay at the increasing failure of his opium-visions to satisfy him: 'I must have a better vision than this; this is the poorest of all. No struggle, no consciousness of peril, no entreaty...' This is truly murder conceived as a fine art, with Jasper's recognition of his failed attempts to achieve its ideal form voicing his artistic dissatisfaction and darkly parodying the frequent experience of the novelist.

What he had relished in the earlier visions, it seems, and now increasingly missed, the vertiginousness of the struggle, the sense of having a human being so closely in his power, locked literally in a life-and-death struggle, also corresponded to a state of mind that Dickens knew well: 'It was a good thing to have a couple of thousand people all rigid and frozen together in the palm of one's hand.'[75] The difference, of course, was that the act in which Dickens sought to achieve it would not be destructive but would evolve a communal opening of the heart in an outburst of emotion. Yet the *means* by which that state was to be brought on often involved, paradoxically, the representation of a killing: the projected murder of Frank by Richard Wardour in *The Frozen Deep*; or the murder of Nancy by Bill Sykes, which became the high point of the public readings. This latter role was one into which Dickens threw himself with extraordinary intensity. His son Charles was disturbed by the sound of violent wrangling outside the house one day and leapt to his feet when the noise swelled into an alternation of brutal yells and dreadful screams. At the other end of the meadow he found his father, murdering the imaginary Nancy with ferocious gestures.[76]

The larger dimension of such intense engagements is indicated, however, by a device invoked for the first, private presentation of the last-mentioned incident. A hundred friends were assembled in St. James's Hall, where curtains and screens directed the eye to a single figure in front. The audience, we are told, were reduced by the final murder scene to a state of white-faced horror, verging on hysteria. As soon as the reading was over, however, the screens were swept aside, to reveal a banqueting table ready to receive them.[77] The urge to push his audience to an extreme and then to draw them into a renewed sense of their genial human unity could hardly be better manifested. Dickens could not undertake such representations, however, without drawing heavily upon his own daemonic powers and so coming to know more of their nature.

Those who knew Dickens at the end of his life commented on both sides of the complex character that resulted. His disposition could be so strongly gay and sunny that even some who knew him well hardly suspected any other side to his character; yet he could also display an extraordinary daemonism. Gladys Storey sums up this aspect of him by saying that, for all the many-sidedness of his character,

> the dominant characteristic lying behind every trait which, with hurricane force, swept through his entire mental and physical being, was his amazing energy, at times demoniacal in its fierceness.[78]

Dickens could acknowledge the havoc wrought by such devotion to his inner energy, but he could not, after a certain point, bring himself to forgo it. And there can be little doubt that in spite of the contradictions which it produced within him, it also provided a golden thread that made sense of otherwise conflicting strains. It brought together his feelings about the necessity of benevolence and warmth of heart, for instance, into a single drive towards an ultimate experience which would make him at one with his audience, sharing a single intense emotion. But one also becomes aware of a growing division within him between the aimed-at wide and discursive sympathy which could range freely over a whole society, placing each member of it in loving relationship with the whole, and the daemonic drive which underlay the whole enterprise. Not only was the murder from *Oliver Twist* presented with extraordinary violence on his part; the question of whether he should go on with it, in view of the possible effects on his health, could simply induce further violence – as his manager found on trying to persuade him to cut them down:

> Bounding up from his chair, and throwing his knife and fork on his plate (which he smashed to atoms), he exclaimed – 'Dolby! your infernal caution will be your ruin one of these days!'[79]

Immediately afterwards, he began to weep and told Dolby that he knew he was right.

In his vehemence Dickens is the exact opposite of the Dean of Cloisterham in *Edwin Drood*. When Mr. Crisparkle says that he has stated emphatically that Neville will reappear in Cloisterham whenever any new suspicion or evidence may arise, the Dean comments,

'And yet, do you know, I don't think,' with a very nice and neat emphasis on these two words: 'I *don't think* I would state it, emphatically. State it? Ye-e-es! But emphatically? No-o-o. I *think* not. In point of fact, Mr Crisparkle, keeping our hearts warm and our heads cool, we clergy need do nothing emphatically.'[80]

Inherent in this is a limited critique of orthodox Anglicanism. Important as it was to affirm the importance of head and heart they were for Dickens not enough. Without the vigorous vitality inherent in emphasis the Church could not, in his view, penetrate the beings of his contemporaries so as to stir the springs of action.

The paradox tightens. For may it not have been that same 'emphatic' drive in Dickens that led him to the decision (taken at whatever point in the planning) that Edwin Drood could not simply disappear, but that he must die? Yet in so deciding he was taking his plot out of the realm of Miss Twinkleton's 'two states of consciousness' or Durdles's absences of self in drunkenness and entering a country where murderous intent could break free from the opium fantasies where it had been cradled, to turn itself into actual, calculating murder – even if the act might still somehow contrive to exist side by side with a continuing love for the murdered man.

Such emphaticism then drives hard against any simple fulfilment of innocence in the novel. Jasper's power has an inner quality of its own, a daemonism like that of the novelist himself which may work in positive independence from the outer intent of the man, showing him new things. The effects upon Rosa of his power, for instance, have been too little considered. She may be afraid of him, but it is also clear that she is fascinated, and in some sense attracted. While Edwin and she are standing outside the cathedral, after she has bought herself 'Lumps-of-Delight' at the local sweet shop, 'the organ and the choir sound out sublimely'. Drood is impressed by the sense of harmony:

'I fancy I can distinguish Jack's voice,' is his remark in a low tone in connection with the train of thought.

'Take me back at once, please,' urges his Affianced, quickly laying her light hand upon his wrist. 'They will all be coming out directly; let us go away. Oh, what a resounding chord' But don't let us stop to listen to it; let us get away!'[81]

An open-minded reader might well infer from this behaviour that Jasper was already regarded, and even partially accepted, by her as a serious rival to Edwin; and there are other ambiguous elements in her behaviour, as Aylmer has pointed out. To say that she even recognizes the nature of the attraction she feels would be to go too far; the curious feature of the affair, however (and one which I think has not been remarked on) is the fact that Jasper's influence should have so powerful an effect in severing her from Edwin. Her fear of Jasper might be expected to drive her to greater dependence on her betrothed, as a refuge from the other man's attentions; yet the opposite is the case. One recalls Dickens's account of her elsewhere:

> Possessing an exhaustless well of affection in her nature, its sparkling waters had freshened and brightened the Nuns' House for years, and yet its depths had never yet been moved: what might betide when that came to pass; what developing changes might fall upon the heedless head, and light heart then; remained to be seen.[82]

The depths have not been moved in any positive fashion, perhaps, but it is hard to resist the conclusion that they have been disturbed by Jasper's emphatic attentions in a manner that has revealed to her – even if quite incidentally – the shallowness of her relationship with Edwin. Since she has no psychic equipment with which to meet and organize this influence, however, the result is a pure fear, which intensifies as Jasper increases his pressure.

In the same way, Dickens notes with acumen that on the day when Jasper's murderous plans are to reach fruition, his skills as a musician are quickened:

> Mr Jasper is in beautiful voice this day. In the pathetic supplication to have his heart inclined to keep this law, he quite astonishes his fellows by his melodious power.... His nervous temperament is occasionally prone to take difficult music too quickly; to-day his time is perfect.[83]

The irony of the situation, which is exquisite, points in more than one direction. Satire of hypocrisy dominates, but the fact that Jasper's powers should be so fully brought out by his demonic intent is also matter for reflection. There are other signs that Dickens was thinking about such strange interplays of power in the psyche at this time; on hearing of the death of his old friend Daniel Maclise in 1870, he wrote,

> It has been only after great difficulty, and after hardening and steel-ing myself to the subject by at once thinking of it and avoiding it in

a strange way, that I have been able to get any command over it or over myself.[84]

To be able to think of something and avoid it at the same time hints again at the double consciousness in Dickens that has already been discussed. It suggests a mental versatility that must have been of great assistance when he had to face, yet not to face, doubtful elements in his own behaviour such as his relationship with Ellen. Jasper's villainy called for supreme artistry, and Dickens was in a unique position to show how that artistry might work. The phrase 'to lay all that ground carefully' that he used to describe his ideal in fiction is precisely the one that is used in the drafts for Jasper, as he prepares for his crime: 'Jasper lays his ground'.[85] But by the same token he was also in danger of allowing Jasper to steal the show. For in a dramatic narrative it is difficult to give a convincing portrayal of innocence triumphing over the daemonic.

The attempt to do so would presumably have relied heavily on the personality of Helena Landless. She must be at once innocent and vitally powerful; she must be, as it were, the moral equivalent of the gold ring which was to survive the quicklime and reveal the identity of the murdered Drood, presenting a vital incorruptibility against which Jasper's powers would finally be powerless. (That she bears some relation to Ellen Lawless Ternan is very likely: the resemblance of names can hardly be accidental; the exact manner in which Dickens's artistic and personal lives bear on each other here is however difficult to assess.[86*]) She must also be seen to outlive, and, in the strictest sense of the word, *overpower* Jasper; it is possible that animal magnetism, the ambiguous quality of which has already been noticed, would also have played a part. It has been seen as instrumental to Jasper's villainy – as, for example, one of the methods which he is using in order to dominate Rosa Bud; Helena Landless, already suggested to be in telepathic communication with her brother, might now have been intended to turn her powers against him to more beneficent effect.[87]

All this belongs to the unwritten part of the novel, however. Even the Victorians, despite their general commitment to innocence, had difficulties in giving that quality the moral pre-eminence which, from their point of view, it should have commanded. Increasingly they tried to encourage healthful expenditure of energy (as in Kingsley's devotion to sport) or even a touch of wild nature (as with their approval of Emily Brontë). What Dickens had come to see, however, was the dark potentiality of such invocations; energies could not only exist side by side with the affections but, if once cultivated apart from human inter-change, consume them and turn them to their own ends. We return to the description of Jasper: 'a look of intentness and intensity – a look of hungry, exacting, watchful, and yet devoted affection' – is always, now and ever afterwards on the Jasper face whenever the Jasper face is addressed in this direction. And whenever it is so addressed, it is never, on this occasion or on any other, dividedly addressed; it is always con-centrated'. The touches of the sinister in those words 'hungry, exact-ing, watchful', focusing the intensity and concentration of Jasper's gaze, are reinforced by the strange impersonality of 'the Jasper face', a face which is 'addressed' – as if by some power beyond itself. (And that hint of an impersonal force is perhaps to be linked with Dickens's use of the present tense in the chapters which show Jasper being carried along to his deed, by comparison with use of the past tense elsewhere which allows us to relax into the comparative innocence of Cloisterham and its everyday charities.) This is the ambiguous imper-sonality of the daemon, which can turn either to good or ill. And in terms of our general argument the juxtaposition of the words 'exact-ing', 'watchful' and 'affection' with the word 'hungry' expresses the terms of this conflict between consciousness and being. The word 'hungry' belongs to the hidden subconscious needs that drive him on to his deed, enlisting the powers of watchfulness and exactingness in the process. The phrase which so baffled Aylmer embodies it with precision, in fact, setting the hunger and exacting watchfulness of the animal waiting to pounce for its prey against human affection of the highest kind. What Dickens is trying to do, if we accept the import of such hints, is to show how a man of intense drive in his very Being could, by allowing that drive total freedom, bring himself to the point of killing the very human being he loves.

And yet his moral consciousness resists. This problem is already evident in the first chapter and the description of the opium-woman. As he watches the 'spasmodic shoots and darts that break out of her face and limbs … some contagion in them seizes upon him', and he is forced to sit down 'until he has got the better of this unclean spirit of imitation'. The morality of his other persona as clergyman evidently subsists in his wish to clear himself of the 'unclean spirit of imitation' derived from the old opium woman's features, which have changed from her grotesque 'nursing-mother' persona to resemble those of the cruel Lascar.

Where else in literature does one come across such a situation, a character drawn towards the acting out of evil by imitation of a character who displays moral ambiguity? Apart from a touch of this in the opening scene of *Macbeth* (a play which gives the title to Chapter 14 in the novel), only one comes to mind: Coleridge's 'Christabel', which Dickens read in 1839.[88] Christabel's unconscious imitation of a lapse to the snake-like in Geraldine's features is for her a sign of danger. All the indications are, of course, that her ensuing struggle will, unlike Jasper's, be successful, a triumph of good over evil.[89] Yet it can still be suggested that Coleridge's attempt to depict the encounter between good and evil in this subtle fashion is relevant to Dickens's novel as a whole, the accompanying problem of showing how innocence may triumph over evil without in some way assimilating itself to it being prominent in both works. Must not innocence engage with the dark as well as the light elements in human experience if it is not to become insipid?[90*] This was even more the problem facing Dickens's own, post-Darwinian age, where the darkest riddle was to understand how a universe in which the highest value was that of love could also be that in which the highest law apparently involved continual, apparently amoral destruction of life.

It was his need to solve this problem, given the customary kindly bent of his mind, that may well have given rise to his 'curious and new idea', the 'difficulties' of which he spoke to his friends, being that it brought with it the problem of showing the triumph of good in his novel in ways which would not be overshadowed by the personality of its chief character: 'a strong idea', as he had put it, 'but difficult to work'. The originality, as has already been pointed out, was to consist in the review of the murderer's career by himself at the close, when its temptations were to be dwelt upon 'as if, not he the culprit, but some other man, were tempted'.[91] But how could the villain enter fully into the consciousness of his former innocence, even by proxy, without awakening the reader's sympathy? Yet to abandon the idea and present Jasper as one *simply* working maliciously would take away the 'originality' of the plot, leaving it as a straightforward descent into evil. The reader would be left simply with John Jasper the villain: there would no longer be any hint of the translucent jasper which had imaged both heavenly man and heavenly city in the writings of St. John the Divine. Had Dickens been content to engineer a simple disappearance and rediscovery of Drood the way might have been open for Jasper to recollect his innocence in remorse, for the wicked man to turn away from his wickedness 'and save his soul alive'; his decision that Drood was to have been murdered removed such possibilities.

During that period Dickens was becoming increasingly obsessed by death and its implications. The contract for the novel included a special clause to deal with the possibility of his death while it was appearing. Even as he wrote it, he became estranged from his son-in-law Charles Collins, whose incapacitation through cancer had cut short his illustrating and brought him to a point where he could neither live nor die, making him increasingly a burden to Katey. A visitor recorded how Dickens's mind seemed 'bent on the necessity of Charles Collins's death', so that even at table he had seen him 'look at him as much as to say, "Astonishing you should be here today, but tomorrow you will be in your chamber never to come out again".'[92]

While he contemplated that static death-in-life with such estranged intensity, Dickens was playing out his own hectic life in death. He threw himself into his readings until his pulse-rate reached 124; during intermissions he would retire into utter exhaustion and then revive himself with weak brandy and water, his doctor being always available in the audience. He was frequently in pain and would speak of 'haemorrhage' and 'irritability' – which yet had 'not the slightest effect on my general health that I know of.'[93] Meanwhile he worked on with intensity at his novel. His son is reported to have described, more than once, how on a country walk the question of *Drood* came up. 'Almost as if he were talking to himself ... he described the murder, standing still and going through the scene in rapid action.'[94] The strange, impersonal energy of that scene exhibits just how close Dickens had come to the extremism of his chief character. And yet, we reflect, he was still telling the story as if, not he, but another man were at its centre.

To say this is to recall Blake's remark that Milton, as a true poet, was of the devil's party without knowing it. His commitment to his own artistic energy had brought Dickens into a country where some criminals also walked, fascinating him by their simple intensity and impersonal single-mindedness even as he recoiled from their acts. He gives us the clue to his dilemma, perhaps, in a parenthetic remark towards the end of his unfinished novel where he comments, of Rosa's inability to understand Jasper,

(for what could she know of the criminal intellect, which its own professed students perpetually misread, because they persist in trying to reconcile it with the average intellect of average men, instead of identifying it as a horrible wonder apart) ...[95]

Again that telling word 'apart': the full resonance of the aside emerges as it is placed alongside those other statements which include the same phraseology – his description of Emily Jolly's story the previous summer as 'a thing never to melt into other stories in the mind, but always to keep itself apart', coupled with his comment to the authoress herself – 'It will always stand apart in my mind from any story I ever read';[96] or his remark eight years earlier to Henry Bulwer Lytton about possible titles for a new story of his:

> As to Title, 'Margrave, a Tale of Mystery', would be sufficiently striking. I prefer 'Wonder' to 'Mystery', because I think it suggests something higher and more apart from ordinary complications of plot, or the like, which 'Mystery' might seem to mean.[97]

Yet if the criminal mind was 'horrible' it was also a 'wonder'. In other words the demonic seemed to be separated by no more than a hair's breadth from the daemonic. To enter with any empathy into the consciousness of a criminal, therefore, was to risk allowing him to dominate the reader's imagination, leaving the forces of guiltlessness dwarfed: such a conflict of interests could lead to complexities that the author would be at a loss to resolve. To Fildes Dickens said 'something meaning he was afraid he was "getting on too fast" and revealing more than he meant at that early stage'.[98] Charles Dickens Junior relates that on their last walk together,[99] his father asked him whether he did not think that he had 'let out too much of the story too soon' and that he assented to this. Dickens himself is reputed to have told Boucicault that he did not know how to end the story; he also spoke to Georgina Hogarth of 'some difficulty he was in with his work, without explaining what it was'.[100] That there were such difficulties is further suggested by the fact that his detailed notes for the novel had already given out, two chapters before the end of the surviving fragment, and that he apparently differed from his previous practice in not writing any notes whatever for the remainder of the book; we may also look at a statement ascribed to Wills concerning his difficulties during the writing of the novel:

> While in the midst of the serial publication of 'The Mystery of Edwin Drood' he altered the plot and found himself hopelessly entangled, as in a maze of which he could not find the issue. Mr Wills had no doubt that the anxiety and subsequent excitement materially contributed to his sudden and premature death.[101]

It is inherently unlikely that a man of Dickens's inventiveness could not have extricated himself from minor difficulties of plot. His dilemma was more like that of Coleridge, who had said some years before,

> The reason for my not finishing 'Christabel' is not that I don't know how to do it; for I have, as I always had, the whole plan entire from beginning to end in my mind; but I fear I could not carry on with equal success the execution of the Idea – the most difficult I think, that can be attempted to Romantic Poetry – I mean witchery by daylight.[102]

If witchery is also the wonderful, Dickens's problem was similar to Coleridge's: what is conceived in wonder can look very different when brought to the light of naturalistic telling.[103] It was also of the same order as Jasper's: to bring about a climax that would be a consummation of the 'Idea' without leaving a sense of disappointment and dissatisfaction. Once again the murderer, the man truly 'apart', was his dark fellow-traveller as artist.

There is also a sense in which the actual movement of the novel increasingly seems to mime Dickens's own mental state, involving a tendency to resolve itself into tableaux. The scene between Jasper and Rosa by the sun-dial (actually made the subject of an illustration as well), is one such, the latest one in the cathedral, with Jasper officiating, the old opium woman shaking her fist at him from behind a pillar and Datchery the easy buffer watching her with shrewd eyes, another – forming as it stands, as Dyson pointed out, a 'not unfitting conclusion' to the whole, unfinished novel.[104] They displayed the uneasy stance of an imagination that had not succeeded in projecting itself easily into conscious or rational onward presentation, working rather through static dramatizations which sometimes reflected back upon themselves bewilderingly. While his artistic consciousness came to rest in a morally acceptable position, his artistic daemon was moving restlessly on and on in hungry and watchful affection for his 'curious idea', an idea which reached to the very roots of his being. Perhaps Pansy Pakenham wrote even better than she knew when she said that *Edwin Drood* was 'not a riddle, but a labyrinth'.[105]

The labyrinth is certainly one of the best images for the strange game of hide and seek that Consciousness plays with Being. Like that other great explorer De Quincey, Dickens was less concerned with the theoretic discussion of psychological issues than with manifesting directly, at a personal and artistic level, a plot that would be faithful to some of the complexities he sensed. To say this is in one sense to confirm the judgement of Dickens's daughter, who remained equally faithful to Charles Collins, whom she nursed until his death, and to her father's memory. In her article on *Edwin Drood*, she maintained that her father 'was quite as deeply fascinated by the criminal Jasper, as in the dark and sinister crime that has given the book its title', and that it was 'not upon the Mystery alone that he relied for the interest and originality of his idea'.

It was not, I imagine, for the intricate working out of his plot alone, that my father cared to write this story; but it was through his wonderful observation of character, and his strange insight into the tragic secrets of the human heart, that he desired his greatest triumph to be achieved.[106]

To succeed completely would have involved reconciling the loving observation that could throw its light over the whole range of normal human character with a presentation of that daemonic force in the heart which was 'a wonder apart'. It would indeed have been a triumph of benignity, and it was probably beyond even *his* powers. Not knowing how to answer the riddle, we turn instead to Carlyle, who wrote some years after his death that beneath Dickens's 'sparkling, clear, and sunny utterance', beneath his 'bright and joyful sympathy with everything around him', there were, 'deeper than all, if one has the eye to see deep enough, dark, fateful silent elements, tragical to look upon, and hiding amid dazzling radiances as of the sun, the elements of death itself.'[107]

For Carlyle's 'elements of death' we might prefer to read 'the glare of a fixed daemonic energy'; in either case the conclusion would be the same. Whenever we approach the labyrinthine problems that made it hard for Dickens to finish *Drood* in the way that he planned, we glimpse contradictions that had penetrated so deeply into his own personality – whether as artist or man – that they could set the organizing Consciousness of his plot-making as a novelist at odds with his very Being.

3
Essaying the Heights, Sounding the Depths, of Being: F. W. H. Myers and Edmund Gurney

Few experienced the tension between an outward consciousness and the sense of an inward, other, 'being' as powerfully as did Dickens, yet his experience answered to a widespread malaise, prompted partly by the widespread and growing veneration of love as a central value. The two powers that moved most importantly in his psyche – the feeling for affectionate behaviour that dominated his upper consciousness and the fascination with violence that moved in his subliminal self – sometimes reinforcing one another, sometimes mutually thwarting, were ultimately held together – even if tenuously at times – by a belief in human benevolence strong enough to amount to a religious attitude.[1*] Disliking the coldness of most religious institutions, he opted for Unitarianism as his religious affiliation[2*] and had little of the respect for the established order that moved Coleridge and his admirers to try to heal the religious divisions in their society while at the same time salvaging Anglican dogma by seeking a larger, more inclusive conception of Being.

The self-division that has here been traced in Dickens mainly as a personal matter, working increasingly in the late fiction, was also obliquely reflected in the surrounding society, which was experiencing divisions of a wide-ranging kind – often to be perceived rather as the confluence of different streams. On the one hand, the logic of progression favouring the expansion of Britain into enlargement of its dominions overseas was reinforced by extension of the suffrage to the male population, so that England was on the brink of turning into the mass, male-dominated society which it would be for the first part of the twentieth century. Alongside this boost of political confidence, on the other hand, the growth of scientific knowledge and the inroads of biblical criticism undermined imperial confidence with internal disquiet.

If the traditional Christian beliefs of their society were not intellectually safe, where was security to be found? A sense of absence and loss
proliferated. Even Darwin's *Origin of Species*, the best-known contemporary disturber of intellectual peace, fed both streams at the same time –
particularly as one reading of its significance, not prominent in
Darwin's own presentation, yet implicit there – would in time attempt
to replace lost metaphysical security by adopting totalitarian solutions
based on eugenic theories.

The conflicting tendencies were reflected in further developments.
Extension of the suffrage produced as its logical consequence the Act
providing for universal education – which was recognized at the time:
Viscount Sherbrooke's comment, popularized as 'We must educate our
masters',[3*] achieved wide currency. The growth of intellectual questioning, likely to be encouraged further by the spread of education, was
then a spur to new thinking. An initial urge to find new ways of presenting traditional doctrines, as for example by extending the
Coleridgean conviction that the very act of commitment to Christian
beliefs would bring with it a corresponding assurance of their truth,
would be further extended into a general approval of intellectual
commitment to causes of any kind – foreshadowing in turn a counter-
tendency to cut the threads of pretence by simple assertions concerning the overriding importance of sincerity. (In the intervening period
of late Victorianism a middle way was in some cases secured by respect
for that quality known to contemporaries as 'earnestness'.)

There was, in the years around 1870, a corresponding shift in the
attitudes of figures who might be considered representative. David
Newsome has listed outstanding Cambridge men of the 1840s, who all
took orders, and contrasted with them the equivalent generation
ranged round Henry Sidgwick thirty years later: some of them sons of
the clergy but all either agnostics or proponents of a hesitant deism.[4*]
The underlying change might be seen as the shift from a culture of
religious acceptance to one of religious criticism.

Attitudes to the unconscious were correspondingly affected. During
the mid-nineteenth century the fascination involved had found
expression in dramatization. Dickens's John Jasper and George Eliot's
Gwendolen Harleth were apt examples of consciousnesses in which the
conflicts that troubled the Victorians could find some form of open
expression, even if they remained unresolved. During the lifetimes of
their authors, however, the potentialities of the unconscious were
coming to be viewed in a less tentative manner. While English ortho-
doxy had been carrying forward eighteenth-century traditions, still

placing its ultimate faith in what was reasonable, Romantic thinkers had explored the sense that further attention to the creative processes might make possible an enlarged view of Reason itself. At the same time, a growing fascination with the occult led to other and more extreme suppositions. In a time of general anxiety, especially as people became aware of the closed universe implied by the new science, it was not surprising if phenomena that brought the possibility of freedom from the intellectual prison-house of mechanized thinking were looked at with favour and hope. The idea that the unconscious concealed access to levels of reality deeper than those available to conscious analysis, now less firmly linked to traditional Christianity – as they had been in Coleridge's later projections – could be explored in its own right.

In the years around 1870 the swirl and convergence of such ideas was particularly strong among young men; some of whom, as already mentioned, were, like the admired Henry Sidgwick, sons of the clergy, looking for an alternative dispensation to direct towards their own intellectual situation the regard for idealizing truth that had straightforwardly informed their fathers' vocation. Among the most important of these was Frederic W.H. Myers, a man of quite unusual abilities, whose father, vicar of Keswick, had been a friend of James Spedding, one of the Cambridge Apostles particularly admired by Tennyson, and had written religious works of a broadening and liberalizing tendency. The younger Myers's early intellectual career, including his achievements as a young classical scholar and his election to a fellowship in Trinity College, Cambridge at the age of twenty-two – followed by his decision a few years later to follow in the wake of Henry Sidgwick's more well-known resignation – I have discussed elsewhere.[5] It was a sign of the times that, like Matthew Arnold, he showed his commitment to the new broadening of intellectual attitudes by joining the recently formed Inspectorate of Schools, in which he served for the remainder of his career.

In these years he was discovering the potency of Darwin's ideas, which had been making their way in British intellectual thought for a decade: in a letter to Sidgwick of 1871 he described him as 'a TIDAL progenitor'.[6] While anxious to play his part in the social and political events that were stirring in England and indeed the whole of Europe, he was increasingly oppressed by the implications of the new thinking and its apparent undermining of human religious hopes. He was particularly affected by an inability to countenance the fact of mortality, which, he said later, dated back to his childhood and his shock when told by his mother that a dead mole he came across during one of their walks was not only incapable of being revived, but without hope of an afterlife, since it had no soul.[7] If the lack of an afterlife were true not only of animals but of human beings – an idea which seemed to be entailed by some of Darwin's arguments – the prospect for mankind presented a bleakness which only strong converse evidence for the immortality of human beings might relieve.

When such possibilities were mooted, however, it was in the spirit of the age that the most stringent evidence should be demanded, as opposed to the expressions of confirmed opinion, supported by anecdote, which too often served instead. 'Intimations' of immortality were no longer enough.

One of the strongest supports for such intellectual rigour came during these years from George Eliot, who seemed to Myers one of the few contemporary writers engaging with the problems of the age at an adequate level. An enthusiastic letter to her in 1872 concerning the recently published *Middlemarch*[8] was followed by her visit to Cambridge and the well-known walk in the Fellows' Garden at Trinity College during which, he recalled, 'taking as her text the three words which have been used so often as the inspiring trumpet-calls of men, – the words God, Immortality, Duty,' she 'pronounced, with terrible earnestness, how inconceivable was the first, how unbelievable the second, and yet how peremptory and absolute the third'. 'Never, perhaps,' he went on, 'have sterner accents affirmed the sovereignty of impersonal and unrecompensing Law.'[9] The point which must have struck him with most deadening force was her dismissal of immortality as 'unbelievable'. If that were so, the fate of human beings must seem undeniably dreary.

Given the bleak outlet offered by the operation of natural science as currently received, on the other hand, it was natural to cling to any evidence that might suggest the operation of laws other than those that had so far been discovered. If one considered the possibility that evolution might be not just a physical process but a spiritual one as well, a counter-movement at work in human beings that was gradually raising them further and further above the animal creation from which they were now generally acknowledged to have sprung, a more optimistic view became possible. To the extent that human beings accepted and co-operated with this process, acting for the sake of the whole rather than out of a simple urge to survive, the workings of divine providence could properly be looked for, not in the mechanisms of the universe as such but in those who were true to this more lofty view, acting constantly out of a disinterestedness that complemented their respect for more selfish needs.

Such considerations led naturally enough to participation in a contemporary concern that might seem relevant to such matters, the current interest in the paranormal and the psychical. If it was in the depths of the unconscious that the motive power of spiritual evolution was to be sought, it became logical to look at such phenomena more sympathetically than had sometimes been the case in the past. Myers became friendly with various investigators.

In view of the potential importance of such matters for a world that seemed dominated more and more by intellectual bondage to simple physical laws, moreover, he also found himself asking after a time whether any single individual could be equal to the task, and whether the time had not come for a group of trustworthy intellectuals to devote themselves to the seeking out and thorough sifting of as much evidence as was available.

Such a group might be charged with the task of examining the question from both sides in a totally disinterested and uncommitted fashion, the aim being either to establish indisputable evidence for the existence of life after death, or to conclude – however reluctantly – that the phenomena involved were after all illusory. During a 'star-light walk which I shall not forget', he put the proposition to Henry Sidgwick, asking him,

almost with trembling, whether he thought that when Tradition, Intuition, Metaphysic, had failed to solve the riddle of the Universe, there was still a chance that from any actual observable phenomena, – ghosts, spirits, whatsoever there might be, – some valid knowledge might be drawn as to a World Unseen.[10*]

Sidgwick gave guarded support, writing to him in 1872,

I sometimes feel with somewhat of a profound hope and enthusiasm that the function of the English mind with its uncompromising matter-of-factness, will be to put the final question to the Universe, with a solid, passionate determination to be answered which *must* come to something.[11]

Myers's own researches were coloured by a strong sense of need and yearning, resulting in part from the childhood incident recorded above and from the loss of his father at an early age. Soon he and Sidgwick were joined by a third figure, Edmund Gurney, whose generosity of spirit and outgoing nature were often commented on by their friends. Unlike Myers, who was never elected, he became a member of the Cambridge Apostles, a fact which is relevant to this study and my preceding one – in one later detail unexpectedly so, as we shall see. George Eliot, who met him during her Cambridge visit, found it difficult to get him out of her mind for days afterwards. (Leslie Stephen – though without evidence, he admitted – believed him to have been the original of Daniel Deronda.[12]) William James was even more explicitly admiring, describing him as 'a magnificent Adonis, six feet four in height, with an extremely handsome face, voice, and a general air of distinction about him, altogether the exact opposite of the classical idea of a philosopher'. He also found in him 'the tenderest heart and a mind of rare metaphysical power'.[13] Walter Leaf spoke of him as the most handsome man he had ever met, notable also for his wit and conversation and showing 'a love of speculative inquiry which made him a master of subtle dialectic'.[14] It is hard to find hostile assessments, in fact, the nearest being Vernon Lee's sharp 'Edmund Gurney is supposed to be marvellously handsome but is to me more like a fine butler with a dash of guardsman'[15] and some of Alice James's acerbic observations.[16]

Gurney also had manic-depressive tendencies. It was as if he had no means of shutting off his energy and aspirations before their intensity turned them into their opposite. This limitation had already affected his fortune in three different spheres. His greatest love had been of music and his widest hope at one time that he could assist the brotherhood of human beings through its agency. Unfortunately, he found that in spite of intense practice, he could not develop the requisite executive skills, and in the end abandoned the idea of a career at the level he desired – though his book *The Power of Sound* (1880) would continue for many years to command respect for its analyses. (William James thought it proved Gurney 'one of the first-rate minds of the time'.[17]) He then attempted a career in medicine, only to discover that for this too he was not suited – a decision probably reached again through inability to develop his practical execution to the highest level: according to Myers, he found that he could do no other than 'leave the bandaging of the actual physical wounds of humanity to those who perhaps sympathized with the sufferer less, but who fastened the bandages better.'[18] Law also proved unsatisfactory: it seemed as if he must always draw back in defeat on finding his appetite for perfection unappeased. Myers came to argue that Gurney's intellectual nature contained 'juxtaposed but scarcely reconciled impulses', instincts largely aesthetic being accompanied by powers that were mainly analytic:

> His dominant capacity lay in intellectual insight, penetrating criticism, dialectic subtlety. His dominant passion was for artistic, and especially for musical sensation.[19]

This more emotional side to his nature was characterized further by an acute sensitivity to pain and suffering. Whether this sprang from abnormal bodily awareness or whether his mental keenness induced an unusual capacity for empathy, it produced a strong interest in matters such as the current controversies over vivisection,[20*] along with an insistence that when the matter of pain entered an intellectual equation it must be regarded not simply as a further factor, to be treated on an equality with others, but as belonging to another order entirely.[21]

Believing that human beings had a natural taste for the best, particularly in music, his favoured art. Gurney also followed Myers's trust in education as a way of dealing with the current cultural changes.[22] Another strong insistence had to do with the contemporary tendency to conduct arguments in simple oppositional terms. In such cases, he would often point out, the adopting of a subtler mode of thinking might replace simple knockdown opposites by a further path, a third way, avoiding the difficulties presented by the other two. Hence the title, *Tertium Quid*, given to a series of studies. In these essays, he offered alternatives to the more dogmatic assertions that often divided men of integrity in their intellectual discussions.

In spite of his general moderating tendencies, however, Gurney's impulse to emotional commitment attracted him towards the investigations being undertaken by Myers and Sidgwick, which promised the chance of exercising his analytic powers to facilitate the solving of the metaphysical questions he regarded as crucial to the time. The most striking of these were associated with Spiritualism, the extraordinary spread of which in North America from 1848 onwards and its subsequent expansion into Europe have been well documented.[23*] Myers and Sidgwick, seeing in the current vogue a splendid opportunity to 'put the final question to the universe', had begun to study some of the people currently claiming to produce paranormal phenomena, including materializations. They visited Newcastle, where a particularly lively group was at work, and brought some mediums to Cambridge for detailed investigation.[24] The results were not conclusive; in particular any acceptance often relied too strongly on the honesty of the participants. Gurney joined them at seances during the years 1874–8, but here too the indications were not decisive.

In an attempt to construct their researches on firmer ground the group moved their concerns from Spiritualism to other fields where unusual experiences were being reported, The associates, who now included the more sceptical Frank Podmore, began gathering reports about abnormal phenomena of various kinds, once again subjecting them to intense scrutiny and eliminating those that did not meet the highest standards. As others joined them, a meeting was held under the chairmanship of Professor W.F. Barrett in January 1882, when it was resolved that a Society for Psychical Research should formally be set up. Myers and Gurney insisted that Sidgwick should be president – a shrewd move, given his intellectual stature and his contemporary reputation for integrity. Despite the withdrawal after a few years of some spiritualists who felt their own sense of assurance was being slighted, the Society prospered,[25] but the leaders soon realized that their work needed to be more properly co-ordinated. Gurney, who had some private means and was still in search of a profession, was prevailed upon to undertake this task as secretary. During the 1880s he was extraordinarily active; among other things he may have been primarily responsible for the proposal that their researches should begin with questions where a positive case to answer seemed to be offered. Six committees were appointed to work in such basic areas: thought-reading, mesmerism, experiments on unusual sensitivity, apparitions, physical phenomena and historical documentation of all these. Gurney himself showed a strong interest in hypnotism; from there he extended his attention to thought transference.

In devoting their attention to these aspects of psychical research Gurney and Myers were partly recognizing the strides that had been made in recent years in the field of hypnotism. They were also careful to point out that hypnotism was not mesmerism, and that critics of the former often displayed their lack of expertise by failing to distinguish the two The scepticism and outright hostility directed against it since the time of Elliotson[26] had recently given way to acknowledgement of its achievements, notably in the work of James Esdaile, who by its means had devised a means of anaesthetizing patients in India. So successful was he, indeed, that his method might have been adopted more universally had it not been for the introduction of chloroform – a means of alleviating pain so unequivocally effective, while also avoiding the moral questions that otherwise posed perils for practitioners, that it was immediately adopted by most doctors.

Among records of the paranormal so far accumulated, some of the most common concerned the appearance of phantasms of living individuals to people who knew them intimately – a phenomenon believed to occur most commonly at a moment of crisis for the person appearing, such as critical illness or death. Gurney set to work to collect every available instance, trying as far as possible to establish how far each witness's account was to be trusted. In 1886, he published what he, along with Myers and Podmore, had so far been able to amass and examine in a volume entitled *Phantasms of the Living*, assuming primary responsibility for the volume and evidently believing that such a large collection of data would inevitably attract attention and might lead to acceptance. The volume was indeed noticed, though, as might also be expected, some who had already shown scepticism about such phenomena looked with a colder eye than he had hoped; above all, they drew attention to the lack of firm corroboration in many of the cases cited – some even remarking that the volume was little better than a collection of ghost stories. When the available records were checked more thoroughly, moreover, one or two narratives, which had seemed at first sight secure, turned out after all to be vulnerable.

Already Gurney's other interests had produced one contact that was to prove important for the Society in the years to come. Oliver Lodge, then giving lectures in mechanics at University College London, came across him when he attended them to improve his knowledge of physics in connection with the work that had already resulted in *The Power of Sound*. By then, Gurney was involved in the researches for *Phantasms of the Living*, and Lodge, who until then had found the whole subject repugnant, began to take an interest – becoming gradually convinced, almost against his will, that the facts uncovered needed to be recognized by sceptical thinkers such as himself. Like Gurney and Myers, he came to acknowledge the significance of hypnotism as a power, entailing as it did acceptance of the fact that consciousness could not be treated as a simple, or single, phenomenon and that once this was admitted the way was open for dispassionate investigation of similar abnormal phenomena.

Lodge was impressed not only by Myers's familiarity with the classics – which among other things gave him a ready range of references when composing messages to be conveyed without their being aware of the content by less well-educated mediums – but by the range of his reading generally, including his awareness of developments in the natural sciences, and his power of invoking analogy and illustration.[27*] His admiration was shared by William James, who visited England in

1883, being already known to Myers through acquaintance with his brother Henry:[28] he later went so far as to claim that Myers had been enabled to recreate his own personality over time, so as to become 'the wary critic of evidence, the skilful handler of hypothesis, the learned neurologist and omnivorous reader of biological and cosmological matter, with whom we were in later years acquainted'.[29] James was invited to join a group calling themselves the 'Scratch 8', who occasionally met in London for discussions and who explored some of the relevant questions from a philosophical point of view. One of them, Shadworth Hodgson, writing to him in the spring of 1887, spoke of the difficulty of achieving a clear conception of 'Mind':

What is 'the Mind'? Res Volatica? or perhaps Volatica alone, a sorceress or Witch?

But be this as it may; – prove that there is such a thing, or any intelligible thing that answers to the word Mind, and I shall welcome the proof with joy, nay eagerness. As it is I suspect it is a mere *façon de parler*, a traditional hum, which has a basis neither in psychological construction nor in philosophical analysis. I have no sort of objection to admit the thing itself, if good grounds can be given for it; and we are now having many prejudices, due to the Aufklärung, dispelled; and being forced to see that there are more things in heaven and earth, Horatio, &c; chiefly by the labours, the pertinacity, of the Psychical Researchers, & among them foremost perhaps of our own friend Ed. Gurney. So for myself, I am in a frame of mind disposed to revision of many judgments, – and this among them.[30]

Even this wary optimism, however, was not altogether shared by the members of the Society itself, who met in November of the same year in sombre mood. Richard Hodgson, an incisive young researcher who had been sent to India to investigate Madame Blavatsky and found good reason to doubt the authenticity of her phenomena, had persuaded other members of her fraudulence: from then on they determined to be still more severe in their appraisal of evidence.[31*] Sidgwick, surveying their results, felt that there had as yet been no breakthrough of the kind they were looking for, and indeed that everything so far discovered in their researches was consistent with eternal death. To quote Myers's account of his view, 'Men would have to content themselves with an agnosticism growing yearly more hopeless.'[32]

In June of the following year, the work of the Society suffered a further and more devastating blow. Gurney, who had gone to Brighton, where several recent experiments had been in progress, was found dead in a hotel room there, a sponge bag covering his mouth and nostrils and a small bottle with some colourless fluid by the bed. At the inquest shortly afterwards, evidence was offered that from time to time he had had recourse to opiates in his efforts to deal with obstinate sleeplessness and occasional neuralgia, and that on the present occasion he must have continued such attempted remedies by taking chloroform. This explanation was accepted, though according to reports in the local paper the jury took a long time to reach a verdict and 'the foreman conducted himself very strangely';[33*] there were subsequent murmurings from some, who believed that it had been not an accident but deliberate suicide. Certainly, the circumstances of the death make it ambiguous – and Gurney may even have intended it to appear so. Cyril Flowers, who dined with him on the evening before his journey to Brighton, wrote, 'I have never seen him in better health and spirits and his conversation was brilliant.'[34] Professor Croom Robertson, who accepted the jury verdict when he wrote his account for the *Dictionary of National Biography*, spoke, on the other hand, of the year or so leading up to his death as a period of 'nervous exhaustion that went on ever increasing',[35*] an account reinforced by Lady Battersea's comment that he had devoted 'his time, his pen, and alas! his strength' to the subject of psychical research.[36*] This links with the other side of Gurney's personality already referred to. In spite of 'the impression of so much force and fire', Myers subsequently reported, Gurney suffered from 'a constitutional lassitude which made all effort distasteful'.[37] He was also subject to moods of extreme depression: in a private letter after his death, Myers related that he 'often wished to end all things'.[38*]

There was a similar disparity in his private life, where he embarked on a marriage which was apparently linked with the concept of 'Being' as it had developed among the Apostles. To casual acquaintances the marriage could seem an enviable one: John Ruskin, writing to Myers in May 1878, sent much love to Gurney and his 'treasure',[39] while G.H. Lewes described her as 'charming' and George Eliot, who visited Cambridge with the Gurneys and subsequently entertained them in London, wrote of her as his 'graceful bride' and told Barbara Bodichon how before her marriage she had 'worked in an exemplary way both to help her mother and educate herself – her father having lost his property and left his family destitute'.[40] Vernon Lee gave a slightly different version of her background, describing her as a gardener's daughter whom he had educated 'Morris-fashion' and as 'a very fine, beautiful young woman, with fine manners'.[41*] Not everyone agreed in seeing the marriage as unreservedly happy, however. Although Kate was evidently a blooming, healthy and attractive woman, she may have found herself out of her depth intellectually in her relations with Gurney and Myers. Certainly, she seems to have been unsympathetic to her husband's time-consuming absorption in psychical research – a very natural reaction in view of the fact that she saw so little of him.[42] Writing about the death the James' sister Alice went further:

> Mr Ed. Gurney's death was a great shock to Wm. I am afraid. I hope it will make him carefull with his sleeping potions. His poor wife was much knocked down at first, the more so from its being a very unhappy marriage, from her own acct. She will however arise à l'Anglaise from her ashes & follow the example of her intimate friend Mrs. Lionel Tennyson. whose history she used to tell me was precisely like her own: Lionel treated his wife shockingly & died about two yrs ago, a yr. ago she came to see me swathed in crape from head to foot & now she is the enraptured wife of Mr Augustine Birrell, author of *Obiter Dicta*, the 3 little Tennyson sons, the youngest about six being sent off to boarding school. They are not as Harry says an affectionate race, but they [have] an endless capacity for renewing their experience on the stormy waters of la belle passion.[43]

Her extended account of the Gurneys' marriage, in another letter, fills out this alternative view, as formed by an unsympathetic observer, and includes a detail that is particularly relevant to the present theme, linking Gurney and his friends, apparently, to the Apostles' idea of 'Being':

> The story of the marriage wh. I heard from a man & several women is this. Some half dozen young men were on the search for *beings*, one of them found a being in a lodging-house in Pimlico, a daughter of a solicitor who had died leaving a large family in poverty. They flocked to see her & Mr Fred Myers who seems to be more of an idiot even than usual persuaded Mr G. to marry her. He wrote to his friends saying he was going to marry a young woman much beneath him but who as *his* wife wd. have a rise in life & larger opportunities, he wasn't in the least happy but happiness wasn't in the least in his line, so that didn't matter. To another friend he wrote making him exclaim 'why Gurney writes as if he were marrying a house maid!' This I know at first hand from the friends. Mr Fred M. joined them in Switz. after a week or two & began 'training' Mrs G. in French manners & the musical glasses, when Mr G. wanted some pruning done he got

Mr M. to do it. Apart from the cruelty can you imagine anything so ludicrous? – – She poor soul, as she said had given her all & got a stone in return! His snubbing of her in public was proverbial; for him it must be said that she was very provocative of it for she talks on all subjects human & divine with supreme infelicity. To have taken the poor, sweet, inept & blundering creature for 'a being' shows an unexacting standard in the British youth. Mr G. was *distinguished* for his fidelity & devotion to his friends & was high-minded in all ways, but not meant by Nature for a husband. They say he wanted to break off the engagement.[44*]

For present purposes the most intriguing element in the account is, of course, the mention of the young men's search for *'beings'*. Unless this is unusual contemporary slang, unknown to Eric Partridge, we see here another offshoot from Apostolic parlance, suggesting that the young men referred to were, at least in part, members who, like Gurney, had left Cambridge and were living in London. If so, the very significance of the ideal they were seeking may have been misapprehended by some of those reporting on it, since the term would suggest a universalizing process in which persons could be valued for their genuine underlying human qualities rather than social position.

Once married, Gurney may have been dismayed to find himself valuing intelligent consciousness in a wife more than he had expected. The most intriguing clue is a simple reference in an earlier letter of his to Myers in March 1877: 'I don't find K.S. escape her own notice vibrating in the memory much, do you?'[45*] Written in Gurney's laconic, allusive manner this is not easy to understand, but assuming that it indeed refers to Kate Sibley, it suggests a rather unflattering initial view of her that must have been suppressed promptly to have produced the May marriage – yet which perhaps returned to haunt him as he gave more and more time to his researches.[46*] On this reading of the matter, the Apostles' conception of 'Being' was here being tested to destruction. The ideal of persuading humanity to move towards improvement by learning to understand their common Being and participate in it (an ideal he himself had perhaps hoped to nourish through his encouragement of communal music-making in East London[47]) had met the rock of finding a domestic partner with whom the dream of shared Being was not to be realized.

Alice James's account was coloured partly by the fact that Kate Gurney, whom in her invalid state she was often trapped into passively receiving, was to her mind, though lovable, something of a bore:

His marriage was from all accts. a most singular blunder, but it must be admitted that however great his faults to her have been she ~~was~~ is singularly calculated to drive a complicated & easily exacerbated organization wild, by her tactlessness & her inconceivable literalness. She is the sweetest of tempered mortals with a perfectly healthy & absolutely British simplicity of construction, exactly like her healthy, blooming, story-less face, labouring under the impression that she has gone thro' the profoundest subtlest & most tragic experience & telling you about it by the hour. The second time I saw her she revealed indirectly her domestic woes & told me her life had been spent on the verge of suicide from the cradle, I believe. Notwithstanding her boring power, one cannot but be fond of her, owing to her singularly generous temper & her cleanly healthy uninteresting beauty. Cleanly, I am afraid can no longer be applied as I am sorry to hear she took to painting herself last winter.[48]

Ironically, it seems likely that at an early stage Kate's attentions to Alice James were encouraged by her husband. After meeting her for the first time, Gurney wrote to James, 'My wife has been greatly drawn to her; but I fear she must have very long lonely hours.'[49] He may well have thought that frequent meetings would be helpful to both women, not grasping that Alice might sometimes have found solitude preferable to Kate's conversation, particularly since, debarred from good health for the greater part of her life, tales of woe from such a flourishing, healthy beauty would have been hard for her to take.[50*] Her revelation that she had lived on the edge of suicide might have evoked more sympathy from her acquaintance had she appeared to have better reason for it.

On this interpretation the Apostles' belief in Being as a concept by which humanity might subsist at a level more important than the cultivated consciousness, a brave ideal at the social level, necessarily presupposed a common sensitivity that might lead to dismal circumstances if imposed on individuals of everyday sense rather than heightened sensibility. It could also be claimed that the required sensibility might be a quality which was in fact the very opposite of 'Being' – if that is thought of as best exhibited in a powerful physical presence. Alice's account to William showed that she felt just this lack in Gurney himself:

I was afraid that you (Wm) wd. feel Mr. Gurney's death as a great loss. But what an interest death lends to the most commonplace, making them so complete & clear-cut, all the vague & wobbly lines lost in the revelation of what they were meant to stand for. Mr Gurney's death apart from his psychical value, was not to be greatly lamented [on his own acct.] as he seemed to have little hold upon life. I only saw him twice but he made an impression of weakness upon me wh. I find is shared by other outsiders. He showed with me an almost feminine irritability, & talked of his low-tonedness & of the great effort all work was to him, & seemed to be little in love with existence [generally].[51]

Her attitude was no doubt coloured by impatience at her brother's interest in psychical research and a desire that he should cultivate its pioneering less. It is also likely, however, that she had encountered Gurney in one of his times of depression. Her account of his 'low-tonedness' and lack of hold on life is strangely at variance with the memory of him which Kate Gurney herself expressed to William James: 'Such a strong personality, such force. I can't believe in it's [*sic*] being gone.'[52] Her undoubted grief at his sudden death (which, nevertheless, did not prevent her from fulfilling Alice James's prophecy by finding solace in a second marriage a little while later[53*]), was shared by his friends. William James, whose admiration has already been mentioned, was particularly afflicted, writing to Henry,

It seems one of Death's stupidest strokes, for I know of no one whose life task was begun on a more far-reaching scale, or from whom one expected with greater certainty richer fruit in the ripeness of time.... He was very profound, subtle & voluminous, and bound for an intellectual synthesis of things much solider and completer than anyone I know, except perhaps Royce ...[54]

To Robertson, (another member of the 'Scratch 8') he wrote:

Poor Edmund Gurney! How I shall miss that man's presence in the world. I think, to compare small things with great, that there was a very unusual sort of affinity between my mind and his. Our problems were the same, and for the most part our solutions. I eagerly devoured every word he wrote, and was always conscious of him as critic and judge. He had both *quantity* and quality, and I hoped for some big philosophic achievement from him ere he should get through. And now – *omnia ademit una dies infesta* – ![55*] The world is grown hollower – but I've already digested the loss, and put myself into the new equilibrium.[56]

Robertson replied in a letter of 9 September,

I knew what you w[d] feel about our irreparable loss in Gurney & have often thought of you in connexion with him since the catastrophe. About my own last intercourse with him I must not now attempt to write. I saw less of him, for one reason or another, this winter than usual. In May when he did again come here (for the last time) he struck me as haggard & worn. I could not easily now have a greater blow than when I opened the paper one day at the seaside and read the dire news. (It came too at a bad time for me, for only 2 days before I had lost a second sister in 3 months). Tomorrow I am to try to set down a few sentences about him for the Oct. No. It has amazed me that a man of his power & performance should have dropt out of sight so little heeded even by so vain a world. Sidgwick, as you may suppose, has felt the loss enough. Myers will pronounce his *éloge* in the next no. of their *Proceedings*. (By the way, Royce seemed to me to deserve more attention than G. gave him; & even what he said I had to extort.) [57]

As they recovered from the shock, members of the Society agreed to divide among themselves the tasks Gurney had been undertaking, including the first work on a census of hallucinations. While the 'metaphysical' valuation of 'being' might lead to a disastrous unworldliness (as in the Gurney marriage) the associated desire to separate various levels of consciousness could be a highly valuable tool in the hands of psychologists, who were free to produce findings free of any religious or metaphysical implications. The consequences were particularly productive for Myers, who produced in these years some of his best writing. The chapters on 'The Subliminal Self', which he contributed to the Society's *Proceedings*, were suggestive not only for their wealth of evidence concerning the non-rational aspects of consciousness, but for the range of metaphors by which he was able to suggest the nature of what lay beneath and beyond them. One of the first to use the expression 'stream of consciousness' – a concept to be even more popular in the coming century – he constantly developed imagery from the physical world to adumbrate further meanings, including for instance the idea that imagery might be stored rather as rainwater was stored in a subterranean reservoir, to reappear in a spring where it would still be possible to find traces of the salts it had acquired in its underground sojourn.[58] While retaining the evolutionary idea that all human instincts and drives could be traced back to their sources in primitive needs, he still reverted to geological imagery, arguing that the various strata of the self had no impassable barriers between them:

> They are strata (so to say) not of immovable rock, but of imperfectly miscible fluids of various densities, and subject to currents and ebullitions which often bring to the surface a stream or a bubble from a stratum far below.[59]

In another version he used similar imagery to deal with the disintegration of personality, arguing that this was not a straightforward breaking up but a 'manifestation (in many cases) of subliminal strata of personality which are rarely accessible except by automatisms of this kind. We are not dealing with the cracks in a plate, but with fissures which, like those of the earth's crust, testify to unknown depths and a volcanic power beneath them.'[60] The manifestations were not always so dramatic, however: intercourse between the supraliminal and the subliminal might be a much less observable process, as with images that escaped the notice of the supraliminal and were retained by the subliminal for only a short time: 'They resemble pebbles which the earthworm sucks into his burrow and re-ejects upon the lawn, rather than an uprushing lava-stream from caves of hidden fire.'[61] With equally subtle scientific imagery he compared advances in the science of psychology to those that had marked the progress of crystallography, which had begun with the measurement of angles and then of planes of cleavage, until the discovery of light polarization had led to study based on the behaviour of the light within. A similar development in psychology, if effected, would serve to detect 'double or multiple refraction within a personality which, to less subtle analyses, seems still a limpid homogeneous whole'.[62] He could view the question in large terms: 'Our supraliminal consciousness is but a floating island upon the abysmal deep' of the total individuality beneath it... '[63] And on the largest scale he could suggest that the great laws which had been found to govern the world, the laws of evolution in biology, of conservation in physics and of uniformity in science at large were now to be joined by another, the law of the Interpenetration of Worlds.[64] Meanwhile the breaking down of the idea that the self was a unity was assisted by the new sphere of telegraphy, which furnished the concepts of duplex and multiplex channels of communication. This new terminology included not only the word 'telepathy' (which Myers himself coined), but also the proposed term 'telaesthesia' (not so success-ful in gaining acceptance). These new attempts to chart the subliminal were making distinct contributions to the matter; only occasionally were they open to question. When he attempted to view the subliminal con-sciousness as a spectrum, for example, his further attempts to see areas corresponding to the infra-red in certain facts of hypnotic suggestion and to ultra-violet in the region of telepathy, clairvoyance, retrocogni-tion and premonition prompt the question whether he might not be provoking misconception by forcing them into a pattern that might prove a Procrustean bed.

At its best Myers's method was intended to lead a reader possessing stamina comparable to his own through various accounts of unusual experiences, classifying each according to its type. Thus he began with a section entitled 'Disintegrations of the Personality', in which he cited cases where a human being seemed to have suffered some form of frag-mentation. Further reports then followed, passing by almost impercep-tible degrees to more and more striking examples. Although no conclusive proof was attempted, the evidence of human survival could, to a reader who had been prepared to follow Myers's exposition sympa-thetically, appear by the end of the book to be formidable, and even overwhelming.

Although there was little by way of controlled experimentation in the approach adopted for such work, Myers and his associates were far from disregarding the need for intellectual rigour; on the contrary, any promising piece of evidence would be examined as stringently as possi-ble. It has become common to mount criticisms of the methods adopted in this first phase, comparing them to their disadvantage with the more tightly controlled experimentation that has come to be taken for granted in parapsychological research. Simply to rely on disparate reports submitted by a range of individuals, however strict the moni-toring, risked descent into anecdotalism. Yet it may be argued that the procedure adopted, however unsatisfactory from one point of view, was reasonable enough given the uncharted nature of the field at the time and the limited resources available. To call for as many reports as possible and then winnow down those received by questioning their reliability scrupulously was to build up a preliminary body of evidence from which further research might be developed. It could indeed be regarded as a useful extension of the inductive method earlier used by the great luminary of their Cambridge college, Francis Bacon.

A more valid criticism is that these earlier investigators were too pre-pared to trust the testimony of individuals whose 'respectability' could be vouched for – individuals who were likely to be, for obvious reasons, members of their own class. If such a person happened to be a clergyman, the balance of trust shifted still further in his favour. When laudable open-mindedness was linked to an innocent and unsuspecting nature, moreover (those who knew Edmund Gurney, for example, remarked that he found it difficult to think ill of anyone[65*]), this might put them at the mercy of a clever person who tried to take advantage. In spite of their wariness, also, these early workers seem to have been confident that they could tell instinctively whether or not someone with whom they were dealing was straightforward. The ease with which conjurors and tricksters can deceive even the shrewdest of observers was clearly understood by Gurney,[66] but whether or not he and others always acted fully in accordance with their scepticism is hard to say.

In spite of such caveats, there remains from these early results a residue of phenomena, reasonably well attested, which is striking. Another point, which the early researchers noted, was that where such phenomena were reported, their incidence tended to be widely scattered in time. Most people reported only one or two such cases during a lifetime; it was common for such observers to comment that they were not normally subject to such experiences. Such events occurred at a moment of unusual crisis, in addition, more often than would be expected from a chance distribution.

Despite some spectacular debacles, as in the Smith-Blackburn experiments,[67] the project of the Society for Psychical Research remains a remarkable and laudable one. It was all the more worthy of respect because in the Cambridge of that particular time, with natural scientists of a most sceptical kind reflecting an English secular intellectual life dominated by positivists such as Frederick Harrison, it required courage and determination to maintain such a venture. At the same time the spread of new scientific discoveries and inventions such as X-rays and wireless telegraphy was creating a new uncertainty about the nature of the universe and encouraging a more questioning climate. Oliver Lodge, for example, forming theories about ether, knew that he would not now necessarily find his speculations automatically rejected by champions of scientific method. Whereas a few years earlier he might have felt compelled to pursue a straightforward career as a professor of physics, he could now be drawn without too much embarrassment into the additional realm of psychical research and so on to the exploration of spiritualism.

Although many contemporaries found the fervour of the group infectious it is not easy, from a later perspective, to form a clear impression of the individuals involved. If Gurney's personality was puzzling, Myers's is still harder to pin down.[68*] When it comes to his work there are certainly separate levels of discourse. While in general his images and analogies from science are enlightening and suggestive attempts to map the nature of a subliminal which is likely to be by its very nature ultimately undefinable, the existence of such a different level, once noted, quietly helps to suggest that part of the region under exploration has an element of sublimity. Both natural and classical motifs assist in such suggestion, which in his writing is often reserved for the end of a chapter, especially in 'The Subliminal Self'. In his peroration to the first there he sees his current enterprise as a fitting conclusion to the scientific enterprise as a whole:

> For nothing is more important to us than the power of extending the bounds of experiment – of ourselves ascending, with steps however slow and toilsome, the Mount at whose foot we have waited so long in helplessness till the voice of thunder came.[69]

These notes of natural and biblical sublimity are directed to the significance of the new investigations as he sees it: human beings are at last turning their observations inward, to their own nature, and, paradoxically, finding there new heights to conquer. At the end of the fourth chapter, likewise, he dwells on the cosmic significance to which, despite their apparent triviality, all these investigations may be pointing:

> do his long-past actions stand about him in his soul's presence-chamber, – ever changeless but ever living – like the golden watch-dogs in Alcinous' palace-hall which Hephaestus fashioned with cunning heart? There is significance, there is dignity, in even the pettiest incidents which seem to link man's secret memory with this chronicle of imperishable things. Poor and brief is all the life he knows; but yet some chapter of that cosmic record is writing itself unceasingly within the bounds of his being... [70]

Wordsworth, in his earlier years at least, would have understood such a concept.

It would, of course, be possible to draw a quite different conclusion from the phenomena Myers was investigating. It might be maintained that their incidence was markedly random and that, in any case, they pointed to nothing beyond themselves. Deeper even than the yearning for immortality in Myers, however, was his conviction of the sublimity of human experience, unpromising though it might at first sight appear. Such considerations illuminate, as well as being illuminated by, the brief cameo portrait of him by William James where, describing how he seemed to change under the very influence of his own inquiries, he sketched the range of Myers's personality:

> Brought up on literature and sentiment, something of a courtier, passionate, disdainful. and impatient naturally, he was made over again from the day when he took up psychical research seriously. He became learned in science, circumspect, democratic in sympathy, endlessly patient, and above all, happy. The fortitude of his last hours touched the heroic, so completely were the atrocious sufferings of his body cast into insignificance by his interest in the cause he lived for. When a man's pursuit gradually makes his face shine and grow handsome, you may be sure it is a worthy one.[71*]

If there were obstacles to the cause, the personalities of the pioneers were equal to them. Writing in 1885 of the difficulties in establishing a similar society in North America Sidgwick offered an acute appraisal of his English fellow-workers and their complementary qualities:

> if it were not for the peculiar combination of reckless independence of Thought & action with laboriousness which characterizes Gurney, & the passion for immortality which rules Myers, I have no doubt our movement would fail similarly.[72]

Even this shrewd assessment did not quite do justice to the differences between the two men, however: despite the community of their preoccupations it can be argued that their objectives were not the same. Gurney was seeking his key in the depths of the human being, trusting that a common source of sociability existed in all, while Myers looked rather for a transcending nobleness, believing it to exist ultimately in the heights of certain rare human experiences and to be sublime. Gurney recognized the existence of such a distinction between them with pinpoint accuracy when he wrote to Myers,

> Your letter was an IMMENSE comfort.... I am glad *you* can do, what I believe *no one* else could do, – perceive how little my appearance of agnostic & gloomy isolation answers to my real inside. The difference between us is that I cannot *make definite* the issues which –

could we know them – might reconcile us to our fates. Meanwhile the *one* thing I can cleave to is the sense of union in the depths – & in the heights if there are any.[73]

At such moments one is reminded of the deep debt to Wordsworth subsisting in both men. Gurney's belief in human nature differed, certainly, from the socialist sympathies that led his colleague Frank Podmore to join the Fabian Society. While assured of its essential goodness he was not likely to join in such moves towards egalitarianism, his position being rather, like George Eliot's, meliorist: he looked for the signs of sympathy in other human beings as a *tertium quid* that could mediate between extremes of optimism and pessimism and elevate their common powers – notably in the appreciation of music – towards realization of their best potential. In this respect he resembled that side of Wordsworth that rooted itself in the conviction that 'We have all of us one human heart.'

Myers came to a not dissimilar position, but from a perspective of height rather than depth, dominated by the intense Platonic love that he had conceived during the 1870s for a young woman, Annie Marshall, who had married one of his cousins. Her tragic death by suicide in the middle of the decade had left him torn by grief, coupled with an overwhelming hope that she had survived and would be reunited with him after death.[74*] While it was a mark of the new rigour surrounding investigation of such matters that his intense desire should be matched by an equally strong determination to deal as stringently as possible with any evidences that might point in such a direction, his desire remained urgent and exalted, introducing an element of fixity into his speculations concerning the subliminal self. Much as he rejoiced in the human complexity uncovered by his experimentations in psychical research the bond with Annie meant that many of his later essays were dominated by a cosmic conception of the power of Platonic love and an aim of discovering the springs of nobility in all human behaviour.

This strengthened the link between Myers and Tennyson, already assisted by their contacts with the Cambridge Apostles,[75*] particularly since Myers had inevitably been aware at every previous stage of Tennyson's current thought and work. The solution that they, thinking in harmony, had found was not equally satisfying to most people in their position. Ruskin, for example, nursed a love for Rose La Touche matching Myers's for Annie Marshall – including the hope that they might after her death be reunited through spiritualism[76] – but disillusionment followed, with a practical-minded sense of the ultimate uselessness of any renewed contact that did not restore the person in the body, actually and physically. Two years before, while Rose was still alive, he had written to Susan Beever concerning Rose's refusal to see him, coupled with her promises of reconciliation in a future life, 'I wanted my Rosie *here*. In heaven I mean to go and talk to Pythagoras and Socrates and Valerius Publicus.'[77] His own concept of being had a more physical content; however intrigued by the possibilities opened up by recent investigations, he could not exert the clerkly scepticism that often enabled Myers and Gurney to balance their eagerness for discovery in psychical research against a perpetual recognition that they might after all be dealing with an illusion. In his case ardour and scepticism excluded one another more absolutely.

Myers's had misgivings of his own from time to time. Although from 1893, when he was convinced by some demonstrations that human personality survived death, he became more forthright in his assertions, questions returned as to the ultimate significance of what was being discovered. Not only might those who were convinced still be left in the plight that prompted Ruskin's complaint, lacking the human assurance offered by simple, solid flesh and blood; messages, too, had the same drawback. However startlingly accurate they might be in particular instances, they tended to be curiously devoid of substantial content. Myers's way of dealing with any resulting unease was to contend that humanity was still at the beginning of a long development, and that these questions needed to be seen against the background of a far longer time span and a cosmic background. The perspectives of evolution could at least be turned to this advantage.

The fact remained that the immediate and recorded results of the psychical researches so far carried out often proved disquietingly banal. Where Darwin's work had been accompanied by a sense of the sublime in the whole process, comparable with the majesty of the gravitational processes opened to view by the Newtonian universe,[78*] the messages that came through mediums were, time and again, disappointingly bathetic. Earlier, Michael Faraday had commented on the results obtained by the medium D.D. Home:

> If the effects are miracles, or the work of spirits, does he admit the utterly contemptible character both of them and their results, up to the present time, in respect either of yielding information or instruction, or supplying any force or action of the least value to mankind?[79*]

Years later T.H. Huxley made a similar remark:

> supposing these phenomena to be genuine – they do not interest
> me.... if the folk in the spiritual world do not talk more wisely and
> sensibly than their friends report them to do I put them in the same
> category.... Better live a crossing-sweeper, than die and be made to
> talk twaddle by a 'medium'...[80]

Another puzzling feature for the investigators was that when the relevant evidence did arrive it was often remarkably discrete. Even when mediums convinced them that they had powers well beyond those normally reported they stood in strange isolation, leaving unanswered the question why, if such powers were important, they should have been granted to such a minute number of the human race.

Whatever unease they might have felt about such matters, including the intellectual quality of messages that purported to come from beyond the grave, however, the curiosity of Myers and Gurney had not been finally dampened. What in the end impressed them was not the triviality of this or that message, but the fact that any at all should come – with all that that claim, if once validated, would mean for one's intellectual conception of the universe and its laws. On one occasion Myers set this out explicitly:

> to my argument it is no disadvantage that the phenomena should
> be rare, and it is a positive advantage that they should be useless. I
> am trying to discover the furthest limits of human faculty; and I
> have already endeavoured to define and study this scattered experi-
> mental inquiry by a wide hypothesis – the hypothesis, namely, that
> the evolutionary process of which we men see the result is not a
> terrene process only, but a cosmical; and that our supraliminal fac-
> ulties, our specialized sensitivities, are but a selection from those
> which we potentially possess – a selection determined by our race's
> terrene history, and the capabilities of organic matter.[81]

This was to use Darwin's sense of sublimity to reassert that of the human being, raising it well beyond anything that the unevolved consciousness could envisage. Once more the divergence of attitude between the two men appears. Gurney found the problem acute in a different way, possessing as he did alongside his stubbornness of logical intellect a fineness of sensibility that could not intellectualize the question of pain and was not to be satisfied by contemporary reassurances concerning the existence of an ultimate justice in the universe. If all ended in mortality, a sense of the suffering and deprivation to be experienced by many without apparent hope of recompense must be overwhelmingly oppressive:

> When we forget pain, or underestimate it, or talk about people 'getting used to it' we are really so far losing sight of what the Universe, which we wish to conceive adequately, really is.[82]

It was this sense that had deterred Gurney from assent to the current fashion for Positivism. It had also been the driving force behind his enthusiasm for psychical research:

> if for the worst and most permanent suffering there were no possible assuagement of hope, if I found in myself and all around me an absolute conviction that the individual existence ceased with the death of the body, and that the present iniquitous distribution of good and evil was therefore final, I should in consistency desire the immediate extinction of the race.[83]

Both he and Myers had felt the effects of the new condition to a degree that is now hard to recapture, since it increased the stress involved in the mid-century hope that the natural and moral might yet be reconciled in a grand synthesis, furnishing an agreed basis for future social and educational programmes. The abstract formulations might just fit Tennyson's *oeuvre*, where they could be read against the background of his total poetic achievement, but in Myers's hands they could seem more effusive, even vapid. Since the weight they had in his own mind as a result of his steadily deepening convictions was not transferred to the reader as ballast, there could not be a sufficient achievement at the verbal level to compensate. Other writers at the end of the century would also try to express an intensity which the words, as received in their society, would not easily bear.

The same problem is sometimes true of Myers's prose. At the conclusion of his autobiographical account, for instance, he maintains that the love of life still burns as strongly as ever in him, being by now 'the love of life elsewhere'. This is to be related to his larger cosmic aims:

> I believe, as against all Stoic and Buddhist creeds, that this temper of mine, however much of chastening it still may need, may yet be that which best subserves the cosmic aim; which helps the Universe

in its passage and evolution into fuller and higher life. To be purged, not dulled, is what we need; to intensify each his own being, a pulse of the existence of the All.[84]

From that aspiration Walter Pater would hardly have dissented; he might indeed have found it a convenient summary of his own celebrated aspiration to 'burn forever with a hard gem-like flame'; even Thomas Hardy, who would doubtless have distanced himself from Myers's enthusiasm for psychical research, would have recognized the terms of the language: his poem 'In a Museum', for instance, with its projection of a bird's lost song as part of the 'full-fugued song of the universe unending,'[85] has the same cosmic sweep, even if his feeling for the sufferings and frustrations experienced in the physical world sets him closer to Gurney than to Myers.

Late nineteenth-century science had in fact made projects of interpreting the universe on its largest scale more fashionable. Even the puzzling uniqueness of various of the psychic experiences, though continuing to be a stumbling-block, was not seen as an insuperable obstacle. William James argued that the apparent contradictions involved in some psychical research should not lead too swiftly to its dismissal, since the observation of anomalies was often the path to scientific discovery. He commented ironically:

Phenomena unclassifiable within the system are therefore paradoxical absurdities, and must be held untrue.... one neglects or denies them with the best of scientific consciences. Only the born geniuses let themselves be worried and fascinated by these outstanding exceptions, and get no peace till they are brought within the fold. Your Galileos, Galvanis, Fresnels, Purkinjes, and Darwins are always getting confounded and troubled by insignificant things. Anyone will renovate his science who will steadily look after the irregular phenomena.[86]

The point was clearly an important and valuable one; yet in the case of psychical research the objection might be raised that when a whole new dimension was being suggested, where none of the existing scientific canons might hold, the situation was different. A further obstacle was that these exceptions could apply so individually to the investigator as to raise in an acute form the matter of observer error. Was one being so arrogant as to suggest that the universe was making an exception for oneself alone? After an arresting seance in Paris during which Annie Marshall seemed to have given extraordinary evidence of her presence,[87*] Myers wrote to Sidgwick,

> My main objection is that I can scarcely believe that the Omnipotent & Benevolent Author of things is as Omnipotent & as Benevolent as all that. And I am a poor worm for him to choose to try it on... [88]

The possibility he had to accept was that the remarkable knowledge shown by the medium might be due to thought-transference from himself; in such cases it was extremely difficult to frame searching questions of fact without knowing what the answers were, or to find any questions where the answer would not already lie in the mind of some person or other. The operation of such a process of transference was of course remarkable in itself, but, as evidence of immortality, totally neutral.

Despite its tendency to fall into modes of effusiveness and sententiousness Myers's poetry was, as one might expect from someone who had written prize-worthy classical verse, invariably accomplished. Some of the poems are memorably moving, particularly when read in the context of the emotions that brought them forth.[89] He was also a sensitive literary critic, particularly responsive to those writers who seemed to him to have appreciated the full demands of the age. Among writings of the recent past he found the work of Swinburne and Morris absorbing,[90] but believed only two poets to have been adequate to the deepest challenges,[91] the first being Wordsworth, whose presence as a still living poet had overshadowed his own Lakeland childhood, and the second Tennyson, who was, of course, producing poetry during most of his own career and who seemed to him to strike exactly the note that the age needed. Whereas he could express unease about the later Wordsworth,[92] he saw in many of Tennyson's later verses a natural development of the poet who had earlier spoken his disquiets in 'The Two Voices'. He was all the more attracted because Tennyson referred to experiences of trance similar to the very ones that he and members of the Society for Psychical Research were investigating:

> It may be that no life is found,
> Which only to one engine bound
> Falls off, but cycles always round.

As old mythologies relate
Some draughts of Lethe may await
The slipping thro' from state to state.

As here we find in trances, men
Forget the dream that happens then,
Until they fall in trance again.[93]

Quoting these stanzas Myers commented,

His analogy from 'trances' has received, I need not say, much re-
inforcement from the experimental psychology of recent years.[94]

Of the later verses he dwelt particularly on 'De Profundis' and 'The
Ancient Sage'[95]* as expressing his 'deepest creed'.[96] 'De Profundis' does
not, as one might expect, echo the grief and yearning in the psalm of
that name but is instead addressed to a young child; the sense that it
comes out of, and returns to the deep is at one with Wordsworth's
stance in the Immortality Ode. Between the extremes that were bat-
tling in the Victorian intellectual scene Tennyson introduces a third
something – the mysterious nature of humanity itself, expressing his
hope that the child will find

Nearer and ever nearer Him, who wrought
Not Matter, nor the finite-infinite,
But this main-miracle, that thou art thou,
With power on thine own act and on the world.

The terms to be found in these closing lines of the poem, 'this
divisible-invisible world', 'numerable-innumerable I Sun, sun, sun',
'finite-infinite Time',[97] may be subtle enough in their thought, but for
many readers they fall under the same potential judgement as some of
Coleridge's early metaphysical verses:[98] the thinking is expressed with
some precision, but is not the kind that is primarily suited to poetry.
The dissociation in Tennyson's mind between the element that created
fine verse and the element that could engage with the subtleties of
thought proves not dissimilar to the quality in his verse that prompted
T.S. Eliot to make it a prime exemplification of his 'dissociation of sensibility'.[99] The connection of this with a mystic strain may have been
what Hallam Tennyson had in mind when, inviting a tribute to his

father from Myers, he asked him to approach the subject 'not from the side of Plotinus, but from the side of Virgil'.[100] Myers, nevertheless, could not easily perceive the limitations of such writing, partly because Tennyson still showed himself a fine poet when he was working in this mode (even if for its quality to be appreciated his poetry had to rely on something of a 'halo effect' from other verses). He admired 'The Ancient Sage' in its mixed acceptance of a pessimistic view of the world and determination to cling to robustness and optimism; but he was even more impressed by Tennyson's indications that his metaphysical assertions were stimulated by paranormal experiences of his own reinforcing his own sense of a subliminal self in human beings, complementary to rational consciousness.

Tennyson's observation that he could repeat his own name until his individuality seemed to dissolve and fade into boundless being, commented on elsewhere,[101*] had been recalled in the course of 'The Ancient Sage':

> And more my son! for more than once when I
> Sat all alone, revolving in myself
> The word that is the symbol of myself,
> The mortal limit of the Self was loosed,
> And past into the Nameless, as a cloud
> Melts into Heaven. I touch'd my limbs, the limbs
> Were strange not mine – and yet no shade of doubt
> But utter clearness, and thro' loss of Self
> The gain of such large life as match'd with ours
> Were Sun to spark – unshadowable in words,
> Themselves but shadows of a shadow world.[102]

Hallam Tennyson was to link this statement with the lines from *In Memoriam* (also quoted in my previous study[103]) in which Arthur Hallam's soul was 'flashed' on his own. There was a similar reference in the poem 'Vastness', to which Tennyson attached a manuscript note: 'What matters anything in this world without full faith in the Immortality of the Soul and of Love?'[104] Whether or not Myers was aware of the existence of this note he would fully have endorsed its sentiment.

In his last years, Myers moved further and further along a trajectory taking him beyond the rhetoric of compromise. His language (like the content to which it referred) continued to blend the established and ordained with the scientifically heuristic. Only to those who fully appreciated the duality of his concerns would such a style seem appropriate. Readers who did respond positively might also appreciate the strength of the force that drove him towards the hope of finding a single-minded assurance in certain areas, but the dominant feature of his discourse, the fact that it looked back as much as it looked forward, rendered it unsatisfactory as an example for future writers and not very acceptable to coming readers. For that reason his critical writings would remain his more generally accessible achievement.

His enterprise involved, moreover, a further logical step, based on recognition of the paradox inherent in evolutionary process. Although development was at its heart, that development could not in the case of living creatures be, by the nature of things, indefinitely sustained, whether in the individual or the group at large, but in physical terms must move inexorably to the inevitable finality inseparable from the fact of death. The feelings of anyone confronting the human condition must be correspondingly ambivalent. One senses a recognition of this ambivalence and its darker side throughout the thinking of both Myers and Gurney.

In Myers's case the predicament is reflected most accurately on the occasions when his art finds imagery of an ambiguity equal to the underlying dilemma. It appears at its best, appropriately enough, in a poem headed simply 'Brighton' since the title almost certainly refers to Gurney's death there: Trevor Hall, seeing Myers as primarily hypocritical and therefore looking for signs of guilt on his part, read it so, believing the poem to be a threnody from 'the conscience-stricken Myers' in return for having persuaded Gurney 'against his inclination and good judgment' to devote his life to psychical research: 'To this labyrinth of fraud and frustration, Gurney had given six years of his life – including, eventually, the life itself.'[105] The reading is, however, at variance with Myers's own testimony in the surrounding narrative, where he acknowledges that Gurney, up to the time of his death, remained uncertain about the possibility of human survival: 'He still held that all proved phenomena were possibly explicable by new modes of action between living men alone.' Indeed, it was after that death, paradoxically, that Myers's own view of survival was clinched into faith – for ever, he claimed – 'by the message which Edmund Gurney, as elsewhere recounted, sent to me from beyond the tomb'.[106] Whatever else Myers may have felt at Brighton, then, it can hardly have been pangs of conscience. There was indeed a hidden piquancy in the fact that an event which was for the Society a disaster, depriving them of their most intelligent researcher, might have contained for the participant himself a decisive, yet tantalizingly hidden answer to their central problem. For the reader, meanwhile the question of suicide – which must always have been a possibility given Gurney's temperament and his various statements on the subject – must remain open. Had he finally given up in despair, resolving that 'to be or not to be' was the question to which he must now demand an answer? Or had exhaustion from the seemingly endless questions of evidence surrounding psychical research led to sleeplessness and pain, resulting, as Myers's brother argued, in a fatal attempt at relief? Or was it just that his driving curiosity had led to an experiment that went wrong? Or had there been a mixture of such causes? The possibilities seem to have continued working in Myers's mind in the years following, multiplying without end and leaving him still in doubt as to Gurney's state of mind on that last night. The incident, which remained essentially sombre, brought out to the full, meanwhile, the ambiguities of Gurney's own career and his courage in seeking the truth. At one extreme his act might have expressed a despair of establishing any certainty about the phenomena he was investigating. If, at the other, as Myers believed, it had ended after all in survival, that outcome threw over his whole career a retrospective grandeur.

The scene of his last act embodied within itself a not altogether dissimilar ambiguity. In Brighton, the remains of Regency society and culture at the time of the Romantic age mingled with evidences of the broad cult of entertainment that was now bringing Londoners in their thousands to its shores – attesting vividly to the unlikelihood that a higher cultivation would ever achieve more than a limited position in this new, post-Darwinian world. Spiritualism would have a brief wider fashion when that world descended into an excruciating war, flourishing, however, only as an answer while such needs were urgent.

Brighton itself, meanwhile, had a further dimension of its own, transcending issues of culture and fashion: the sea. In looking out to it there, presumably with the questioning about Gurney renewed in his mind, Myers was appropriately facing what had been a prime image of Being for Wordsworth and others, and for himself also a copious source of imagery. In one of his essays, musing on France's failure in his time to offer a clear prophetic message, he recalled some wistful words from Emile Littré, despairing positivist, who recorded how, looking out at the sea from his nearby room, he would think of the Trojan women who 'Pontum adspectabant flentes [gazed at the sea weeping]'. Myers commented:

> Fit epigraph for a race who have fallen from hope, on whose ears the waves' world-old message still murmurs without a meaning:

while the familiar landmarks fade backwards into shadow, and there is nothing but the sea.[107]

Such nihilistic implications of the sea and the 'world-old message' of its waves are expressed again, only to be implicitly questioned, in his poem:

Brighton

1

Her brave sea-bulwarks builded strong
    No tides uproot, no storms appal;
By sea-blown tamarisks the throng
    Of idlers pace her broad sea-wall;
Rain-plashed the long-lit pavements gleam;
    Still press the gay groups to and fro;
Dark midnight deepens; on they stream;
    The wheels, the clattering horses go.

2

But that wave-limit close anear,
    Which kissed at morn the children's play,
With dusk becomes a phantom fear,
    Throws in the night a ghostly spray: –
O starless waste! remote despair!
    Deep-weltering wildness, pulsing gloom!
As though the whole world's heart was there,
    And all the whole world's heart a tomb.

3

Eternal sounds the waves' refrain;
    'Eternal night,' – they moan and say, –
'Eternal peace, eternal pain,
    Press close upon your dying day.
Who, who at once beyond the bound,
    What world-worn soul will rise and flee, –
Leave the crude lights and clamorous sound,
    And trust the darkness and the sea?

This was evidently not a work written out of guilt. It reflects with some accuracy the question that remained from the two men's complementary, if Quixotic, attempts to make issues of the paranormal directly available to scientifically organized consciousness – whether it was Gurney's sense that the secret of Being could be sought in the depths, attesting the ultimate nobility of the universal human heart, or Myers's that it was only discreetly accessible at present – likely to be glimpsed, if at all, from the heights of certain sublime moments of experience. In Gurney's case, any sense of universal Being had been put in question, it seems, by rueful recognition that his own wife failed to fulfil what his idealistic hopes had looked to find in a 'being'. Neither he nor Myers appears to have found this a disabling flaw for their thinking in general, however – though the failure was sometimes reflected obliquely in their worries and those of other psychical researchers concerning the 'class' of some of their subjects, as will be seen again. In spite of the work of Myers and others as school inspectors many presuppositions and implications of universal education had not yet been fully considered.

Myers was more concerned with his friend's nobility of attitude and what his achievements might portend for the potential of human nature than with the significance of a particular failed marriage so far as the Apostles' ideals of 'beings' were concerned. Looking out at Brighton over the sea, that great symbol of Being, he had placed himself in an appropriately emblematic position, his final question concluding in a sense of its mystery, approached at one and the same time from the heights and from the depths, and – as often in Wordsworth's poetry and his own – haunted by a sense of possible sublimity.[108]

The mystery remained just that, nevertheless. His poem might represent a culmination, but it could in no manner signal a conclusion. In the years following, accordingly, others would want to find their own ways of exploring the problems involved.

4
James, Heidegger, Sartre, Havel: More Versions of Being

After Gurney's death Myers turned increasingly to William James, who had been particularly attracted by Gurney's mixture of open-mindedness in the face of new work and his hard-headed scepticism in evaluating its results.[1] Like all three of the Cambridge pioneers in psychical research, James was the son of a clergyman, though in his case the Swedenborgianism of Henry James Senior had meant that he was not intimately involved with the orthodox religious establishment of his country. Indeed, in view of Swedenborg's claims concerning the supernatural, he must have been more exposed to belief in the paranormal than was common in the Anglican establishment. Any tradition that might have passed to the three from the central Apostles concerning the nature of Being would have reached James mainly through Myers's idea of the 'subliminal self', which he regarded as initiating an exploration until then not seriously undertaken.[2] The existence of a psychical entity in each person more extensive than that individual knew was the aspect of the concept that most excited him: 'The Self,' as Myers had put it, 'manifests through the organism; but there is always some part of the Self unmanifested; and always, it seems, some power of organic expression in abeyance or reserve.'[3] The idea that the Subconscious Self might therefore be 'an intermediary between the Self and God'[4] offered a means of approaching, however tentatively, some of the problems encountered in interpreting religious experience. It also, however, raised further questions which were increasingly being raised: those of human incompleteness and the inadequacy of the rational consciousness.

In recent years Myers himself had been showing a steadily increasing assurance concerning the validity of psychical phenomena, insisting to

James that their work was of the greatest importance for the future – partly because it might solve problems raised by Darwin:

> Remember that in spite of our individual inferiority to Darwin, our collective work is far more important than Darwin's; – more important in so far as the evolution of a boundless spiritual future is more important than the evolution of a finite terrene past.[5]

In reply, James wrote of the possibility that, with his 'singular tenacity of purpose' and 'wide look at all the intellectual relations of the thing', Myers might himself live to be 'the ultra-Darwin'.[6] (After his death he commented that he had 'a genius not unlike that of Charles Darwin for discovering shadings and transitions, and grading down discontinuities in his argument.'[7])

In the 1890s their collaboration was affected by further factors, particularly the emergence in Boston of Leonora Piper, the most successful of the mediums to be investigated at the time. Tellingly for the pioneers, Richard Hodgson, who had played a central role in discrediting Madame Blavatsky, found it hard to undermine her authenticity. Followed by James, he had come to believe that they had at last found a medium fully worthy of scientific investigation. For Myers, the discovery of her powers proved particularly momentous. In September 1893, a sitting with Mrs Piper at James's house (transmitted, it seemed, by her control, 'Phinuit'), convinced him that he was truly in touch with the dead Annie Marshall, internal evidence, meanwhile, suggesting that a message mediated by her from Gurney was also genuine.[8*]

In herself Mrs Piper was not attractive. Even Myers, in spite of her apparent success with Annie, saw it as a paradox that the agent of such delight should be 'that insipid Prophetess, that tiresome channel of communication between the human & the divine...'[9*] Yet he remained convinced that through her unlovely ministrations a revolution was being wrought that would be of the first importance. Alice James, who, like Myers, found Leonora Piper's personality distasteful, was less impressed, not sharing his belief that her presence was worth patient endurance for the sake of the tidings she brought. On the contrary, believing, as her father had done, that in transactions between the individual soul and the divine *no* intermediaries were needed, she found the 'revelations' for the most part insufferably banal. 'I do pray to Heaven,' she wrote in her journal shortly before her death, that the dreadful Mrs Piper won't be let loose upon my defenceless soul. I suppose that the thing 'medium' has done more to degrade spiritual conception than the grossest forms of materialism or idolatry: was there ever anything transmitted but the pettiest, meanest, coarsest facts and details; anything rising above the squalid intestines of human affairs? And oh, the curious spongy minds that sop it all up and lose all sense of taste and humour![10]

Her wish was not, however, to be granted, at least if credence is given to a report from her brother Bob, in December 1893, the year following her death, that her presence was made known (along with that of her father, mother and a brother) in a sitting he undertook with Mrs Piper. When he asked the presented Alice how it was that having thrown discredit on spiritualism during her lifetime she was now prepared to talk through a medium, she replied, 'We all think differently now. You must not (with emphasis) think of us as we were but as we are.'[11]*

Myers, meanwhile, despite efforts to preserve a detached attitude, became more convinced that the important breakthrough had come. His letters to William James, increasingly less guarded, were imbued with a note of exultation: he was no longer inhibited from using the very language of spiritualism:

> Mrs Piper is all right – and the universe is all right – and people will soon pay up money to S.P.R. – and an eternity of happiness and glory awaits you – and I am sure Mrs James would agree to much in this letter – and the dear spirits are hovering around us in the Summer Land.

He was less worried now about the small number of the researchers involved, being convinced that in the new epoch that was about to open, human knowledge would be so transformed that a tide of support would set in, just as it had done only a few years previously for Darwin. He resorted to a cross between seriousness and humour which could take account of the scepticism of his contemporaries by adapting the language of the New Testament and his own favourite Virgil, transposing it into a high-toned sardonicism of his own:

> has there ever been, in any truly historical age, such a ray of hope and glory thrown upon the world before? Let us preach Piper and the Resurrection, none making us afraid!

> ... Sleep on now and take your rest! oculisque et pectore noctem
> Accipe! – there still lies many a deed before you, ere you pass to the
> arms of Phinuit in the Summer Land![12*]

In response to James's praise of his 'tenacity', he wrote,

> do not compliment me on tenacity: any more than you praise the
> male frog who does not relax his embrace when his head is cut off. I
> am – as you surely know – no more than an insatiable lover of life
> and love, to whose earthly existence a kind of unity is given [by his]
> passionate effort to project his life and love beyond the tomb.
> This is not ethical, but organic.[13]

The import is clear. He believed that the growing evidence of human
survival now being discovered would provide the breakthrough that
humanity needed if it was to break the bounds of a death-haunted universe. In the process, his own consciousness and inner Being, would,
by this new vision of the world that he felt opening out around them,
be restored to organic unity and find themselves at one. By 1897 he
could write of being so happy that he was 'in danger of losing strength
and fibre among soft affections and prosperities of earth and a too
luxurious and contented hope of heaven', tracing in himself 'the
growth of the characteristic vices of the new era of revelation; –
a tendency to a quietism without sanctity and a gnosticism without
intellectual effort':

> As the great deliverance approaches for me, I find myself already
> watching with a sombre exaltation the symptoms of decay, and
> saying inwardly; –
> But since the longed-for day is nigh,
> And scarce a God could stay us now; –
> till the anticipation takes me prematurely from labour into a world
> of dreams.[14]

In 1899 his assurance was reinforced by contact with another
medium, Mrs Thompson, who made known to him the approach of a
spirit 'almost as bright as God', who 'spoke words w[h] left no doubt of
her identity'. Having given more details of Mrs Thompson's experiences he went on to speak of his autobiographical sketch, which James
was at that time the only person to have read, and its account of his
dealings with a spirit who was 'as high as aught but my own limited

heart & mind can grasp'.[15] By now he felt that Annie Marshall had a quality of the divine that made her fit for worship. It was not surprising that in December he could write from Italy,

These are great days! With the possible exception of the Christian era itself, I can think of no such expansive illuminative moment in the story of mankind.[16]

What did James make of all this? He was sufficiently impressed by Myers's conviction to make sure of being with him at the time of his death soon afterwards. Suffering from heart trouble after an attack of influenza, Myers had been told by a medium that he had not long to live and turned with increased urgency to his work, including the long book he had been constructing from it. The prophecy of the period remaining to him proved overoptimistic, however, and he died on 17 January 1901. With typical zeal he had agreed with James that whichever of them died first should try to send a message to the other as he passed over; James went to Rome to be with him, in the hope that the time of his death might be marked by some phenomenon worthy of record, but without success.[17*]

James's own letters in the 1890s had had little to say in the way of direct comment on Myers's growing assurance. He was concerned with practical matters relating to his presidency of the Society for Psychical Research, not to mention the politics of the time, which at one point threatened war between England and America. When in his longest letter of the period he urged Myers to produce his book on the subliminal consciousness, he included advice about his style of presentation:

I am more and more persuaded that times are ripe for you to make a great impression. But publish the volumes separately, tone down your transmundane enthusiasm in the first one, and reserve all lyrical outbursts for the last page of the second, where they will crash in with full effect, the reader having been unsuspectingly led up from one step to another until at last the full view bursts upon his vision, and he finds that he must take it in.[18*]

Although the death of both Myers and Sidgwick left his position as a psychical researcher more isolated, he remained firm in his belief that the very novelty of systematic research into psychical phenomena made the need for an open-minded and receptive attitude all the more pressing. He was sufficiently impressed by Mrs Piper's powers, for example, and by the arguments in Myers's *Human Personality and its Survival of Bodily Death* (a full version of his researches to date which his widow, aided by friends, published in 1903) to be annoyed by scientific contemporaries who would not even consider the evidence, declining to attend testing sessions which he tried to arrange for their benefit.[19] In spite of his own sceptical tendencies, recent developments had convinced him that existing assumptions were at least worth questioning. Having acknowledged how miserable it was for truth to be confined to presumption and counter-presumption, 'with no decisive thunderbolt of fact to clear the baffling darkness', he then made an assertion on his own part:

> For me the thunder-bolt has fallen, and the orthodox belief has not merely had its presumption weakened, but the truth of the belief itself is decisively overthrown.

In order to upset the law that all crows were black, he pointed out, it was not necessary to prove that *no* crows were not; simply to prove that one single crow was white would be enough. He continued,

> My own white crow is Mrs Piper. In the trances of this medium I cannot resist the conviction that knowledge appears which she has never gained by the ordinary waking use of her eyes and ears and wits. What the source of the knowledge may be I know not, and have not the glimmer of an explanatory suggestion to make, but from admitting the fact of such knowledge I can see no escape. So when I turn to the rest of the evidence, ghosts and all, I cannot carry with me the irreversibly negative bias of the 'rigorously scientific' mind, with its presumption as to what the true order of nature ought to be.[20]

In spite of this he could not easily extend the breadth of his sympathies to cover the other celebrated medium of the period, Eusapia Paladino, a peasant woman from the Mediterranean who was producing feats that so impressed some European researchers as to make them rush across the continent to study her achievements. In the end, during a visit to Cambridge, she was caught indulging in trickery and in accordance with their rules the members of the Society for Psychical Research resolved to have no more to do with her. In spite of such disquiets, however, other researchers, including some distinguished scientists,[21*] were convinced of her powers; she herself, meanwhile, still insisted that her results were genuine and that since it was natural to her to produce them by trickery if that was the simplest way open, it was the responsibility of researchers to devise means of preventing her from taking short cuts. She remained a controversial figure.

James's academic attitude included, like that of his English counterparts, an infusion of loftiness: when a figure such as Eusapia appeared, it could be contended that as a peasant her closer relationship to the earth and so to the sources of true originality might have facilitated her psychic skills yet if common assumptions concerning her social status were accepted they suggested that she might be not averse to indulgence in low practices. A sense among these early pioneers that to be convincing, the subliminal self should show itself to be *noble* once again suggests itself. In this case, at all events, William James's scepticism retained its tenacity, but he commented on the 'tragi-comic suggestion that the whole order of nature might possibly be overturned in one's own head, by the way in which one imagined oneself, on a certain occasion, to be holding a tricky peasant woman's feet'.[22]

The collecting of all that he had to say on the subject of psychical research generally, whether in formal lectures or private letters, shows how much he wavered in his attitude, between a scepticism that came readily to someone trained in American and Harvard intellectual traditions and an open-mindedness that echoed Myers's enthusiasm. In the early years of the twentieth century, two factors drew him strongly towards the spiritualist side of the argument. One, mentioned earlier, was the sheer impressiveness of Myers's achievements and comportment in the last few years of his life.[23] The other was the continuing success of Leonora Piper in convincing others of her psychic skills. It was not simply a matter of Bob James and messages from a purportedly chastened Alice; even Henry was impressed by Mrs Piper's apparent access to unique knowledge of the family's affairs. Yet in the event William James's final statements on the subject corresponded with those of Sidgwick, who said a year before his death that if anyone had told him at the outset of his enquiries that after twenty years he would be in the same state of doubt and balance as when he started, he would not have believed them, yet that that was no less than his position. Recalling this, James agreed: 'For 25 years I have been in touch with the literature of Psychical Research, and I have been acquainted with numerous "researchers".... Yet I am theoretically no "further" than I was at the beginning; and I confess that at times I have been tempted to believe that the Creator has eternally intended this department of nature to be *baffling*...'[24] Both men's experiences of psychical research, in other words, mirrored almost exactly Coleridge's comment on hypnotic phenomena nearly a century earlier: 'Nine years has the subject of animal magnetism been before me ... I remain where I was ... without having moved an inch backward or forward.'[25]

One consequence of William James's interest in psychical research was an enhanced intentness on bringing out the more practical aspects of his philosophy, as for example in his development of pragmatism. In doing so he ran foul of his old friend Shadworth Hodgson, who, after reading *A Pluralistic Universe*, took him to task:

> if you can only refute the 'thin' Oxford intellectualism, as you call it, by means of some such pragmatic assumption as this of a 'preferred' attitude, I for one cannot think much of your reputation, though I am very far from being one of your 'intellectualists'. I am as little of an intellectualist, in your sense of the word, as you are.
>
> In my humble opinion, the very meaning of such terms as attitude, individual, self, universe, being, existence, feeling, will, thought, perception, soul, mind, ego, &c. &c. &c., is what philosophy has first and foremost to ascertain. To do this it must analyse, and that without assuming any particular piece of knowledge as representing known fact – what? Why, consciousness itself, awareness itself.... No philosophy, in my humble opinion, deserves the name, which does not endeavor at least to base itself on the analysis of consciousness without assumptions.[26]

The idea of any discontinuity between consciousness and Being was evidently foreign to Shadworth Hodgson, for whom it remained the straightforward task of the conscious mind to analyse, without preconceptions, the nature of being itself, placing it in the same category as other ideas of the kind. Awareness of the problem was to grow during the century, however, exacerbated by the sense that traditional philosophical methods did not offer an adequate answer to the questions that were now becoming prominent. As results of the comprehensive work on psychical research accumulated it became clear that the quest for cast-iron proof was doomed to failure. Evidence from a few sources might be startling, but experiments set up to repeat them then proved impracticable, destroying the possibility of developing valid scientific methods. If psychical phenomena existed, it seemed, their operation was largely wanton, lawless, unpredictable, not therefore to be allowed the kind of status accorded to scientifically established 'facts'. The latter might need to be reinterpreted according to new theories and new evidence, but in themselves their existence was verifiable and replicable – over and over again if necessary – in a way that that of psychical phenomena was not. It gradually became clear to some that whatever the truth of the matter, the attempt to establish psychical research on a firm scientific basis was likely always to be thwarted by this simple difficulty.

Such questions were soon to be overtaken by matters that would change the very perspective from which they were viewed, as the events of the First World War challenged the intellectual fabric of Western civilization directly. Ironically, they also gave a boost to psychical research itself, as tens of thousands of the bereaved sought assurance that their lost loved ones might still in some way have survived. One or two of the researchers themselves, such as Sir Oliver Lodge, who was convinced that his dead son remained in contact,[27] believed that further confirmation was being produced. But this, for obvious reasons, could not be regarded as a permanent, and certainly not as a welcome resource; the actual survivors were more likely to turn from such sources of possible consolation to revulsion against the whole course of events that had caused their current desolation. Questions concerning life after death were dwarfed by a new sense of the need to enhance the life that preceded it.

When they looked for a viable use of scientific methods the sober, disillusioned minds of the post-war era turned more readily to the psychological theories of Sigmund Freud. Myers had in fact been one of the first to draw attention to his work, though his favourable comments had not been altogether reciprocated. As a thinker who rejected the 'oceanic consciousness' proposed by his friend Romain Rolland (a concept which was later to be drawn on profitably by some in interpreting texts such as Wordsworth's Immortality Ode),[28] Freud was not likely to regard with favour writing that looked to the workings of the subliminal self for clues to the metaphysical nature of Being. As one writer has put it, he saw the unconscious as

> a kind of territory in which lay the 'repressed': certainly not the hidden being, since that was no more than an illusion, but an area which could be found many forces that went to make it up – in particular the notorious threefold Ego, Id and Superego into which the forces of the self could be split.[29]

Freud's use of the term 'primary' (not, of course, in Coleridge's sense), when describing consciousness, created problems for writers such as Arthur Koestler, another explorer of unconscious powers, who was anxious to avoid confusion with unconscious mentation. In Freud, the primary process was, he claimed, 'devoid of logic, governed by the pleasure principle, apt to confuse perception and hallucination, and accompanied by massive discharges of affect'. 'It seems,' he continued, 'that between this very primary process and the so-called secondary process governed by the reality principle, we must interpolate a whole hierarchy of cognitive structures, which are not simply mixtures of primary and secondary, but are autonomous systems in their own right, each governed by a distinct set of rules. The paranoid delusion, the dream, the daydream, free association, the mentalities of children of various ages and of primitives at various stages should not be lumped together, for each has its own logic or rules of the game.'[30]

Koestler's sense of an incompleteness in Freud's theoretical framework was shared by some other thinkers. In Germany, Martin Heidegger had followed the lead of Edmund Husserl in attacking what they termed 'psychologism'. As professional philosophers they were anxious to protect their intellectual practices yet were also alive to current issues. While some writers had been dwelling on the dangers of over-developed consciousness in producing an unhealthy neurasthenia, or worse,[31*] Heidegger was taking a radical step which in one sense recalled Coleridge and other earlier thinkers of his kind: to invert the normal precedence between consciousness and Being and proclaim the supremacy of the latter. It was an ordering to be sustained in his own manner for the rest of his career.

That career had remarkable consistency, which could also be associated with a powerful sense of locality. Born in a small town in Swabia, he never went very far from his native Black Forest; nevertheless, he always thought of himself as engaged on a 'way', or 'journey', including 'wanderings when all shores stay distant'.[32] When struggling with a difficult idea he would take the path out of town and go into woods where the abundance of great trees afforded a sense of correspondence to the changing seasons of his own life:

The trees seemed to fathom quite naturally what poets and thinkers and thinkers struggled desperately to say with words: to be oneself authentically requires that one both reach into the heavens and down into the earth.[33]

For him, 'rootedness' was, in other words, a key image. In the same way, his favourite poet was Johann Hölderlin, a poet of his own region

who seemed to achieve an utterance outside the conventional discourse of the academic culture that surrounded him. Like Coleridge
again, he proved fertile in neologism, producing new words for what
he had to say whenever needed – particularly if he thought that the
use of familiar ones might actually mislead, obscuring what he was
trying to express.

Heidegger's criticism of current trends, his insistence that Being was
not to be discussed simply theoretically, but out of the situation in
which human beings find themselves, proved particularly important.
In the sphere of psychoanalysis the trenchancy of his ideas struck
home with particular force for some readers, particularly the critique
he directed against assertions that most psychoanalytic theory was
based on scientific 'naturalism'. If, as was assumed, the psyche was
totally in accord with the rest of nature, it would only be necessary to
find and point out the sources of any apparent conflicts for them to be
eliminated. From a theological point of view this created difficulties,
clearly, since if human nature is in a fallen state it is not enough for
the flaws to be discovered and eliminated by a simple act of will: there
is need for the intervention of some kind of super-natural power.

So far as succeeding thinkers were concerned, a major benefit of his
critique was to raise the question of authenticity and inauthenticity in
behaviour. This was a distinction to be developed further by Jean-Paul
Sartre, but Heidegger would no doubt have challenged an application
that was connected with insistence on the supremacy of personal
consciousness. Such an attitude was open to the objection that by
always aiming to make Being conscious, the cultivation of authenticity
was in danger of intensifying self-consciousness – which then ran the
risk of becoming inauthentic in a different manner. It is a danger that
Heidegger himself foresaw, speaking of an 'extravagant grubbing about
in one's own soul which can be in the highest degree counterfeit'.[34] For
him Being was not to be confused with personality.

In approaching this implicit debate one must allow for changes in
the situation over the centuries. Since it is to be assumed that in any
recognizable version of themselves humans have always been conscious, it might well be maintained that in earlier periods of civilization consciousness and Being were more closely integrated, as humans
expressed themselves more directly out of their inner selves, with a
consciousness that was more transparent. Those who, like Heidegger,
bypass comparatively modern developments, moving behind the
developed Cartesian consciousness of their contemporaries in the hope
of recovering such a purer integration of consciousness in, say, the

time of Aristotle, run the risk of ignoring important other factors, such as the sophisticated evolution of political consciousness; Heidegger's dealings with the current political situation of his day, which, as is well known, furnished the most controversial element in his career, might be thought to have suffered from just such a psychological naïveté, leading to a blinkered political vision. The crisis that led him to turn away from Catholic dogma took place in a crucial political phase in his country, the winter of 1918–19, yet the letter he wrote to his most intimate colleague concerning the decision was about the repression he felt as a philosopher; there was no mention of the world-shaking events then taking place – the end of the war in which he had served (helping to prepare poison gas attacks and gaining promotion to the rank of lance-corporal shortly before the coming of the Armistice), the Bolshevik Revolution, the end of the Hohenzollern dynasty, the proclamation of a socialist republic in his homeland, or the outbreak of civil strife.[35] It is hard to believe that he was not moved by such events or by the sense of national humiliation that pervaded Germany following the terms of the peace agreement, or that this did not affect his initial attitude to the rise of authoritarian movements. In these years, he was certainly concerned by social issues: he came to reject 'global technology' as the power that was undermining human values in the Soviet Union and the United States alike and urged that the only hope for humanity lay in recovering 'the beginning of our spiritual-historical beginning' – which meant going back to what had been initiated by the Greeks.

The discrepancy between the early projected shape of Heidegger's career and his later stance of criticism was included within the contradiction that ensued, between his position as a philosopher and seeker after truth and his overwhelming acceptance of the assumptions of the National Socialist Party – which involved the leap of believing that the Führer was about to deliver the manifestation of Being that the age demanded and that in the new era he himself was destined to be a central intellectual guide. Given the state of Germany at the time, it is not altogether surprising that he should have been attracted by a movement that presented itself as offering such resolute courses of action. What is more unexpected, however, is that he should have been so ready to take on the rest of the National Socialist programme so uncritically. It was one thing to proclaim that 'the German people must choose its future and that that future was bound to the Führer',[36] or to proclaim him as 'a man of unprecedented will' who would ensure that his people would 'find again their organic unity and greatness',[37] it was quite another to follow that loyalty so uncritically as to swallow Hitler's militarism and anti-Semitism, secretly denouncing a colleague who had been a pacifist during the First World War and another who, he said, had an active Jewish connection.[38] This, after all, was the man who had earlier refused to persist with the promulgation of Catholic dogmas that would have interfered with his freedom to teach and question as a philosopher. His attitude, however, well in line with a previous statement of his concerning the growing influence of the Jews in German intellectual life, was taken to the point where he spoke of 'a dangerous international alliance of Jews' and declined to direct the doctoral dissertations of Jewish students.[39] Within a year of these events he had resigned his Rectorship, having found that his authoritarian conduct of it had brought serious trouble and that the overtures to his projected role as the Party's philosopher were being cold-shouldered; he would soon decide that the Nazi belief in 'total mobilization', so far from leading the fight against global technology that he had urged, was realizing it in a form worse than was being produced in either the Soviet Union or the United States.[40] Yet he never fully renounced his support for the Third Reich; after the war he was prohibited from teaching and was granted emeritus status in 1951 only after intervention from his university.

The chief paradox was that this philosopher of Being was himself riven at the core of his own being in a manner that evidently resonated with others of his generation who were no more capable of appreciating or understanding their affliction. Like many of his contemporaries, he had grown up in a settled environment that had seen no changes in living memory greater than those brought by Bismarck's *Kulturkampf*. From his village environment, it had been the natural progression for a gifted child to proceed into the kind of education that would enable him to study for the Catholic priesthood; proceeding in this trajectory he had been seen as a rising star of the Church, eloquent in his defence of traditional positions. It was the irruption of the First World War, with its manifestation of what war was like in an industrial society, that opened his eyes to the surrounding crisis and the need for a totally different manner of human thinking if the challenge were to be met. The crisis was further elaborated in his personal life when he met and married a Protestant, and also came to realise that he could no longer act as a Catholic philosopher if that entailed accepting the obligation to teach Catholic dogma. Yet although he acquired a new respect for Luther, he was to discover, like many before him, that it was not possible to question the religion of his forefathers without embarking on a much longer voyage. By the autumn of 1929 he was writing to Elisabeth Blochmann that, when deep roots have been put down, the past of human experience must always be returned to. 'But this return is not a passive taking over of what has been, but its transmutation. So we can only abhor contemporary Catholicism and all that goes with it, and Protestantism no less so...'[41] In the following section of his letter he showed, however, that he was ready to make further, less blanket discriminations. Compline must be more reward-ing than the High Mass, for example, since there the essential 'other-ness' of night was acknowledged, countering the assumption of modern human beings that it was simply an addendum to the day.

In view of his political record it is surprising that he achieved and maintained his high reputation as a philosopher. It was obviously in part a matter of his technical prowess, yet this was not, perhaps, the whole story. The many philosophers who beat a path to his door did so, it may be argued, because they too were responding to the incom-pleteness in contemporary philosophy that he had sensed. By concen-trating so obsessively on Being, he kept attention focused on the shortcomings of an approach which other philosophers were all too ready to resolve into conventionally framed questions.

In the coming years he would reinforce his opposition to contempor-ary Christianity, looking for the Being that lay behind all its manifesta-tions, exercising a particularly strong appeal to thinkers who valued intensity and commitment. To those who attended his late lectures, we are told, it was impressive simply to hear him ask, in his distinctive voice, 'What does it mean to think?' In these years his stress was always on the need in philosophy to question. Petzet described how, at the end of his lecture series on 'The arts in the age of technology',

> When Heidegger closed with the now-famous proposition 'Asking questions is the piety of thought', a never-ending storm of applause erupted from a thousand throats.[42]

In his later years he subsisted in an uneasy equilibrium between a sense in his audience that the practical results of his wartime activities could only be deplored and their respect for a man who had pursued his calling as a thinker with such unswerving persistence. The final contradiction lay between his barely expressed acknowledgement that he had been guilty of errors[43*] and his unwillingness to face them in detail without underestimating their magnitude and in some cases being willing to distort the record. In spite of all his criticisms of dogmatic Christianity he remained deeply attached to the church of his fathers, which in late life he claimed never to have left. Although the authorities would have preferred it if he had walked through the door of his native church in the robes of a penitent, that was not to be: in the end he went to his grave there in a subdued funeral ceremony, honoured nevertheless as 'perhaps the greatest seeker after truth this century has known'.[44] A more just assessment, if merciful enough to spare him the penitential garment and respectful of his intellectual distinction, would still have required him to face, fairly and squarely, many facts about his previous political conduct; only so could he have truly merited the robe of a great 'seeker after truth'. Heidegger is, in fact, one of the most enigmatic of the figures to be dealt with in connection with the present theme. In spite of his apparent relevance, his very self-distancing from current psychology meant that he tended to avoid close discussion of consciousness, treating the matter instead in more strictly philosophical terms and exploring the implications of the human tendency to ignore questions of Being. Much of his work belongs within the strict range of technical philosophy and need not concern us here. It is the window it opened on more practical issues that gives it relevance in the present context.

The interest in practical issues calls up Richard Rorty's critique of Heidegger's argument that if you begin with Plato's motives and assumptions, you end up with some form of Pragmatism. Since he respects Heidegger, yet does not think Pragmatism a bad place to find oneself in, he resolves to investigate the statement further, devoting himself particularly to what he sees as the inherent attitude betrayed by Heidegger, his attempt to defend the poets against the philosophers. He quotes Heidegger's poetic words, 'Being's poem, just begun, is man' and continues by asserting that the project that emerges is to present metaphysics as an inauthentic form of poetry, 'poetry which thinks of itself as antipoetry, a sequence of metaphors whose authors thought of them as escapes from metaphoricity'.[45] This kind of poetry would be exemplified in Heidegger's eyes by the writings of Hölderlin, with its nostalgia for a Greek civilization in which the gods held sway: a very different order from the rationally and technologically directed culture of the twentieth century. There is a certain appropriateness in the idea of Heidegger, the failed priest, responding so strongly to Hölderlin the failed clergyman, still leaving an irony in the fact that a poet who refined and pressed the Romantic consciousness to the limit where it toppled over into madness should have had such a response from a philosopher who spent his life exploring the alternative possibility of an escape by vaulting from consciousness into the realm of Being and viewing the world from that angle.

A different course was followed by Jean-Paul Sartre, who, like Heidegger, found psychoanalysis unattractive, and was indeed sceptical about the whole question of the unconscious, but who was more happy with traditional philosophical assumptions. All questions, in his view, must ultimately be settled through analysis of the developed consciousness by that developed consciousness itself. In this respect he remained an unflinching Cartesian. It was, ultimately, a question of power: to take the psychoanalytic view of the unconscious seemed to involve accepting an individual's lack of control of his or her own actions. The reaction was typical of a graduate from the École Normale, where philosophy was the undisputed sovereign subject. For a Cartesian the logic might seem impeccable; it also assumed that in the relationship between consciousness and being, no real discrimination was possible: consciousness must be the founding and preceding power. Any sense that Being might have its own part to play in the relationship was automatically excluded, as was the potentiality that it might be involved even in the concept of authenticity – which thus becomes simply subject to analysis of the workings of the individual's rational mind. In these circumstances Simone de Beauvoir, who accepted his superiority as a philosopher while casting herself in the alternative role of novelist, emerges as playing a similar part to that of Coleridge's in relation to Wordsworth – bowing before a strong intellectual identity while herself possessed of a ranging and discursive intelligence that could include insights into aspects of being not to be demarcated by a dominating consciousness. Toril Moi recognizes this when, invoking Coleridge's adjective for Shakespeare, she complains that no critic contemplating Beauvoir's gift for self-projection would still, it seems, be prepared to write of her as 'myriad-minded Beauvoir'.[46] It may even be the case that their examiners glimpsed something similar when, trying to discriminate between Sartre and her, they commented that Sartre was the better philosopher but that she '*was* philosophy'.[47]

The parallel between Heidegger's philosophy and Sartre's deserves to be probed further, since their common interest in questions of Being and authenticity might at first sight seem to place them in the same category. Little could be further from the truth, however. Heidegger's concerns had a strong centripetal element: despite his emphasis on selflessness one is always aware of the manner in which his statements move in and in upon themselves in an endless circling of self-referral.

That this circling does not turn into a vortex is due to Heidegger's belief in a central essence in every human being. 'We receive many gifts, of many kinds,' he writes. 'But the highest and really most lasting gift given to us is always our essential nature, with which we are gifted in such a way that we are what we are only through it. That is why we owe thanks for this endowment, first and unceasingly.'[48]

Sartre, for whom the term 'Being' was also crucial, came to feel precisely the opposite. In the 1930s he was sufficiently interested by what he heard of current philosophical movements to go to Germany and study with Heidegger, but unlike his mentor he found himself sceptical concerning an 'essential nature' in human beings. In his view they had no innate qualities, no permanent nature, but gradually created a nature for themselves as a result of their own actions. It is easy enough to see how this position was then supported when he and others saw how people of a supposedly firm identity would, in the heat of decision, act in a quite different manner from that which their previously supposed 'essential nature' might have led one to expect: the time of the Second World War and the German Occupation was a fertile period for such observation. In political terms it also meant that he emerged with a less ambiguous political reputation than Heidegger's, never having been misled by the allure of doctrines that promised an early realization of Being at a national level.

In his further thinking about such matters Sartre was prepared to foreground the term 'Being' – as, famously, in the title of his study *Being and Nothingness* (*L'Être et le Néant*). The word that appeared more frequently in his general writing, however, was 'existence'. Where Heidegger wished to go behind later Western philosophy and particularly behind Descartes, rooting himself in the ontology that he believed to have been developed by the early Greeks, Sartre never escaped the later influence; indeed, in certain respects he could be thought of as an ultimate Cartesian man. The description in *L'Âge de Raison* of Matthieu's thought-processes reads like one of a state he knew well:

Matthieu began to open gently like a wound; he saw himself exposed and as he was: thoughts, thoughts about thoughts, thoughts about thoughts of thoughts, he was transparent and corrupt beyond any finite vision. Then the vision vanished...[49]

Sartre's early development displayed a subjective consciousness that was determined to realize itself in just those terms. His major distinction, between Being-in-itself and Being-for-itself (*Être en soi* and *Être pour soi*), relied firmly on the supposition that the second is distinguished from the first by the presence of consciousness. In accordance with his beliefs he took issue constantly with the Western intellectual tendency to predicate its philosophy on the assumption that human consciousness looked back to an essence, or essences, preceding all existence; his own, opposite, assumption being, famously, that existence preceded essence. The human being found itself flung into the world and forced to make of its existence what it could. In Sartre's belief there was no God, nor were there the human essences, presupposed in a Platonic version of religion, that would support belief in a controlling Deity. In their absence, human beings must be viewed as naturally endowed with freedom and needing to make responsible use of it.

Since it is one of the attractions of Sartre's writing that his philosophical thinking was so intimately involved with his own life his autobiographical study, *Les Mots*, is of central significance as an account of the sources from which his distinctive philosophy sprang. Its narrative structure is given resonance by the allegorical story, introduced at one point, of a small boy who creeps into a train bound for Dijon and falls asleep without money, ticket or even identity card. Roused by the ticket collector, he is forced to redeem the situation by confabulation, concocting a story of the crucial importance of his journey to Dijon, while assuring himself that as long as he keeps talking he will not be thrown off the train. The ticket collector, meanwhile, remains totally silent. This, we grasp, is emblematic of Sartre's own position: cast into life without a father and existing between an elderly grandfather and grandmother and his mother, Anne-Marie – on the one hand admired as the centre of attention in the little circle, on the other reminded constantly by the adults' attitude that his views counted for nothing – he was gradually forced into the belief that he had no authority for travel, no identity. The sense of his condition was crystallized in his relation to Monsieur Simmonnot, his grandfather's collaborator, who lunched with them each week. When asked about various personal matters – his musical likings, his holiday preferences, his earlier memories –

he would pause for thought and let his mind dwell on the granite-like mountain-range of his tastes. When he had obtained the required information, he would communicate it to my mother in a detached tone, nodding his head. What a happy man he must be!, I thought, to wake up joyfully each morning and survey, from some Sublime Point, his peaks, ridges, and valleys, and then stretch himself pleasurably as he said: 'This is me all right: I am Monsieur Simmonnot whole and entire.'

As for himself,

> The stones in the Luxembourg Gardens, Monsieur Simmonnot, the chestnut trees, Karlémami were all beings. I was not. I had not got their inertia, their depth, or their inscrutability. I was *nothing*: an indelible transparency.[50]

There *was* a world available to him, however. It was opened first when his grandfather made him free of his library and when the women of the household subsequently indulged his romantic imagination by introducing him to works of adventure. There he could assume an identity, however imaginary, as the courageous adventurer who sacrifices himself to rescue the heroine. He also glimpsed the possibility of realizing himself by writing – analogous, in a sense, to the boy's compulsive need to make up a story for the silent ticket collector. But he was also to grasp another truth about himself: that it was his destiny for his identity to be realized not in stasis, but in movement. In this new phase of self-awareness he was showing himself to have entered a stage similar to the condition which the equally identity-challenged Shelley had reached in his final attraction to the sailing-boat *Ariel*. Sartre's enfranchisement differed, however, from Shelley's driving 'in the evening wind, under the summer moon, until earth appears another world'.[51] When later, as part of a series of aptitude tests in 1948, he was asked to say which gave the greatest impression of speed among various cards that he was shown – a galloping horse, a walking man, a flying eagle or a motor boat springing forward – he chose the motor-boat:

> The reason for my choice came to me immediately: when I was ten I had had the impression that my prow was cleaving the present and wrenching me away from it; since which time I have been running, am still running. Speed is conveyed, to my eyes, less by the distance covered in a specific lapse of time than by its wrenching power.[52]

His sense of Being as realized in movement is reinforced later in a moment in the Luxembourg Gardens when, after running and drenching himself with sweat, he sits down at his mother's insistence and finds himself fixed into a relentless boredom that seems to root him to that particular spot – until he gets up under an equally powerful compulsion to run again at full speed to the end of the avenue. But when he turns round nothing has changed. From this renewal of non-being he can now release himself only by returning to the library and picking up a much-read book, when the experience of nullity will be replaced at once by restoration of the familiar grouping in which he is three people: himself, reading, the famous novelist he will be and the descendant who will one day appreciate his achievement:

> I do not stir or glance at the show. I carry on my reading like a good boy, the lights eventually go out and all I can feel is a rhythm, an irresistible urge. I am unmooring, I have unmoored, I am moving forward and the engine is purring. I experience the speed of my soul.[53]

This revised version of Being has various effects. First, any vestigial Platonic basis for his thought, by which he possessed an original form of Being, disappears, to be replaced by the presumption that his Being consists in movement, as if he is now confident of it only when it is in motion. Yet physical movement does not altogether do the trick: what he ultimately needs is the sense of movement as it is found in reading. Secondly, it follows that what might be thought of as his personality will necessarily be in a perpetual process of change, with the result that instead of having what might in another person be regarded as an abiding 'character' there will be rather a constant proclivity to treachery:

> In vain I have put myself wholly into what I undertake or given myself unreservedly to work, anger, or friendship; in a moment, I shall deny myself. I know this, and want it and I am already betraying myself, in the heat of passion, by the joyful anticipation of my future betrayal.[54]

In this self-recognition Sartre perfects the development that was initiated when thinkers such as Thomas Hobbes began to appreciate the implications of a world in which the ultimate reality must be approached not as solid substance but as motion. But where that realisation was formerly restricted to physical movement, as when Wordsworth's 'Lover' moved in trance-like motion on horseback towards his 'Lucy', only to experience later the devastating knowledge that by her unexpected death she herself had now become one with the gravitational movement of the whole world, so Sartre came to see that the human being was, equally, 'seizable' only in terms of change and movement.

It was, in one sense at least, something he had always known since childhood:

> doubt never crossed my mind: trotting along, chattering, fascinated by what was going on in the street, I never stopped renewing my skin and I could hear the old skins falling one on top of the other. When I went back up the Rue Soufflot, I felt at each step, as the dazzling rows of shop-windows went by, the movement of my life, its law and the noble mandate of being unfaithful to everything.[55]

Yet even so, the death of his Platonism was necessarily slow. There came a day when he thought idly of God and found with a mild surprise that he was no longer there; even later the Holy Ghost, guarantor of his career as a great novelist, also disappeared. But the vanishing of these metaphysical pillars did not involve the disappearance of the personality they supported, for that was already a non-entity. What they had created remained in its own right, a personality always ready to reassemble at any moment; Sartre now knew that he could go on living under the assumption that he was a chosen one until he chose for himself to be otherwise.

In view of his background, he was nevertheless an unusually complex and interesting example of mid-twentieth-century humanity. He might exist as a human projectile, but had at the same time inherited, inescapably, a quite distinctive personality, associated with his original rootedness in a post-Revolutionary French culture which, as embodied in his family, was already deeply anachronistic. Human beings of the next century might look on in wonder but would not be able to repeat the particular moment of culture that he embodied: for them only the presumption that being is identifiable with a conscious response to change and motion would remain.

All this creates a problem for Sartre as novelist. *La Nausée* presents, from beginning to end, the situation of its hero, with a corresponding sense of the opacity presented by those with whom he deals. Over and over again the dominating presence is that of Roquentin and his streams of consciousness, rendered with psychological subtlety. The result is that there can be no novel in the more dramatic sense, with strong patterns of interaction between characters. At the end, Roquentin does indeed envisage the making of a fine work of art, prompted by his love for the song 'Some of these days', which has convinced him of the worth of the composer and the black woman who sang it; from it he derives a final hope that he might rival their achievement by writing a novel:

> you would have to guess, behind the printed words, behind the pages, something which didn't exist, which was above existence. The sort of story, for example, which could never happen, an adventure. It would have to be beautiful and hard as steel and make people ashamed of their existence.

This would be a very different novel from the one we have just been reading, though that could be said to revolve around and be haunted by just such a concept of art – which is a perfecting of the rational state that Raquentin embodies. In the novel there is at least one other significant personage, Anny, but between them there is no real relationship. Even when he finally re-encounters her, late in the work, the reader is made emphatically aware of her own subjectivity, which attracts but also baffles Roquentin as he tries still – with little success, it seems – to read her.

There is, of course, no firm specification of the rules to which a novel must conform to be valid, but some critics would find a lack in a novel which does not include intersubjective activity between characters. Iris Murdoch, who as critic and novelist was well placed to judge Sartre, commented shrewdly on this deficiency, contrasting Sartre's attitude with that of George Eliot, who shows Dorothea Brooke coming to grasp that her desiccated husband, like all human beings, still had 'an equivalent centre of self, whence the lights and shadows must always fall with a certain difference'.[56] As she points out, 'The grasp which his characters have of each other seems flimsy if we compare it with the joyful and terrible apprehension of each other of, for instance, Anna Karenina and Vronsky' – the reason being, she suggests, that in the presentation of his characters he endows them with 'an excess of lucidity and transparency'.[57] This is to the point: and of course what is being so presented in a pure form is their consciousness. There is no suggestion of their having Being in any solid sense, for in Sartre's terms any such acquisition could only be as seen in terms of existing and choosing. The artist that Murdoch finds most nearly equivalent to him is Virginia Woolf, with her vision of life as 'a luminous halo, a semi-transparent envelope surrounding us from the beginning of consciousness to the end'.[58] The difference in the case of Woolf, as we shall see later, is that she did not exclude the possibility of a relationship between consciousness and Being, so that the 'luminous halo' could be closer to forming an essential part of the character's existence – whereas for Sartre it would be bound up with transition. The potentiality not dealt with in his writing is that of a full human relationship not only between two consciousnesses, but also between two 'Beings', each of whom may experience the other not as a restraint on their freedom but as an opportunity, whether for discovery, appreciation and delight or for apprehension and terror. The term 'Being' will still be unsatisfactory if it suggests anything like a rigidity of character; for that reason George Eliot's term 'centre of self' is better in this context. But the existence of such a stable centre in other people continues to be the assumption from which most proceed – even if its stability is no more than that of a nucleus, constantly lending form to the appearances which they in their turn present to others.

It is implicit in this argument that when we try to deal with a human 'Being' we find ourselves trying to apprehend neither a fixed character nor an ungraspable cluster of energies but an *intermundium* between the two modes. It is for this reason that Sartre is so fascinated by words, which are the closest we come to approaching experience in a manner that offers the possibility of 'making sense'. Yet the bias of his mind is such that he will always lean towards their mobility rather than their offers of permanence; just as his personal emphasis will always be on himself in the act of writing rather than on the study of what emerges. Throughout his career he was notably careless of the fate of what he had written, once it reached the page. In *Les Mots*, on the other hand, he muses at one point on the fantasy that his first book will cause a scandal, after which his work will remain unpublished, until in the end the chance discovery of a manuscript, unknown to him, brings him fame.[59] (In his last years the fulfilment of the prophecy took quite an opposite form when a friend reported how he had looked at what Sartre had tried to write following a late operation and was heartbroken to find it totally illegible.[60])

Most typically, Sartre's feeling for mobility took the form of endless, unresting journeys across the real world to uncover injustices wherever they were to be found in order to write about them. With the aid of newly developed air travel, he was able to visit countries in Africa and the Far East. His concerns were equally basic; for him the clearest form of injustice was to be found in the practice of torture. As he travelled he came to see that the most pure form of action might in fact be reaction. Where for Heidegger Being resolved itself into a pure essence, for Sartre it became an existence of moving energies that could be realized only in response to other moving energies, under the aegis of a consciousness that recognised very few moral sanctions, the inadmissibility of torture in any human context being a notable exception. Heidegger might retreat to his forests, Sartre might keep in motion, 'impatient as the wind', but neither man glimpsed the sense of a Being in the very life of nature that had for a time enwrapped their Romantic English predecessors.

The most recent figure to be considered here, Václav Havel, developed a conception of Being that was closer to Coleridge's in certain respects, including a tendency on occasion to emerge as an anti-philosopher. So far as they belong to a tradition, the roots of his thinking are with Heidegger, and with the European exploration of existentialism and phenomenology, particularly as mediated through the seminars of Jan Patocka.[61] However, Havel himself warns his readers that he is not using his terms with philosophical rigour: 'I am not a philosopher,' he writes, 'and it is not my ambition to construct a conceptually fixed system.'[62] His writing is to be read rather as the record of a lived inquiry: he would no doubt have joined in the applause that greeted Heidegger's 'Asking questions is the piety of thought'.

Whereas Sartre's ideas developed against his experience of Nazi domination, which gave him a sympathy with the communism it sought to destroy, Havel's sense of Being was shaped radically by encounters with communist totalitarianism: as a firm opponent to the repressive regime in Czechoslovakia, he suffered long periods of imprisonment for speaking out. Various of his writings during the period, gathered in the volume *Living in Truth*, bore witness to his acuteness in observing how the party operated during this period to keep a whole country under domination. The deeper nature of his concerns emerges in another set of his writings, the *Letters to Olga*, written to his wife during the periods when he was in prison between 1979 and 1982. To read these is to learn the exact process by which he came to his own concern with the question of 'what we are and what we are capable of becoming'.

In 1977 an incident took place which deeply affected his thinking for some years afterwards. Under detention by the authorities, he was undergoing interrogations that were leading nowhere. It occurred to him one evening to put in a request to the authorities which he thought he worded very cleverly, contriving to ask for release while saying nothing that he did not believe or that was not true. It was a gesture worthy of the Good Soldier Schweik. For some time nothing happened; but then to his surprise he was told that in all probability he would be set free and that 'political use' would be made of his request. At that moment he realised that he had, in fact, been guilty of an act of self-betrayal, and that however cleverly he had phrased his request it would be read as a sign that he had reneged on his former principles and said what the authorities wanted to hear in order to get himself out of jail. His resulting crisis of political conscience involved asking more urgently questions that had already been present in some of his plays, concerning the nature of our individual existence and where it is to be located. This inquiry lasted all through the second period of imprisonment and is the subject of many letters – letters all the more remarkable for the fact that he was prohibited by the prison authorities from discussing the conditions in which he found himself, which must therefore when one is reading be imagined by way of what is otherwise known. But even when this knowledge is absent from the mind they present the moving spectacle of a human being trying to interpret his existence under conditions of considerable stress. More than either Heidegger or Sartre, he showed himself capable of rigorous moral self-judgement. In a later speech, accepting an honorary degree in Jerusalem,[63] he commented on his own persistent sense of guilt –

> a profound, banal, and therefore utterly vague sensation of culpability, as though my very existence were a kind of sin. Then there is a powerful feeling of general alienation, both my own and relating to everything around me, that helps to create such feelings; an experience of unbearable oppressiveness, a need constantly to explain myself to someone, to defend myself, a longing for an unattainable order of things, a longing that increases as the terrain I walk through becomes more muddled and confusing.

In this respect one is again reminded of Coleridge, throughout whose writing, from 'The Eolian Harp' to his 'Epitaph', unexpected outbursts of guilt well up. Coleridge once said that he could not recall a time when he had not been 'preyed upon by some Dread ... from fear of Pain, or Shame'; on another occasion he filled out his own initials as 'Sinful, Tormented Culprit'.[64] His attitude to his own guilt was less consistent than Havel's, however, wavering constantly between such severe self-examination and extraordinary feats of self-deception.

Both Coleridge and Wordsworth had anticipated Havel in feeling the need to put their discussions concerning questions of Being to practical use. Living in similarly troubled times, they left behind speculations on the 'one Life', endeavouring instead to overcome the manifest vacillations of contemporary society by working for the establishment of fixed principles in political life. While serving as a secretary at Malta, Coleridge was led to praise his superior, Sir Alexander Ball, as one who had exhibited admirable independence of mind:

> never was a man more completely uninfluenced by authority than Sir Alexander Ball, never one who sought less to tranquillize his own doubts by the mere suffrage and coincidence of others. The ablest suggestions had no conclusive weight with him, till he had abstracted the opinion from its author, till he had reduced it into a part of his own mind.[65]

This characteristic informed all Ball's political actions. In Czechoslovakia, similarly, a prime reason for the respect in which Havel came to be held was a sense of his personal qualities, as displayed in his quiet stand throughout the years of repression. He was not particularly strident in opposition, simply firm. As someone said of him, he managed always to speak as if censorship did not exist, his main concern being to present a disinterested account of the lack of liberty in his society.

His mixture of independence and moral principle emerges again in the speech he sent in acceptance of the peace prize he was awarded in Germany in 1989, at a time when he was still unable to accept it in person.[66] The discourse is particularly striking by reason of its emphasis on the power of words: sharing George Orwell's fascination with the manner in which they can be manipulated in addressing those who do not attend to them too directly he spoke of the way in which the word 'peace' had at times become almost meaningless in view of the violence that had been countenanced in its name; he also dwelt on the fate of the word 'socialism'. A word expressing ideals for which people were at one time prepared to die had in latter days become one that simply provoked laughter if invoked as a reason for undertaking a particular course of action, however worthwhile it might otherwise seem to be.

During his meditations on these matters, his perception of the problems and paradoxes of the current state of things also led him to express awe concerning the more general power that words can exercise. The move towards endorsement of the Western way of life that was associated with the underground movement in Czechoslovakia, later to come into the open, was perfectly understandable, given the greater freedoms that it sanctioned, yet the exercise of that freedom might easily produce no more than the exchange of one kind of materialist system for another. The market, in other words, might prove to be as powerfully authoritarian as was a centralised system of government, the only difference being that in the new case it would not be possible to hold anyone directly responsible for its actions.

Havel did not stop at social and political protest. His urgent and immediate concerns prompted him to affirm the word's social power:

I live in a country which, 21 years ago was shaken by a text from the pen of my friend Ludvik Vaculík. And as if to confirm my conclusions about the power of words, he entitled his statement: 'Two thousand words'. Among other things, that manifesto served as one of the pretexts for the invasion of our country one night by five foreign armies. And it is by no means fortuitous that as I write these words, the present regime in my country is being shaken by a single page of text entitled, again, as if to illustrate what I am saying: 'A few words'.

Yes, I really do inhabit a system in which words are capable of shaking the entire structure of government, where words can prove mightier than 10 military divisions, where Solzhenitsyn's words of truth were regarded as something so dangerous that it was necessary to bundle their author into an aeroplane and transport him. Yes, in the part of the world I inhabit the word Solidarity was capable of shaking an entire power bloc.

Caught into a totalitarian situation, Havel declared that the word with this power had it because it was also the word of truth: he was thus affirming his conviction that, in the end, human beings would always be bound to attend to it. He could not pursue that connection far, however, without asking who or what guaranteed that truth; this involved him in exploring more intricate questions, again close to those that, once again, had fascinated English Romantic predecessors such as Coleridge at the turn of the nineteenth century. After the first heady days of the French Revolution the actions of the revolutionaries, with their rationalism and their worship devoted to the Supreme Being, had come to look as despotic as those of the Bourbons they had overthrown. In face of this intractability, Coleridge had asked the same question as Havel – what is it that gives distinctiveness to human beings and inspires faith that they will not submit to systematic oppression for ever? And his attempts at finding an answer had brought him back in a similar way to the mystery of the Word.

In his case that sense of mystery took more than one form. Earlier it had been a product of his own imaginative experience as a poet, reflecting the strange process by which words seem to rise up from some unknown source within. In its simplest form it answered to a phenomenon experienced by artists who initiate a work only to find that the creative processes at work are not entirely under their own control. The theme was particularly attractive to him during his early years, when he was still working through the idea that there might be something to be learned from all religions, those that seemed to be founded on pantheism as well as those which were founded upon belief in a transcendent deity.

During this period he was evidently fascinated by the existence of such extraordinary resources of creativity in the mind, which not only helped explain the power of the word but suggested that it might be very much more, even a key to nature and the divine. Such speculations carried obvious dangers: to see the process by which words were created as corresponding in some sense to the divine creativity was to risk a charge of extraordinary presumption. In his later writings he dealt with them by grounding the word more solidly in the Word of St John's Gospel, the divine Logos that was in the beginning and through which all things were created. Increasingly his aim was to return his readers to awareness of their own imaginations, where he believed that they could discover, in humility, a hidden affinity with the Word of Christianity that was the authoritative and driving presence behind all human words.

Havel developed a similar fear of making over-ambitious claims for the human mind. He closed his acceptance speech with some remarks about European civilisation and 'the imperceptible transformation of what was originally a humble message into an arrogant one' – our belief, in other words, that we are capable of understanding totally our own history:

> Having learnt all those lessons, we should all fight together against arrogant words and keep a weather eye out for any insidious germs of arrogance in words that are seemingly humble.
>
> Obviously this is not just a linguistic task. Responsibility for and towards words is a task that is intrinsically ethical. As such,

however, it is situated beyond the horizon of the visible world, in that realm wherein dwells the Word that was in the beginning and is not the word of Man.

The affirmation invokes the same verse of St John's Gospel as Coleridge's; at the same time, there is little sign that Havel had returned, as his predecessor did, to the fold of orthodox Christianity: it is rather as if he was reading Christianity in the mode of a great allegory, representing the larger life of human beings. Trying to convey his attitude to philosophy he dwelt on the fact that although his own sympathies tended to lie with the Judaeo-Christian order of belief they were not limited by that:

To be more specific it seems to me foolish, impossible and utterly pointless, for instance, to try to reconcile Darwin with Christ, or Marx with Heidegger, or Plato with Buddha. Each of them represents a certain level of being and human experience and each bears witness to the world in his own particular way; each of them, to some extent and in some way, speaks to me, explains many things to me, and even helps me to live, and I simply don't see why, for the sake of one, I should be denied an authentic experience of whatever another can show me, even more so because we are not talking here about different opinions on the same thing, but different ways of talking about very different things.[67]

One virtue of this mediating position is that it preserves those who hold it not only from undue arrogance but also from blinkered devotion. Havel has a long passage about the way in which an authentic philosophy grounded in Being can easily slide into a sense of conviction to be described only as fanaticism. This he believes is the trap awaiting those who

cannot resist the attractive force of self-deception, the kind that hides self-surrender to existence-in-the-world beneath the illusion that it is a particularly radical form of orientation toward Being. The essence of this idea is the notion that transferring primordial self-transcendence from the boundlessness of the dream to the reality of human actions is a one-shot affair, that all you have to do is to 'come up with an idea' and then blindly serve it – that is, create some intellectual project that permanently fixes and fulfills the original intention – to be relieved of the duty and effort of constantly aspiring toward Being: for in its place there is a handy substitute – the relatively undemanding duty of devoted service to a given project.

That state he goes on to identify in terms of a familiar condition, akin to the fanaticism that Coleridge (who more than once distinguished positiveness from certainty[68]) discusses in more psychological terms.[69] The true sense of Being, as perceived by both Havel and Coleridge, was less easily seized – so mysterious, indeed, that it was easily mis-identified by restricting one's vision to a single facet or a single movement.

Another speculator on identity, Vladimir Nabokov, was equally critical of such reductionism, insisting that he himself could not be summed up by any neat summation, whether of his upbringing or of his genes:

the individual mystery remains to tantalize the memorist. Neither in environment nor in heredity can I find the exact instrument that fashioned me, that anonymous roller that pressed upon my life a certain intricate watermark whose unique design becomes visible when the lamp of art is made to shine through life's foolscap.[70]

It is a brilliant metaphor for the sureness, yet elusiveness, of Being when thought of simply in terms of personal identity – expressing with accuracy how it is hardly, if ever, to be seen directly and can therefore only be elucidated by special means. Nabokov thus escapes the twin dangers of seeking an imagery of Being either, like Heidegger, in a rooted tree and a forest, or, like Sartre, in an endless transience. It is another way of suggesting that it can be appreciated by human beings only through the twofold nature of the Word – which in turn can be fully apprehended only by adopting a similar versatility of the mind.

Coming to terms with Being involves, in other words, a corresponding double-guardedness, a subtlety of mind that will not allow itself to be contained by a simple fixed image at one extreme or by the lure of infinite energies at the other. It is for this reason that the concept of the Word is so necessary to it, existing in the consciousness as a perpetual reminder of its twofold quality. Another reminder is to be found in the nature of life itself, which in Havel's case draws him into territory where the earlier Coleridge had also travelled. He is fascinated by the idea of the 'collective spirit' of humanity:

none of us knows what is lodged in our subconscious, what archetypal experiences we've inherited from thousands of years of human
existence, what tortuous ways they follow before finally surfacing in
our 'existential praxis'. Even less do we understand the mysteries of
the 'psychic field': what if individual existences are really only
nodes in a single gigantic intersubjective network?[71]

Or, as Coleridge had put it in an early poem,

> ... what if all of animated nature
> Be but organic Harps diversly fram'd,
> That tremble into thought, as o'er them sweeps
> Plastic and vast, one intellectual Breeze,
> At once the Soul of each, and God of all?[72]

The reasons for Coleridge's abrupt rejection of this statement in the
next lines of his poem and for his subsequent turning away from any
belief that might encourage a pantheistic view in favour of a Christian
stance that would mediate between tradition and innovation are
illuminated by considering Havel's embracing of human responsibility
through development of a sense of guilt and by his increasing sense of
reverence for 'the Word'.

On a larger scale, Havel devotes a sequence of his letters to meditations on the relationship between what he calls the 'order of life' and
the 'order of death', a topic closer to that which had engaged Coleridge
and Wordsworth at the turn of the century. He asserts that 'the
meaning of life' is 'not only unlike information or a commodity that
can be freely passed on, it isn't even 'objectively' knowable or gras-
pable as a concept', continuing:

> Though we cannot 'respond' to it in the traditional sense of the
> word, nevertheless, by longing for it and seeking after it, we in fact
> indirectly confront it over and over again. In this regard, we are a
> little like a blind man touching the woman he loves, whom he has
> never seen and never will.

When Coleridge was describing in 1802 the qualities that were
required of a poet he wrote '... a great Poet must be, implicitly if not
explicitly a profound Metaphysician. He may not have it in logical
coherence, in his Brain & Tongue; but he must have it by Tact...' – one

of the instances he gave of such tact being 'the Touch of a Blind Man feeling the face of a darling Child'.[73]

Other writers have shared this sense that what matters most to them is a sense of physical life itself. P.N. Furbank has described how E.M. Forster conveyed the impression that above all he lived the imaginative life: 'It was, to him, the rule and aim of his existence and was entwined with his sense for what – for want of a better word – he called 'life'. He felt as if, on occasion, he could see through to 'life': could hear its wing-beat, could grasp it not just as a generality but as a palpable presence.'[74] This sense of life as something which could be apprehended in its fullness by a person possessed of sufficient sensitivity, demanding in its process a full engagement of the physical senses, lay deep in English Romanticism; deriving first from early work by Coleridge and the Wordsworths. Modified by the acute introspections of Coleridge and the natural observations and moral reflections of all three it had initiated a distinctive yet complex sense of Being which, I have previously argued, could exercise its influence on their successors, affecting writers who ranged from De Quincey to Tennyson. The present volume has shown how it could extend its tentacles even into the work of a writer as 'unintellectual' at first sight as Dickens. Presenting an alternative to the more straightforward philosophical thinking of Heidegger and Sartre and extending beyond even the more literary intuitions of a Havel, it would continue to show its presence in English and American writers of the twentieth century – particularly those who remained in any way in touch with earlier English Romantic thinking.

5
Woolf's Moments; Lawrence's Daemon

When she first read Lawrence, Virginia Woolf was not attracted, the few works she sampled seeming to her inadequate. Returning to look at it more seriously in 1931, after his death, she was immediately struck by the power of the novel she then chose, *Sons and Lovers*. 'The book,' she wrote,

> excites, irritates, moves, changes, seems full of stir and unrest and desire for something withheld, like the body of the hero. The whole world – it is proof of the writer's remarkable strength – is broken and tossed by the magnet of the young man who cannot bring the separate parts into a unity which will satisfy him.[1]

She was evidently troubled by an art that seemed so sure of itself, yet which was completely unlike her own: 'whatever we are shown seems to have a moment of its own. Nothing rests secure to be looked at.' Her comment serves to emphasize what was distinctive about her own idea of 'the moment': that it did rely on establishing such a point of stability. She had evidently failed also to appreciate what he was doing, attributing the restlessness she found in his art to his social background, his desire to move from a working-class to a middle-class setting, without seeing how intimately it was involved with his sense of the nature of life itself. This was strange in view of her devotion to Roger Fry, who insisted on the difference between an organic and a mechanical view of things, but it helps to elucidate her conception of 'the moment', which she had explored, along with the whole problem of bringing time into consciousness, in various essays and fictions. Early in the Second World War she gave a lecture to the Workers' Educational Association in which she spoke of the ways in which novel-writing had changed, assigning much of the responsibility for the alteration to the ways in which earlier writers had been not only settled in their security and basic assumptions, but aware of the limitations within which they could write – the 'box of toys', as she put it, which was there for them to play with – whereas writers since then believed that anything was justified in pursuit of the truth of their experience.[2] Such statements concerning the nature of fictional (and indeed all artistic) production were linked to her thoughts concerning the relationship between conscious and unconscious processes: drawing on an analogy between the way in which a day of crowded and tiring experience can, after a time, become clarified by memory into a more significant pattern, she spoke of the writer's way of dealing with experience:

> After a hard day's work, trudging round, seeing all he can, feeling all he can, taking in the book of his mind innumerable notes, the writer becomes – if he can – unconscious. In fact his under-mind works at top speed while his upper-mind drowses. Then, after a pause the veil lifts; and there is the thing – the thing he wants to write about – simplified, composed. Do we strain Wordsworth's famous saying about emotion recollected in tranquillity when we infer that by tranquillity he meant that the writer needs to become unconscious before he can create?[3]*

The process is in fact an equivalent to Wordsworth's 'spots of time',[4] where there is the same experience of activity followed by passivity in the midst of which the creative experience rises up as if by magic, the difference being that in *The Prelude* the activity is as often physical as it is mental. Between the wars she had written a number of autobiographical reminiscences for the Memoir Club, where she made statements still more relevant to the concerns of the present book. Her theory was that in life there were certain experiences, which she described as 'moments of being' (roughly equivalent, it might seem, to Joyce's 'epiphanies'), which impressed themselves with a sense of heightened reality.[5]

In these sketches she also wrote of two of her earliest kinds of experience, without clarifying exactly how they differed for her, except to say that some she thought of as ecstatic, some as rapturous. Her description of the first kind revolves around memories of early morning at St Ives:

> Sound and sight seem to make equal parts of these first impressions. When I think of the early morning in bed I also hear the caw of

rooks falling from a great height. The sound seems to fall through an elastic, gummy air; which holds it up; which prevents it from being sharp and distinct. The quality of the air above Talland House seemed to suspend sound, to let it sink down slowly, as if it were caught in a blue gummy veil. The rooks cawing is part of the waves breaking – one, two, one, two – and the splash as the wave drew back and then it gathered again, and I lay there half awake, half asleep, drawing in such ecstasy as I cannot describe.

The second kind of experience was more positively sensual, a mingling of apples, gardens, bees, flowers and leaves, creating a voluptuous blend that seemed

> to hum round one such a complete rapture of pleasure that I stopped, smelt; looked. But again I cannot describe that rapture. It was rapture rather than ecstasy.[6]

What, in her eyes, was the difference between rapture and ecstasy? She does not characterize them further here, but it is notable that the one kind seemed characterized by a certain hollowness, corresponding perhaps to the sensing of an equivalent emptiness in her own being, while rapture undoubtedly brought a sense of fullness.

As she attempts to explore the complexity of these experiences further, moving forward in time, she describes a remembered descent into pure passivity:

> I was fighting with Thoby on the lawn. We were pommelling each other with our fists. Just as I raised my fist to hit him, I felt: why hurt another person? I dropped my hand instantly, and stood there, and let him beat me. I remember the feeling. It was a feeling of hopeless sadness. It was as if I became aware of something terrible; and of my own powerlessness. I slunk off alone, feeling horribly depressed.[7]

Equally, however, she could experience extreme satisfaction, as once in the garden at St. Ives:

> I was looking at the flower bed by the front door. 'That is the whole,' I said. I was looking at a plant with a spread of leaves; and it seemed suddenly plain that the flower itself was a part of the earth; that a ring enclosed what was the flower; and that was the real

flower; part earth; part flower. It was a thought I put away as being likely to be very useful to me later.[8]

At other times such experiences could be of horror, her most vivid memory being of a Mr Valpy, who had been staying at St Ives and who, she later overheard her father saying, had killed himself.

The next thing I remember is being in the garden at night and walking on the path by the apple tree. It seemed to me that the apple tree was connected with the horror of Mr Valpy's suicide. I could not pass it. I stood there looking at the grey-green creases of the bark – it was a moonlit night – in a trance of horror. I seemed to be dragged down, hopelessly, into some pit of absolute despair from which I could not escape. My body seemed paralysed.[9]

At this point she turns to discuss the relationship between these moments and her creativity, arguing that despite the fact that the first and third proved so numbing the felt need to explain them was in the long run energizing to her, since the second, rapturous kind had given her a firm conviction that all these experiences afforded an insight into the existence of a 'real thing behind appearances' which she could make real by putting into words – leading to the greatest pleasure known to her:

It is the rapture I get when in writing I seem to be discovering what belongs to what; making a scene come right; making a character come together.[10]

This, it seems, is the true difference that rapture makes. Ecstasy is simply a visitation, unbidden and unworked for, whereas rapture involves an outward pressing of some kind, in accord with certain experiences of satisfaction. It belongs to a realm that has nothing to do with the experiences of everyday, on the other hand, which belong to what she has just called 'non-being'. Drawing on her memory of a single day, for example, she has been remembering how she had read Chaucer and Madame Lafayette's memoirs, and observed the colour of the willows on her walk, but also how these vividnesses had been embedded in much more that was 'non-being', 'a kind of nondescript cotton wool'.[11] This indiscriminate mass, she believes, actually veils what is revealed in moments of shock or rapture –

that behind the cotton wool is hidden a pattern; that we – I mean all human beings – are connected with this; that the whole world is a work of art; that we are parts of the work of art. *Hamlet* or a Beethoven quartet is the truth about this vast mass that we call the world, But there is no Shakespeare, there is no Beethoven; certainly and emphatically there is no God; we are the words; we are the music; we are the thing itself. And I see this when I have a shock.[12]

In some respects her 'moments of being' could equally be termed, in the expression favoured by Hardy, 'moments of vision'. One recalls her 'intuitive notion' – mentioned in 'A Sketch of the Past' –

the sensation that we are sealed vessels afloat on what it is convenient to call reality; and at some moments the sealing matter cracks; in floods reality; that is, these scenes – for why do they survive undamaged year after year unless they are made of something comparatively permanent? Is this liability to scenes the origin of my writing impulse?[13]

The most striking feature of this is its bent towards an objectivizing of reality, a disinclination to recognize that her experiences may after all be subjective, projected on to the external world. She could also contemplate such matters more dispassionately, however, as when, in the same memoir, she considered in succession three characters whom she remembered with a sense of wholeness. These characters, whom she regarded, she said, rather in the way that Dickens might see minor ones in his fiction, had reached this wholeness, she thought, because they had died when she was still young, so that there had been no need to make any later adjustment to accord with her later perceptions of them. It was as if once they were removed from the world of continuous and present perception they could round themselves into firm 'being', free from any artistic necessity to be considered further.

Her various statements deserve additional attention, as providing important clues to what is crucial elsewhere in her art. They help to explain, for instance, why, as she herself acknowledges, she could not easily describe the world of the ordinary to the level achieved by writers such as Jane Austen or Tolstoy. It also gives a new view of Being, one that regards it as accessible to consciousness at some level yet existing in a dimension different from any considered so far, since she refuses to acknowledge the existence of creative individual geniuses, let alone a God. Such a view looks forward to the world of the post-modern, which may reach different conclusions, but from similar presuppositions.

Virginia Woolf was one of the first to perceive the fuller implications of the post-fiduciary world that had been initiated by the controversies of the mid-nineteenth century. Her father, while acknowledging it with sorrow, had still lived according to a morality associated with Christian precepts; as she grew up into the world he and like-minded doubters had framed for her, she recognized it more clearly to be a world from which ultimate signposts and marks had been removed, even if closer ones were retained.

The 'moment', at first sight a source of stability in her universe, was, one comes to appreciate, the shifting stage on which her problems were dramatized. How could it be made definite, when its very essence was to be otherwise? The central problem was to grasp the difficulty of sustaining a sensitive existence within the flux of the time-process. In dealing with it she tried several methods. *Mrs Dalloway,* with its attempts to seize characteristic moments, was perhaps her most successful attempt, exemplified in the sketch near the beginning:

> For Heaven only knows why one loves it so, how one sees it so, making it up, building it round one, tumbling it, creating it every moment afresh.... In people's eyes, in the swing, tramp, and trudge; in the bellow and the uproar; the carriages, motor cars, omnibuses, vans, sandwich men shuffling and swinging; brass bands; barrel organs; in the triumph and the jingle and the strange high singing of some aeroplane overhead was what she loved; life; London; this moment of June.[14]

How to encapsulate such a variety of sense-experiences into a single whole which would yet have a recognizable coherence, this was her task, her labour.

Inasmuch as it was a question of authority it was being pursued also by T.S. Eliot, though in a different manner: traumatized, like Lawrence, by the horrors of the First World War, he resolved instead to look back to the permanent elements in civilization that had been negated by the events leading up to it. In particular he wanted to eliminate the cult of individual personality that had characterized much Romantic writing. There was for him no point in probing the being of the individual in the hope of gaining insight into the nature of Being, for the individual, as such, was necessarily alienated from it, ineluctably flawed and blameworthy. The writer must therefore concentrate attention on the monuments of civilization, the great classics that had resisted the ravages of time: there, if anywhere, would be found the clues to reality. Even a drama such as *Hamlet*, which posed the very question 'To be or not to be', must be judged an artistic failure. The search for a true objectivity, a fully valid authority, would lead even further back, notably to writers such as Virgil and Dante.

Virginia Woolf was less convinced by the need for authority. With a father who was at one and the same time a leading 'authority' and a profound questioner of 'authority', she found it more rewarding to explore the territory between the two versions. She was also a radical observer of the ways in which, for her society, 'authority' reflected the masculine. In the course of time Eliot came closer to agreement at least in one respect. His interest in political authority might run into the sands as the negative effects of fascism became more evident, yet if anything his suspicion of any basis for it in the individual increased. If, as with Middleton Murry, it was respected as the 'inner voice', it called for dismissal:

> The possessors of the inner voice ride ten in a compartment to a football match at Swansea, listening to the inner voice, which breathes the eternal message of vanity, fear, and lust.[15]

If there was to be any revelation to the individual it must be sought (and here he agreed with Virginia Woolf) in the 'moment'. Not, however, a 'moment of being': for him there was no such thing. A 'moment of vision' possibly; but in that case a vision beyond the individual and the individual's normal means of organizing experience, elusive as the unconscious it illuminated when caught by

> the hidden laughter
> Of children in the foliage
> Quick now, here, now, always...

That was the point he had reached in 1935. As the years passed, bringing with them the full horrors of Nazism and Fascism, the authority of the 'timeless moment' grew to be something that transcended even the best of European and even world writing, to be apprehended,

if at all, by the saint – for only the saint could renounce individual
being and so discover the secret of true Being:

> In order to arrive there,
> To arrive where you are, to get from where you are not,
> You must go by a way wherein there is no ecstasy...
> In order to arrive at what you are not
> You must go through the way in which you are not.[16]

This is the opposite of Woolf's moment: ecstasy is specifically
excluded. Being demands the renunciation of individual 'being'. Even
while her vision was being transposed into a more complex version in
Between the Acts, moreover, his was extending, to apprehend, in its own
way, the nature of human time. No longer was the timeless moment
given the absolute authority which made ridiculous 'the waste sad time
stretching before and after'; there was also a place for redeemed time:

> Not the intense moment
> Isolated, with no before and after,
> But a lifetime burning in every moment
> And not the lifetime of one man only
> But of old stones that cannot be deciphered.[17]

In the end, in *Little Gidding*, the last of the *Quartets*, he succeeded in
wedding the intensity of the moment out of time to his sense of the historical in time by way of his feeling for the seventeenth-century English
Church. Here he could bring together two kinds of 'moment' – the
instantaneous, unseizable, timeless moment and that which emblema-
tizes the history of all lives in the fact of death – in a single statement:
'The moment of the rose and the moment of the yew-tree | Are of equal
duration'. He continued:

> a people without history
> Is not redeemed from time, for history is a pattern
> Of timeless moments.

Burnt Norton could now be returned to for a hint, at least, of what
paradise regained would be like:

> At the source of the longest river
> The voice of the hidden waterfall

> And the children in the apple-tree
> Not known, because not looked for
> But heard, half-heard, in the stillness
> Between two waves of the sea.

Again, this is not Virginia Woolf's moment; it corresponds rather to Blake's paradox: 'Between two moments bliss is ripe'. Between two waves of the sea the stillness might give, if only negatively, a sense of the moment, showing how it might be apprehended *within* the kind of experience he describes, but for Eliot the moment itself cannot be *caught* in the manner attempted by Woolf; indeed the core of this poem turns out to lie not in time or the timeless but in fire – the very fire that annihilates individual being:

> The dove descending breaks the air
> With flame of incandescent terror
> Of which the tongues declare
> The one discharge from sin and error.
> The only hope, or else despair
> Lies in the choice of pyre or pyre –
> To be redeemed from fire by fire.

While Lawrence's impersonality results directly from the attempt to reach back into instincts shared with the animal, allowing them to work in the consciousness unimpeded, Eliot's comes from a concentration on the objective elements in writing, accentuating in consequence elements such as style.

Virginia Woolf lighted on a third way of impersonality, the result, not of negating the personal with Eliot, nor of withdrawing into the depths of its constituent vitalism with Lawrence, but of transcending the personality, while including all its elements, by greater comprehension within a given group. A key text here is Bernard's late soliloquy in *The Waves*, reflecting on his relationship to the friends whose experience he has shared:

> And now I ask, 'Who am I?' I have been talking of Bernard, Neville, Jinny, Susan, Rhoda and Louis. Am I all of them? Am I one and distinct? I do not know. We sat here together. But now Percival is dead, and Rhoda is dead; we are divided; we are not here. Yet I cannot find any obstacle separating us. There is no division between me and them. As I talked I felt 'I am you.' The

difference we make so much of, this identity we so feverishly cherish, was overcome.[18]

By the time she came to write her last novel, such problems were no longer simply artistic puzzles, but had become overwhelming. Everyday life was now so obtrusive that she could no longer transform it into appeasing words. In her journal she asked whether in these unpropitious circumstances she shouldn't at least finish her current project, 'Pointz Hall', if only 'by way of an end': 'The end gives its vividness, even its gaiety & recklessness to the random daily life.'[19] Gillian Beer has argued that this element in the current scene helps to account for the particular – and, in the circumstances, unexpected – quality of lightness that characterizes the work she was engaged on during the subsequent period of stress and completed as *Between the Acts*:

Pastimes – gossip, play-acting, sociable meals – may make tolerable the inevitable passing of time, because they suggest that there is time in abundance. That fiction of time-to-spare becomes more important in periods of crisis.[20]

Instead of the large themes that had given coherence to her previous major achievements: the personality of Mrs Dalloway, the aspiration towards the lighthouse, the even larger, more encompassing vista of waves under the sun, there was now simply the more limited scene of the country house (viewed against a backcloth of the whole of human history but still itself, a building in its current condition) and the local pageant, emphasizing the very fictiveness of the novel that contains it. Miss Latrobe, organizer and composer of the pageant, trying to give some sense of meaning to the world she is presenting – or at least to make an audience conscious of the need to try and understand – stands in for the novelist herself, and her awareness of a readership which will find it difficult to give any meaning to such an offering beyond the limitations of their own concerns. It was as if she had decided, for the purposes of this current work, to switch off her larger artistic consciousness and give herself instead to the immediate possibilities that could be discerned.

In one sense this is much her most ambitious novel, for whereas she had previously tried to fence off this or that particular area of concern, trying, for example, to find a successful scheme and scene of symbols or, as in *The Years*, to present an interpreted chronology, here she tried to give play to everything: pastoral description could coexist with strongest premonitions of the coming war. It was, in fact, the least interpretable moment of English twentieth-century history: no one could tell whether they were facing enemies who might still be faced down by the exertion of resoluteness or about to experience the ultimate in destruction, consummating all that had been foreshadowed in the previous world conflict. The lack of certainty brought personal fragility; Rodmell, where they were living, was in the direct path of bombers and potential invasion, while Leonard Woolf's Jewish lineage virtually guaranteed the worst of fates for both of them if Nazi forces should sweep across the country.

Between the Acts was both dwarfed and energized by being created within this context. It could also be multifaceted, many perspectived. In some ways, Woolf was liberated by her situation into a larger tolerance. In her 1940 lecture she acknowledged how much literature might be seen to have been impoverished by the confinement of writers hitherto to an educated class, entailing a limitation in their ability to tell the full truth. She was particularly impressed by a letter in a periodical from a mother whose child, through wartime conditions, was having to attend the local village school and thoroughly enjoying it, but whom she wanted to enjoy the academic benefit of a public school education in due course as well.[21] The effect of her enlarged attitude was exemplified in her fiction by her treatment of the clergyman, Mr Streatfield, in *Between the Acts*. In earlier novels he, as a local clergyman, would have been attacked or mocked or – most likely of all – ignored. Here he emerges as a practical, helpful member of the community, even if his attempt to offer a summing up of the play presents him as a somewhat ridiculous figurehead for it:

> What an intolerable constriction, contraction, and reduction to simplified absurdity he was to be sure! Of all incongruous sights a clergyman in the livery of his servitude to the summing up was the most grotesque and entire.[22]

That is how, after the others' pirouettes in historical fancy dress, he must appear, wearing a garb dating from another century. Only the sight of the tobacco stains on his raised forefinger introduces a human touch to mitigate the effect, making him more acceptable, familiar as a piece of church furniture.

And despite his perceived irrelevance to the whole scene, the words he utters are not in the end entirely ridiculous. Far as they may fall short of an appropriate response to what has been effected, they include an attempted grasp of human unity that draws together everyone there. He expresses also a fitting intellectual humility, matching, perhaps, something that Woolf herself has learned in face of the threat to the local community. And at the end of his groping beneficence he turns back, of course, to the immediate practicality: the need to install electric light in the church (which we know from our privileged hindsight to be about to be rendered most impractical for the time being, at least, by the coming wartime blackout).

Between the Acts, viewed from the same privileged position, is remarkable for its lack of larger patterning, its disregard of possible perspectives. It is as if the wartime need to emphasize human equality in the face of threatening tyranny has invaded and overpowered other contourings. Most notably, there is an open-endedness. Although there are references to actual events, the reader suspects that the details could not be tied down exhaustively to particular, identifiable sources. Instead of producing strong parallels to current actions, similarly, Isa's stream of consciousness has a tendency to trail off into irrelevance.

There is something of the same effect in the concluding dispersal of Virginia Woolf's own personality. It is as if the efforts of outgoing imagination that had characterized her writing, constantly forming themselves into new patterns like flocks of birds in flight, finally took over her whole being, until she could no longer ballast herself with a controlling identity, caring little if her physical form passed into non-existence. The mastery shown in *The Waves* by Bernard had given way to the facelessness feared there by Rhoda.[23] In that state she was incidentally predicting the very condition of subsequent fiction, where, taking the impossibility of perceiving ultimate patterns of meaning as their starting-point, authors would care less about such stabilities.

Some kind of stability was necessary, however. We have already seen how Sartre, faced with the task of relating the writer's consciousness to a state of Being always conceived in terms of mobility, needed to fall back on words as his ultimate resource and appeasing sustenance. For Virginia Woolf in her last phase, even that consoling presence was ceasing to be valid: the relationship was coming to be one of trying to relate her consciousness to a state of Being that was in continuous disintegration. In that sense her 'moments of being' would truly remain Hardyesque 'moments of vision', retaining always the marvellous, diaphanous quality that her admirers valued in her most, but always, and now tellingly, incomplete.

D.H. Lawrence, by contrast, was looking for the nature of Being in a different way, one which involved during his early period a quest for the integration of himself as model, leading to projection of a pattern of the kind for society as a whole. The new note that he was to strike marked among other things a means of emancipation from a literary world that was dominated by graduates of Oxford and Cambridge. The new state schools that had provided Myers with his living as an inspector following the Education Act were now producing writers of their own – Arnold Bennett, H.G. Wells, John Galsworthy. As a gifted man whose parents spanned the cultural divide between traditional working-class culture and the new aspiring lower middle class, Lawrence was well qualified to join them – despite Virginia Woolf's reading of his work, as we have seen, entirely in terms of social aspirations from the first to the second. She herself came of a family where university education had been the norm, yet where her father had excluded himself from remaining at Cambridge by reason of his inability to accept the religious beliefs required there, while she was automatically excluded by her gender. The vicarious initiation provided by her brothers' experience had done little or nothing to palliate the slight of her exclusion. She had this, at least, therefore, in common with the members of the new generation, even if her heredity kept her more closely in touch with older traditions. When T.S. Eliot described Lawrence as displaying the 'crippling effect upon men of letters of not having been brought up in the environment of a living and central tradition', F.R. Leavis protested against the unfairness of his account: the nonconformist chapel of his time, he contended, had been 'the centre of a strong social life, and the focus of a still persistent cultural tradition'; in addition, Lawrence had been able to make full use of the opportunities available by then at a provincial university.[24] He had also been able, one might add, to visit Cambridge himself and make his own sardonic comments on the leading figures he met there.[25]

Yet such attempts to align him with predecessors in the English tradition still leave open the question why, in spite of an immediately attractiveness, he is not easy to apprehend in his wholeness, so that even after reading well-informed studies, the reader is left unsatisfied, feeling that something essential has escaped the net. This is not an effect of the necessary exclusions to be expected when reading good criticism; it is, rather, a sense that some of the statements made about Lawrence's work turn out not to be fully justifiable. Large claims have been made for Lawrence as a social realist, for example. With his picture of English provincial society in *Sons and Lovers* and his deeper probing in *The Rainbow*, he can be seen as a protagonist of those who believe the full strength of English culture to lie in the traditional values of its working and lower middle classes, and his frankness in sexual matters as having made a welcome call for larger honesty in English cultural life. Yet no one who knows British society well would claim that either *The Rainbow* or *Women in Love* presents a true picture of it as a whole, in any 'naturalistic' sense. It is accurate on important points. The detail of the social background is usually correct, sometimes brilliantly so, but what takes place against that background belongs rather to the artist's imagination. The picture of the Brangwens contains elements of implausibility; nor would one go for an accurate commentary on the mining industry to *Women in Love*: neither management nor workers would be likely to recognise themselves fully. From a different point of view, feminists have found his portrayal of women deficient and misguided. And even though Leavis makes the case for an unusually subtle and complex intelligence, manifest in the intensity of his best writing, we find ourselves wondering in turn about the appositeness of his title, *D. H. Lawrence: Novelist*: when the usual criteria of novel criticism are applied to Lawrence's fictions, they do not automatically emerge in the first rank. His handling of characters or of plot is often rather loose; and if we take as a guide the range of human insight displayed, there is still room for disappointment. One critic has pointed out that in his major novels, it is usually the impersonal that triumphs.[26]

As it happens, however, it is that very word 'impersonal' that gives the best clue to his aims as a novelist, and their relation to his attempts to seize the nature of that elusive 'Being', existing beyond direct consciousness, that is the theme of this study. There is a sense, indeed, in which the word can be taken seriously in terms of his own personality and associated with a paradoxical element in the numerous biographical studies. In his own life, Lawrence could be deeply engaged with companions – often polemically so.[27] The resulting arguments and battles are absorbing. Yet when we turn from them to the work that he was producing at the same time, a disparity emerges. There was an intensity in his human relationships, just as there was an intensity in his writing, but they were not of the same kind or devoted to the same objects. He could sometimes draw upon incidents from real life in his novels, yet increasingly the impression created by the novels is that their central running thread consists not of events, or even of people, but of an internal debate being carried on in his own mind.

Certainly, he had begun at an early stage to move towards a distinctive view of the world, setting himself apart from those around him. While participating spiritedly in the life of his family and the group of friends who constantly visited them, he was evolving his own sense of things. He would have disclaimed any straightforward ordering of his ideas, since this was alien to his purpose. Writing to his fiancée Louie Burrows in 1911, he asserted that he would never be able to share all his ideas with her, but conceded that 'it's a philosophy that, shared, would be aggravated to abstruseness and uselessness'.[28] Occasionally, however, he could be a little more forthcoming. Writing in December 1909 to a lecturer at Nottingham, Ernest, nicknamed 'Botany', Smith, he had said,

Life seems to me barbarous, recklessly wasteful and destructive, often hideous and dreadful: but on the whole, beautiful ... I owe you a debt. You were my first live teacher of philosophy: you showed me the way out of a torturing crude Monism, past Pragmatism, into a sort of crude but appeasing Pluralism...[29]

The terms here are not lightly chosen; they were particularly topical during the period when he was awakening mentally. To discover what he meant by a 'torturing crude Monism', for example, we may turn to a book which he is known to have read as a young man,[30] Ernst Haeckel's *The Riddle of the Universe at the Close of the Nineteenth Century*. Published in England in 1900, this was influential among those who were trying to come to terms with the world created by nineteenth-century science. Haeckel's position was of straightforward monism: he believed that the natural order was the sole reality of the universe, and that the aim of human beings must therefore be to understand that nature, together with man's part in it. Haeckel was so excited by the developments of science, in terms not only of Darwin's theories but of the extraordinary profusion among living things that was simultaneously being revealed by the microscope, that he felt confident in assigning such centrality. Writing from within German society, he saw himself aligned with those who were fighting against Catholicism, extending the Protestantism of the Reformation into this final phase where Nature could take the place of God and where morality, though necessary, would be seen as embodying principles of human conduct deduced from knowledge of nature itself and fashioned in conformity with what was to be discovered there.

Such a philosophy carried the compulsiveness of a firm logical body of thought: it also represented a development from those doctrines of

Kant, influential throughout the nineteenth century in Germany, which found their most succinct formulation in his description of a gazing up to the stars in the sky or a contemplation of the moral law within one's own nature and discovery of the same majestic order in both.[31] Haeckel adopted a similar duality of thinking, which in the Kantian version had provided a firm basis for the position of a writer such as George Eliot, but simplified it further. For him an alternative view was enough: to look up to the starry heavens above and down to the wonders revealed in the depths of the microscope.[32]

Why should Lawrence have found so simple and understandable a position 'crude' or 'torturing'? Presumably because, despite its immediate attractiveness, it wound human beings more firmly into a sense that they were held in the grip of inexorable laws. The cruelties, as well as the wonders of nature, must then be seen as inescapable. Haeckel's book ends with a quotation from Goethe:

> By eternal laws
> Of iron ruled,
> Must all fulfil
> The cycle of
> Their destiny.[33]

However invigorating these lines so long as one thought of that destiny as an upward progress, they offered little consolation to those who found themselves *victims* of the natural order. Lawrence's reference to his subsequent 'pragmatism' suggests that he found one answer to this problem in William James, another favourite writer of his youth.[34] James's principle that in philosophy an allowance must be made for the validity of personal experience – that if, for example, the hypothesis of God's existence worked for someone, that person was justified in believing it – helped to liberate his readers from the bonds of law by simply transferring the focus of their attention to individual human experience.

When Lawrence refers to his further movement into a 'crude but appeasing pluralism', similarly, it is likely that he is referring to James's recent *A Pluralist Universe*, which, published in 1909, the year of Lawrence's letter to Smith, had the avowed aim of asserting that

> However much may be collected, however much may report itself as present at any effective centre of consciousness or action, something else is self-governed and absent and unreduced to unity.[35]

This argument offered some way out of the monist suggestion that when one comes down to 'reality as such, to the reality of realities, the actual state of things in which we live',

> everything is present to *everything* else in one vast instantaneous co-implicated completeness and nothing can in *any* sense, functional or substantial, be really absent from anything else: all things interpenetrate and telescope together in the great total conflux.[36]

James's goal, in other words, was to deliver human beings from the sense of living under the shadow of a vast absolute which imprisoned them in its categories, and restore them to a universe where they could, legitimately, deal with each situation to the best of their abilities and in the light of the ideas available to them at the time.

Lawrence's acknowledgement that 'Botany' Smith had helped him reach this latest position suggests that his progress had been assisted by something more than a sequence of philosophical arguments. Indeed, it may legitimately be supposed that the subject Smith taught had to do with the matter, and that the crucial incident in *The Rainbow* where Ursula Brangwen, while in the college laboratory, has a new insight into the meaning of existence, may have been based on an actual experience of Lawrence's own, fostering this 'pluralism'.

Ursula, it may be recalled, has been listening to the argument from a colleague against any need to suppose the existence of mystery in the universe, which on the contrary, she holds, is completely explicable as a complex of physical and chemical activities. At this point Ursula turns to the nucleus of the creature she is examining under the microscope and asks herself what its 'will' might be. 'If it was a conjunction of forces, physical and chemical, what held these forces unified?'

> What was its intention? To be itself? Was its purpose just mechanical and limited to itself?
> It intended to be itself. But what self? Suddenly in her mind the world gleamed strangely, with an intense light.... she had passed away into an intensely-gleaming light of knowledge. She could not understand what it all was. She only knew that it was not limited mechanical energy, nor mere purpose of self-preservation and self-assertion. It was a consummation, a being infinite. Self was a oneness with the infinite. To be oneself was a supreme, gleaming triumph of infinity.[37]

Her grasp of this complementary principle, enabling her to see how the perception of a cell existing in its own infinity offers a more complete key to the significance of all life, including human life, than more mechanist explanations gives a decisive turn to her thinking and her attitude to life. This is an existence in common which can paradoxically allow each self to flourish in its own individuality – and in the process guarantee the full quality of its separateness. The meditation carries, indeed, a weight quite disproportionate to the run of the narrative in the novel as a whole, since the revelation that has been described governs much of what is to happen from then on until its conclusion. In the same way, and equally disproportionately, Ursula's strange behaviour towards her lover Skrebensky, first giving herself to him passionately, then rejecting the prospect of marrying him, is to be understood in terms of a few brief sentences in which he is revealed to her as no more than the 'complexity of physical and chemical activities' in which her colleague had invited her to see the operation of the whole world:

He seemed completed now, He roused no fruitful fecundity in her. He seemed added up, finished. She knew him all round, not on any side did he lead into the unknown.[38]

This is the other side of the same coin. Ursula's behaviour might seem simply wanton unless one is attentive to the logic of what is happening to her, which seems to demand a sharing of her perception.

In one sense the intuition that Lawrence was exploring resembled Heidegger's starting-point. To say of a cell 'It intended to be itself' was akin to the latter's assertion of primacy to the validity of the statement 'it is itself'. Much the same can be said of Tom Brangwen's experience, as related earlier in the novel:

during the long February nights, with the ewes in labour, looking out from the shelter into the flashing stars, he knew he did not belong to himself. He must admit that he was only fragmentary, something incomplete and subject. There were the stars in the dark heaven travelling, the whole host passing by on some eternal voyage. So he sat small and submissive to the greater ordering.[39]

Here was an art that moved to the limits of the normal orderings of space and time in an attempt to render the multivalent experience of Being itself, offering a poetic context for the *ständige unganzheit,* the 'continuing incompleteness', of which Heidegger wrote.[40]

The paradox here is of the same order as that which underlies Coleridge's principle, 'Every Thing has a Life of it's own, and we are all *one Life*',[41] where the biological analogue rests on a speculation that the whole of animated nature might consist of organic harps, trembling into thought at the impact of 'one intellectual breeze,| At once the Soul of each, and God of all'.[42] Yet there was an important difference. As soon as one moves beyond Coleridge's formulation to the larger context of his thought, one sees that he was surrounding it with assumptions concerning the nature of human affections. The joint perception of the life in each and the one life in all ministered to Coleridge's belief in the sovereignty of love: it was that that provided the link between the two kinds of perception and informed every individual act of perception of either kind. For Lawrence, by contrast, as the remainder of *The Rainbow* shows, the experience is rather one of isolating and distancing. Intimacy and sympathetic affection are not concepts that one readily associates with him: affection when it comes has a sardonic overtone, and often does not come at all.

There are strong indications that in the years following, Lawrence often felt himself in an unreal world, surrounded by human beings living according to false gods and false ideas. His main problem, in fact, was often to retain a profitable contact with human society at all, whether in actuality or in the writing of his novels. This extended even to his most intimate relationships. Despite his closeness to Frieda, there were elements in his outlook that he could not feel she shared. Shortly after they were married, he wrote, in a moment of semi-humorous bitterness, 'Would I had married a microscope: I could have kept my eye on it and my heart in my pocket, and been called blessed' – a statement which, in view of what was said above, may have had more literal meaning than one would at first suspect. While fulfilling his need for a vital physical relationship, the marriage to Frieda was in other respects dislocating to him as an imaginative artist. There is a telling incident in *Kangaroo* when Lovat's wife asks him,

'Who is there that you feel you are with, besides me – or who feel themselves with you?'

'No one,' he replied. And at the same moment he looked up and saw the rainbow fume beyond the sea. But it was on a dark background, like a coloured darkness. The rainbow was always a symbol to him – a good symbol: of this peace. A pledge of unbroken faith, between the universe and the innermost. And the very moment he said 'No one,' he saw the rainbow for an answer.[43]

Lawrence's reference to the rainbow as 'a pledge of unbroken faith, between the universe and the innermost' places him with unexpected directness in a tradition again leading back to the early Romantics, this time to Wordsworth's lines beginning 'My heart leaps up when I behold / A rainbow in the sky'. The source of 'natural piety' which Wordsworth had celebrated there was just such a 'pledge of unbroken faith'.

By Lawrence's time, the connotations of a 'natural faith' had become a part of the sub-Romantic ethos. Encouraged by certain elements in Wordsworth's poetry, notably the lines in 'Tintern Abbey' describing

> that serene and blessed mood
> In which the affections gently lead us on, –
> Until, the breath of this corporeal frame
> And even the motion of our human blood
> Almost suspended, we are laid asleep
> In body, and become a living soul:
> While with an eye made quiet by the power
> Of harmony, and the deep power of joy,
> We see into the life of things[44]

various nature writers had come to find their own version of an 'unbroken faith, between the universe and the innermost', revealed in moments of peace and harmony. Such moments aligned themselves with Woolf's; once again, however; they were in the end moments less, as she claimed, of Being, than of vision. It was a tradition that Lawrence at once knew well and distrusted. A moment of the kind occurs in *Sons and Lovers* when Paul and Miriam go to see a wild rose bush on a quiet summer evening:

> In bosses of ivory and in large splashed stars the roses gleamed on the darkness of foliage and stems and grass. Paul and Miriam stood close together, silent, and watched. Point after point, the steady roses shone out to them, seeming to kindle something in their souls. The dusk came like smoke around, and still did not put out the roses.[45]

For Miriam it is a moment of communion and worship in the midst of nature. Paul shares that sense to some extent, but also feels 'anxious and imprisoned': as soon as he is away from the scene and her, he begins to run as fast as he can. Indeed the whole story of *Sons and*

Lovers can be read as that of a young man who finds himself forced to leave the attractions of such psychical experiences behind and move into another area, delighting in nature's vital energies rather than its moments of trance. ('Turning sharply, he walked towards the city's gold phosphorescence.... towards the faintly humming, glowing town, quickly.'[46]) Being is now being interpreted in terms of energy, and affirmed. It is a complex process, however, since it involves a turning away from the context in which his relationship with Miriam had been artistically productive as her intensity brought out what was implicit in his bond with his mother:

From his mother he drew the life warmth, the strength to produce; Miriam urged this warmth into intensity like a white light.[47]

He would need to discover a new way of gearing his intellectual intensity to the life-energies of the world about him before he could regain his identity as a creative writer.

Lawrence's use of the rainbow image must be seen in similar complexity. His introduction of an actual rainbow into his novel of that title is sometimes criticized as sentimental – naturally so to anyone familiar with its use, say, in Pre-Raphaelite painting. The rainbow of *Kangaroo*, similarly, is presented as a *visual* image, revealing itself against a dark background and across ruffled waves, 'a tall fume far back among the clouds of the sea-wall', and recalling for Lovat a time when in the midst of a dismal scene with pouring rain he had seen a rainbow spanning Sydney Harbour – 'A huge, brilliant, supernatural rainbow, spanning all Sydney'.[48]

For Lawrence it is not the straightforward sight of a rainbow as such that is comforting, however – though that consolation may be there too, an awareness that there is little in the order of things that might lead logically to the expectation of seeing anything so beautiful in nature. In a manuscript passage that Lawrence would not have known, tracing the 'analogy betwixt | The mind of man and nature', Wordsworth recalled, similarly, an occasion when he saw a scene of fierce tumult during a storm on Coniston, 'Mist flying up and down, bewilder'd showers, | Ten thousand thousand waves, mountains and crags, | And darkness, and the sun's tumultuous light', – and then, over all, a 'large unmutilated rainbow ... Immovable in heav'n ... With a colossal stride bridging the vale'.[49] Yet in reading such a passage we are aware of undertones which counterpoint and give further definition to an image of peace that is regarded typically as 'Wordsworthian' – if only the use of the word 'stride'. In *The Prelude*, typically, the experiences in which such images of tranquillity are impressed on the heart regularly follow times of unusual energy or directed attention: it is in the relaxation from effort, not in some straightforwardly passive state, that the experience of revelation comes.[50] The resulting sense of a total process preserves such passages from charges of sentimentality or softness.

Lawrence's adoption of the rainbow image also involves invocations of energy and carries their implications further. In *The Rainbow* Ursula's final vision is that, despite the sordidness of the earth's current inhabitants, 'the rainbow was arched in their blood and would quiver to life in their spirit' leading 'to a new germination, to a new growth'.[51] Here, as elsewhere, one is conscious of striking resemblances between the personalities and experiences of Lawrence and Wordsworth: there were similar forces in the two men but they were being apprehended and organised differently. Wordsworth, although passionate, was fearful of the effects of his energy; yet he was even more wary of delivering himself into a fixed or static universe of law. He seized with relief upon the mediating elements in the natural world to which his affections could hold. Lawrence, on the other hand, while attracted by such a cult of affection, also felt stifled by it, breaking out to find his natural world of discourse in those expressions of energy, which Wordsworth treated with reserve. It was at the moment when he could sense his own imaginative energies in unison with those in nature that he felt most at home in the world, most intimately related to its Being.

This was not simply a matter of his artistic thinking. In personal terms, it made him a divided man. Within his own family circle when young, and in that circle as it extended itself to immediate friends, he could be extremely affectionate. But in more solitary moments, and in his growing awareness of nature, he found himself rebelling against the nineteenth-century ideal of relationships so based; hence the crucial tension in the relationship with Jessie Chambers. His visits to her home at Haggs Farm made him aware of the full range of natural life, its cruelty and harshness as well as its charms and tendernesses; he also became aware that, if he were looking for points of correspondence between the natural and the human, those differing factors in external nature could speak to very different elements in the psyche. It was one thing for the affections to be nourished by contact with nature on a calm summer evening, quite another for human instincts to find themselves in rapport with the instincts of wild creatures. Wordsworth had solved this problem by presupposing that the proper time to cultivate the life of instinct was in childhood and youth; once adulthood and the sphere of moral responsibility were entered the picture changed. Lawrence could not agree. In his pluralistic universe, the role of the instincts, particularly in sexual life, was altogether more significant. The relationship with Jessie Chambers was the stage of a cruel drama, therefore. Jessie was his ally in his search for identity as a writer: supporting him against the other 'Pagans' in Eastwood and his mother, who believed that if he were to achieve fame as a writer he would be lost to their little society. She therefore fought against their cultivation of him, keeping his work and encouraging him to submit it for publication.[52] But the same process of cutting himself off from his own group, which she encouraged, was also setting up a division in himself between that affectionate, intellectual self which was drawn to her and the instinctual, sexual self which could not be satisfied by such a relationship. The first signs of such a tension appeared as early as 1906, during the summer before Lawrence's entry into college. He formulated it to Jessie in terms of his lack of sexual feeling for her, defining it in his replying to her expressed desire to love him as a 'complete whole', 'I am *not* a complete whole. One man in me loves you, but the other never can love you.'[53] While he apologised to her for the 'perverse' element in himself, it is clear that he was also coming to see that that perversity might represent an important element in his whole nature. And the recognition of his two natures was not confined to himself. Ford Madox Hueffer (later Ford), for example, who knew him best in the years 1909 and after, contributed a similar impression:

if the God Pan did look at one round a trunk one might well feel as one felt when the something that was not merely eyesight peeped out at you from behind Lawrence's eyes.

For that was really what the sensation was like – as if something that was inside – inhabiting – Lawrence had the job of looking after him. It popped up, took a look at you through his pupils and, if it was satisfied, sank down and let you go on talking…. Yes it was really like that: as if perhaps, a mother beast was looking after its young. It was not so bad an impression, founded as it was on the peculiar, as if sunshot tawny hair and moustache of the fellow and his deep set and luminous eyes. He had not, in those days, the beard that afterwards obscured his chin – or I think he had not. I think that on his holiday he had let his beard grow and, it having been lately shaved off, the lower part of his face was rather pallid and as if invisible, whereas his forehead and cheeks were rather high-coloured. So that I had had only the impression of the fox-coloured hair and moustache and the deep, wary, sardonic glance ... as if he might be going to devour me – or something that I possessed.... Always at first, for a second or two, he seemed like the reckless robber of hen-roosts with gleaming eyes and a mouth watering for adventure and then, with the suddenness of a switched-off light, he became the investigator into the bases of the normal that he essentially was.[54]

Various of Lawrence's own statements at this time suggest a similar analysis. In May 1910, when it seemed as if he might after all be willing to marry Jessie Chambers, he wrote to Helen Corke about the feeling of inertness which this recognition induced. 'I seem to have no will: it is a peculiar dull, lethargic state I have never known before.'

> Till Saturday I shall merely wait in lethargy: I can do no other. Yet I have a second consciousness somewhere actively alive. I write 'Siegmund' – I keep on writing, almost mechanically: very slowly, and mechanically....
>
> Muriel will take me. She will do me great, infinite good – for a time. But what is awake in me shivers with terror at the issue.[55]

At the end of that year, when he had become engaged to Louie Burrows, he wrote to her in different terms, emerging more aggressively now on behalf of his writing self:

> I am very much afraid indeed of disappointing you and causing you real grief for the first time in your life. It is the second me, the hard, cruel if need be, me that is the writer which troubles the pleasanter me, the human who belongs to you. Try, will you, when I disappoint you and may grieve you, to think that it is the impersonal part of me – which belongs to nobody, not even to myself – the writer in me, which is for the moment ruling.[56]

To other people he put the point differently again, making it clear that he foresaw a marriage in which Louie Burrows would have only a partial share of him. To his sister Ada he wrote: 'Don't be jealous of her. She hasn't any share in *your* part of me. You and I – there are some things which we shall share, we alone, all our lives: you know, also, that there is more *real* strength in my regard for you than there is for Louie.'[57] In this case he was thinking primarily of his mother's death and of their previous experiences with his father, which, he thought, had given them a more tragic view of life than Louie, with her own, better-knit family, could possibly imagine. This was not the only area Louie failed to share, however, as a letter to Helen Corke makes clear:

> The common everyday – rather superficial man of me really loves Louie. Do you believe that? But do you not think the open-eyed, sad critical, deep seeing man of me has not had to humble itself pretty sorely to accept the imposition of the masculine, stupid decree. There is a decree for each of us – thou shalt live alone – and we have to put up with it. We may keep real company once in our lives – after that we touch ... now and again, upon someone else – but do not repose.[58]

The rest of the letter shows that his ideas rested upon a further ideology: that the mechanical laws of life and of nature were made for 'the unseeing, unintelligent mass', but that it was also possible to 'step out of the common pale' and find new intuitions dominant. He returned to the matter in July, speaking to Jessie of his love and its nature: 'Some of you I should always love. Then again, I must break free. And I *cannot* marry save where I am not held.... I love Louie in a certain way that doesn't encroach on my liberty, and I can marry her, and still be alone. I must be so, if I marry – alone in soul, mostly...'[59]

The realignment of himself which Lawrence was trying to make is not difficult to understand. Having recognised himself to be, with Jessie, a divided man, he had still hoped to preserve a relationship of intensified sensibility with her, leaving his instinctive self and his creative self to look after themselves. But after his mother's death he knew this to be impossible: to live wholly in such a sensibility would be to perpetuate a part of the relationship with his mother which, after her tragic death, he could never re-enter. Instead, he was now trying an opposite expedient: a relationship of physical fulfilment with Louie Burrows which would neither tax his sensibility nor restrain him from continuing with artistic creation.

Neither relationship could be satisfactory. In his writing, after all, which was now to be conceived as essentially impersonal, he was trying to reconcile affectionate sensibility and instinct; to confine himself to one rather than the other would leave his writing impoverished. With Louie, moreover, the 'passion' was coarse-grained: there was little subtlety in her vitality. If he had married her, he would have

been false to the intelligence which had informed the deeper perceptions in *The White Peacock* – an implicit sympathy with the broad,
unrefined vitality of George Saxton being matched by a still more
evident recognition of its shortcomings.[60] Once again there was an
incompleteness, a sense of infidelity to a larger sense of Being.

There had been times when he could ride happily on the crest of a var-
iegated personality, as when, in the early days of his relationship with
Louie, he had written, 'I wish you'd tell me which of my epistolary styles
you prefer: the gay, the mocking, the ironic, the sad, the despairing, the
elevated, the high romantic, the didactic, the emphatic, the bullying, the
passionate, the disgraceful or the naive, so that I can be consistent'.[61]
The death of his mother and its aftermath had increased his sense of self-
division, however, and one suspects that the attack of pneumonia at the
end of the year was either connected with – or at least subsumed within
itself – the resulting psychic conflicts. By early February, he was writing
to Louie to break off their engagement on the grounds of ill health. Soon
afterwards, Ada Lawrence wrote to her urging her to accept the situation.
She referred to the 'flippant and really artificial manner' which Lawrence
had recently adopted, having commented: 'It's surprising how very
much changed Bert is since his illness, and changed for the worse too, I
think.'[62] Whatever one makes of all this, it is evident that Lawrence had
found himself in a false situation which he was trying to escape. In the
process, he seemed to himself to be 'a sort of impersonal creature,
without heart or liver, staring out of a black cloud'.[63] Yet once again
there were swift turns of reaction. A fortnight later he was back in
Eastwood making love light-heartedly at a dance; six weeks later still he
had fallen in love with Frieda Weekley.

The love for Frieda represented a further reorientation of himself, for
the first time enabling the passionate element in his personality, which
empathised with the instinctive in nature, to find full expression. His
subsequent letters were full of delight at a new freedom and at the
wonder of his love. But this new kind of relationship was not without
its own divisiveness; he and Frieda fought as well as loving, and the
emergent dark side to his personality which Ada had noticed issued
from time to time in blind rages, lending a shadow to some of his subsequent pronouncements about human affairs. To give rein to the
instinctual might at times be a liberation of Being, but it could also
issue in fierce destructiveness.

This is not the place to trace all the complexities of Lawrence's later
personality, however, the concern here being rather to trace his more
impersonal career as novelist and thinker and to recognize the part

which awareness of his subconscious powers continued to play in keeping alive a note of incompleteness – including a sense that his own Being was not fully engaged if it could not give rein to his 'daemon'. In January 1912, for example, just before the end of his engagement to Louie, he wrote to Edward Garnett:

> I can never decide whether my dreams are the result of my thoughts, or my thoughts the result of my dreams. It is very queer. But my dreams make conclusions for me. They decide things finally. I dream a decision. Sleep seems to hammer out for me the logical conclusions of my vague days, and offer me them as dreams. It is a horrid feeling, not to be able to escape from one's own – what? – self – daemon – fate, or something. I hate to have my own judgments clinched inside me involuntarily. But it is so.[64]

'What tosh to write. I don't know what ails me,' he continued; but it was certainly not an isolated reflection: many years later, in 1928, he returned to the theme when he wrote a preface (not to be published as such) for his *Collected Poems*. There he talked of certain poems which he had begun writing at about the age of twenty, which haunted him and made him feel guilty.

> In those early days – for I was very green and unsophisticated at twenty – I used to feel myself at times haunted by something, and a little guilty about it, as if it were an abnormality. Then the haunting would get the better of me, and the ghost would suddenly appear, in the shape of a usually rather incoherent poem. Nearly always I shunned the apparition once it had appeared. From the first, I was a little afraid of my real poems – not my 'compositions', but the poems that had the ghost in them. They seemed to me to come from somewhere, I didn't quite know where, out of a me whom I didn't know and didn't want to know, and to say things I would much rather not have said: for choice ...
> To this day, I still have the uneasy haunted feeling, and would rather not write most of the things I do write – including this note. Only now I know my demon better, and, after bitter years, respect him more than my other, milder and nicer self.... I must have burnt many poems that had the demon fuming in them. The fragment *Discord in Childhood* was a long poem, probably was good, but I destroyed it. Save for Miriam, I perhaps should have destroyed them all. She encouraged my demon. But alas, it was me, not he

whom she loved. So for her too, it was a catastrophe. My demon is not easily loved: whereas the ordinary me is. So poor Miriam was let down. Yet in a sense, she let down my demon, till he howled. And there it is. And no more *past* in me than my blood in my toes or my nose is past.[65]

That last reference to the blood is a reminder that Lawrence's belief in the demon was associated with his sense of a 'blood-consciousness' in the body, a belief expressed memorably in a letter to Bertrand Russell of December 1915:

Now I am convinced of what I believed when I was about twenty – that there is another seat of consciousness than the brain and the nerve system: there is a blood-consciousness which exists in us independently of the ordinary mental consciousness, which depends on the eye as its source or connector. There is the blood-consciousness, with the sexual connection, holding the same relation as the eye, in seeing, holds to the mental consciousness. One lives, knows, and has one's being in the blood, without any reference to nerves and brain. This is one half of life, belonging to the darkness.[66]

Quoting this letter nearly forty years later, Russell commented: 'This seemed to me frankly rubbish, and I rejected it vehemently, though I did not then know that it led straight to Auschwitz.'[67] In expressing himself so vehemently he may have been recalling some expressions of extravagant hatred in Lawrence's other letters of the time, resulting from his black moods during the First World War. The true context of Lawrence's work was very far from Nazism, however. In Germany between the wars, references to a blood-consciousness were to be linked closely with militarism and aggression, expressing themselves through the technology of war, whereas Lawrence's philosophy was the direct opposite: it was based rather on a vision of independent growth in individuals and free communication between them, grounded in his intuitive sense of the inward life of nature and criticising those forces of industry and war which followed a mechanical and inhuman logic of their own. The individuality of Lawrence's position is more evident in an earlier statement to Ernest Collings, which links naturally to those speculations about the self over the microscope that had appeared in *The Rainbow*:

My great religion is a belief in the blood, the flesh, as being wiser than the intellect. We can go wrong in our minds. But what our blood feels and believes and says, is always true. The intellect is only a bit and a bridle. What do I care about knowledge. All I want is to answer to my blood, direct, without fribbling intervention of mind, or moral, or what not. I conceive a man's body as a kind of flame, like a candle flame forever upright and yet flowing: and the intellect is just the light that is shed onto the things around. And I am not so much concerned with the things around; – which is really mind; – but with the mystery of the flame forever flowing, coming God knows how from out of practically nowhere, and being *itself*, whatever there is around it, that it lights up.[68]

This line of thinking reappeared from time to time in later works. In his essay on John Galsworthy, for instance, written in 1927, he drew a distinction between the social beings who inhabited the Forsyte novels and real, individual human beings:

It seems to me that when the human being becomes too much divided between his subjective and objective consciousness, at last something splits in him and he becomes a social being... . the core of his identity splits, his nucleus collapses...

This basic quality is 'the essential innocence and naïveté of the human being, the sense of being at one with the great universe-continuum of space-time-life, which is vivid in a great man, and a pure nuclear spark in every man who is still free'.[69]

His anatomization of the current relationship between individuals is a worthy successor to Blake's lament that 'since the French Revolution Englishmen are all Intermeasurable One by Another Certainly a happy state of Agreement to which I for One do not Agree':[70]

When I stand in the presence of another man, and I am my own pure self, am I aware of the presence of an equal, or of an inferior, or of a superior? I am not. When I stand with another man, who is himself, and when I am truly myself, then I am only aware of a Presence, and of the strange reality of Otherness.[71]

His location of Being in 'being at one with the great universe-continuum of space-time-life', despite its close resemblance to Heidegger's, is still closer to Coleridge. The 'one Life within us and abroad' in the lines added to 'The Eolian Harp' – a presence also in many of the conversation poems – manifests itself very openly in *The Ancient Mariner*

(though from the first, Coleridge had drawn back from its full implications, as threatening pantheism). Lawrence can hardly have been
unaware of such overtones in the poetry, which he read enthusiasti-
cally in his youth. Jessie Chambers recalled how during the winter of
1908 they walked over frozen snow to the ruins of Beauvale Abbey. 'It
was a day of brilliant sunshine, and the three of us perched in a tree
that leaned over a pond, while Lawrence read Coleridge's *Christabel*.'[72]
From time to time he adopted well-known lines from *The Ancient
Mariner*: in 1928, for example, he recalled the year after his mother's
death as one in which 'everything collapsed, save the mystery of death,
and the haunting of death in life'.[73] The Mariner's vision of the water-
snakes ('Blue, glossy green and velvet black, | They coiled and swam;
and every track | Was a flash of golden fire') has a vividness which
looks forward directly to Lawrence's language; or one may recall his
lines in 'Snake': 'And I thought of the albatross, | And I wished he
would come back, my snake'.[74*]

The counter-Romanticism that is here at play could never be more than
one element in Coleridge's work, however: it could not, for example, be
allowed to challenge belief in the moral law. Lawrence's statement, 'with
should and *ought* I have nothing to do',[75] would have been impossible to
him. As a result such strands in his work ran out eventually into private
conversations, isolated notebook entries, footnotes to published works,
and a timidity resulting from his guilt-laden relationship to the Supreme
Being. Lawrence, by contrast, begins his explorations at the point where
Coleridge leaves off, being willing to contemplate unafraid the fact that a
full relationship between the unconscious powers in the human mind
and those in nature will take account of things such as pure sexual desire
– or of violence as well as calm.

He could do so more readily because in his time the element of sensibility in Romanticism had been overplayed to the point of being
played out. The cultivation of states of entrancement had led to the
'dreaming woman',[76*] that typical figure in the society of Lawrence's
time which he found so disturbing, negating as she did the possibility
of more vital and energetic relationships between men and women. In
the same way he found the negative quality in *A Passage to India* at
once authentic and inadequate: 'The day of our white dominance is
over, and no new day can come till this of ours has passed into night.
Soit! I accept it. But one must go into the night ahead of it. So there
you are.... Only the dark ahead and the silence into which we haven't
yet spoken our impertinent echoes.'[77] The Being that lay in the future
was indicated elsewhere by him as not at all static: 'the still, white

seething, the incandescence and the coldness of the incarnate moment: the moment, the quick of all change and haste and opposition',[78] triumphing over the quest for 'Significant Form' which he excoriated.[79] As his own death grew nearer, however, his faith in such an 'incarnate moment' would modulate into the more tentative imagery of 'Bavarian Gentians', where the energy of the flower becomes a torch to guide him into the darkness,[80] an emblem of vital Being that was beautiful but fragile – and intimating in its ambience something of the increasing greyness which he felt to be surrounding the play of energies in the world at large.

There was, inevitably, an innocence in his attitude, as would appear when its implications were developed further by a poet such as Ted Hughes. His deepest vision, however, the one that had inspired the laboratory scene in *The Rainbow*, remained as a presence that might survive to guide his successors. 'The Flying Fish', a story written in 1925 at a time when he felt himself 'near the borderline of death',[81] plays cleverly around a single theme: that human beings in the white civilisations live in a 'lesser day', ignoring that 'great day' which is also the great deep from which they have drawn and to which they must return. The hero is himself called Day, coming from a family of Days who have lived in Daybrook for generations. He is on his way home from the decadence of his life in South America to take over the family house. What he sees on the voyage focuses the story's themes: the unfinished account of his voyage to the 'little day' of Western civilization ends with the greyness and nausea experienced as the boat passes through the oily-grey sea; but earlier, lying alone in the bows, the man has seen first how flying fishes 'on translucent wings swept in their ecstatic clouds out of the water, in a terror that was brilliant as joy, in a joy brilliant with terror' – and then, on the third day, a school of porpoises,

> mingling among themselves in some strange single laughter of multiple consciousness, giving off the joy of life, sheer joy of life, togetherness in pure complete motion, many lusty-bodied fish enjoying one laugh of life, sheer togetherness, perfect as passion.... And it left him wonderstruck.[82]

His sight of flying fish leaping together comes as a final revelation of a Being unrealised by humans.

> This is the purest achievement of joy I have seen in all life: these strong, careless fish. Men have not got in them that secret to be

alive together and make one like a single laugh, yet each fish going its own gait. This is sheer joy – and men have lost it, or never accomplished it.... It would be wonderful to know joy as these fish know it. The life of the deep waters is ahead of us, it contains sheer togetherness and sheer joy. We have never got there.[83]

The language that Lawrence uses here is spirally repetitive in the manner of much of his prose, recalling what 'Botany' Smith had told him long before – that he was *obsessed* rather than *possessed* by his ideas.[84] The method of the whole story, with its interlocking of the idea of 'the greater day' through various elements in space and history, enables him to put that obsessive quality to unusually good use, however, in making it an imitative form for the interplaying movement of the flying fish themselves. Perhaps in producing that vision of interweaving energies he was recalling, consciously or subconsciously, Coleridge's similar vision of energies in the play of the water-snakes – just as Coleridge himself, voyaging afterwards to Malta, had seen a myriad of insect activity in the shadow of his ship as a manifestation of *'being'*.[85] Sartre's devotion to moving energy was here fulfilled and superseded by apprehension of the mysterious nature of Being in such elusive, dancing formations. For Lawrence the vision of 'The Flying Fish' marked his concluding assurance of powers existing beyond the reach of the limited consciousness fostered by the technological civilisation which he had come to loathe – powers which he felt sure would yet survive it. The flying fishes indicated, if only through their diffuse, flying energy, a level of Being that might fully complement the incompleteness created by the organizing consciousness of Western man. Where Virginia Woolf had been content to find her 'moments of Being' in experiences of enhanced vision, Lawrence had developed from his own visionary perceptions to what might be better termed visionary movements of Being. In the course of time, what he had discovered would be taken up by others – most notably by Ted Hughes.

6
Sylvia Plath and Ted Hughes: The Hazards of Incompleteness

Of the twentieth-century figures considered so far, Sartre's attempt to propitiate his sense of non-being by identifying Being with motion was to prove the most accurately prophetic in terms of future developments. The twentieth century would see a world more and more given to transport and communication, while stability, increasingly, would be a quality handed over to nostalgia and the heritage industry. In political terms, by contrast, Sartre's tireless journeys to all parts of the Western world in order to identify and excoriate injustices would be offset by his blind refusal to credit reports of the ills affecting states under communist totalitarianism.[1] For his own part, Simone de Beauvoir has related how he was unwilling to admit that he had any identity connecting him with the past, and indeed rarely reminisced at all;[2] his commitment to motion as Being was in itself, however, a form of identity, displaying, paradoxically, in relation to her a kind of fixity that contrasted with the flexibility of her own outgoing disposition.

In recognizing this, we reach a final pivotal point for the discussion as it has emerged. 'Being', which was in the 'Romantic' section of this study conceived as a largely metaphysical conception, linking the individual either to the divinity or some all-embracing Reality, has in more recent times come to be a term focused primarily on the individual alone, and particularly on the sense of his or her personal identity. Despite this shift of emphasis, however, both senses have continued to be present. More importantly, the notion of Being itself, as a complement to the rational consciousness, comes to be seen as itself essentially riven. Between them Woolf and Lawrence had demonstrated the two polarities involved, the one exploring a sense in which it could be presented as visionary, of 'the moment', while the other conceived a sense in which it was expressed primarily in the vital (and lasting) energy of the human psyche. The dominant literary relationship in England at the mid-century, between Sylvia Plath and Ted Hughes, developed this polarity further, while also relating back to the primary attempts to explore the distinction between Being and Consciousness which is the larger subject of these studies. At a first look, the distinction between the two might indeed strike one as a simple contrast between the respective qualities: Hughes, with a monolithic stability of character seeking to link himself with similar past figures to form a chain of tradition, might seem like an archetypal proponent of Being, while Plath, with her wide-ranging intellectual gifts and restless urge for experimentation, would serve as a good emblem of developed Consciousness. This would be to underestimate the subtlety of the situation, however, for it would assume that Being was always a matter of solidity and stability, Consciousness of instability – both suppositions being open to question, as we have seen. Given the intricacies of behaviour that have been noted, particularly in the last chapter, it is better to think of two modes, involving different *kinds*. Consciousness need not always, for instance, be thought of as opposed to Being; if exercised powerfully enough it can amount to an alternative version. This was indeed true of Plath, whose intellectual intensity could strike anyone who came across her by the memorably forceful impression she made: Dorothea Krook, for instance, recalled a first sight of her in the lecture room:

> I noticed a conspicuously tall girl standing in one of the aisles, facing toward me, and staring at me intently. I was struck by the concentrated intensity of her scrutiny, which gave her face an ugly, almost coarse expression, accentuated by the extreme redness of her heavily painted mouth and its downward turn at the corners. I distinctly remember wondering whether she was Jewish.[3]

Her intensity of reaction caused her on occasion to ignore norms of civilized behaviour, leaving a bitter taste for the people involved: it ranged from a rather absurd bout of incandescent rage when she discovered that her friend Jane Baltzell Kopp, encouraged by finding ink markings of hers in a book she borrowed, had added a few of her own in pencil and then omitted to erase them,[4] to occasions of frosty behaviour, as recalled by Lucas Myers, Olwyn Hughes and, above all, Dido Merwin.[5] It is equally evident that she had an extraordinary physical sensitivity, exemplified by her reaction at the time of the Rosenbergs' death:

> at exactly nine o'clock she looked at me in horror and said, 'Now it's happening,' meaning the Rosenberg execution. She stopped and

held out her arms to me and there were, raising up on her arms from her wrists to her elbows, little bumps. Soon, they sort of bled together like welts from burns. Obviously, Sylvia was experiencing burns all over her arms in empathy for the Rosenbergs who were – she believed – being electrocuted at that moment.[6]

She had in fact mistaken the time of the execution, so that it could only have been a case of unusually strong imaginative empathy, but that does not make its effects less striking. Her reaction when Hughes killed a grouse to put it out of its pain[7] provides another example.

Those who criticize such extreme behaviour are also inclined to point to a touch of the impersonal as well, corresponding to an apparent failure to enact human relationship in the poems – a tendency to speak when necessary only through a single, first-person voice. Behind such forcefulness of impact, however, there was a hesitancy, an unsureness of central purpose, which also ran through her life as a constant theme. Her early journals show awareness of her own fragmentation and her search for a man who would answer to it. She confessed a 'desire to be many lives' but also mused, 'I need some boy to be captivated by my appearance. ... Then I need someone real, who will be right for me now, here, and soon.'[8] In 1953, she wrote that for her there needed to be a 'thou':

> otherwise there is no i because i am what other people interpret me as being and am nothing if there were no people.[9]

In spite of apparent self-confidence she had already been forced to acknowledge her own vulnerability, as in her description of a momentary state of loneliness:

> It comes from a vague core of the self – like a disease of the blood, dispersed through the body so that one cannot locate the matrix, the spot of contagion.[10]

'The loneliness of the soul in its appalling self-consciousness, is horrible and overpowering –' she wrote just afterwards.[11] Even two years late she had advanced little: 'I know what I like and dislike; but please, don't ask me who I am. "A passionate, fragmentary girl," maybe?'

In her alienation from herself, including her sense of facelessness, there was a resemblance to Virginia Woolf's Rhoda in *The Waves*.[12*] Woolf's writings were in fact the ones that she reacted to most positively in her early career, coming to identify her and Lawrence as her

two most important predecessors. After reading *The Rainbow* enthusias-
tically she wrote:

> the flow of my story will take me beyond this in my way – arrogant?
> I felt mystically that if I read Woolf, read Lawrence (these two, why?
> Their vision, so different, is so like mine) I can be itched and
> kindled to a great work: burgeoning, fat with the texture and sub-
> stance of life: this my call, my work: this gives my being a name, a
> meaning: 'to make of the moment something permanent'...[13]

In times of afflatus she felt she could outdo Woolf:

> Also, images of life: like Woolf found. But she: too ephemeral,
> needing the earth. I will be stronger: I will write until I begin to
> speak my deep self, and then have children, and speak still deeper.
> The life of the creative mind first, then the creative body. For the
> latter is nothing to me without the first, and the first thrives on the
> rich earth roots of the latter.[14]

This double aim was not in the event to be fulfilled, though during the
time when she was cultivating country life in Devon she seemed at times
to be moving towards it. It is not easy for a modern woman to reconcile
her intelligent consciousness with a vegetative existence, whatever the
potential richness, and Sylvia Plath could not escape the restlessness of
contemporary culture, which Virginia Woolf had traced in Lawrence.
Again, it was these two writers who seemed her best guides:

> how does Woolf do it? How does Lawrence do it? I come down to
> learn of those two: Lawrence because of the rich physical passion –
> fields of force – and the real *presence* of leaves and earth and beasts
> and weathers, sap-rich, and Woolf because of that almost sexless,
> neurotic *luminousness* – the catching of objects: chairs, tables & the
> figures on a street-corner, and the infusion of radiance: a shimmer
> of the plasm that *is* life. I cannot and must not copy either.[15]

Beyond Lawrence's power, beyond Woolf's luminosity, she was aiming
for something more like completeness of Being; but that came to rely for
her on the success of her relationship with Hughes. When she first
encountered him in Cambridge, in February 1956, she believed that she
had met the first man who was capable of giving physical form to her
earlier dream, writing of him to her mother as 'the only man I've met yet

here who'd be strong enough to be equal with'. 'Strong' was perhaps a mark of misprision at the level of self-knowledge – which her mother, who was to remark after death, 'Sylvia's tragic flaw lay in her own very weak ego',[16] may have found it hard even then to accept. What she did have in abundance was energy and intensity of insight, which for the time being were quite enough to carry her through. She could at times, indeed perceive her own position as forceful: 'I must find a strong potential powerful mate who can counter my vibrant dynamic self: sexual and intellectual ...',[17] while being shrewd enough to recognize the potential unreality of such aspirations. Below the level of determined achievement there subsisted the combination of Being and consciousness which could produce such insights yet also make her mercurial in temperament and mood. This was so particularly in her early student days, when successive boyfriends were left baffled and bewildered – often because, while they were attracted to her physically, she did not feel that they appreciated, or reciprocated, her other gifts. By the time she reached Cambridge in 1955, this had changed: she had come to know a young man, Richard Sassoon, who matched her intelligence and with whom she could regard herself as being in love. In the following spring, however, a day or two after she met Ted Hughes and had her first, gloriously drunken and violent encounter with him, Sassoon rejected her plan to meet in France, prompting desperate expressions of love and later a vain walking of the Paris streets in search of him. To the casual reader of the *Journals* it is perplexing to read, alternately and intermingled, outbursts of yearning love for Sassoon and outbreaks of passionate desire for Hughes, but these make sense once it is recognized that while her love for Sassoon was a matter above all of her conscious intelligence, her desire for Hughes ran deeper, springing from a hunger for his solider version of Being.

This recognition must also throw light on the subsequent development of her relationship with Hughes, whom she married soon afterwards, in June. He struck her as answering to her dynamism, yet lack of personal stability in the manner that she had tended to displace on to an ideal mate:

Let's face it, I am in danger of wanting my personal absolute to be a demigod of a man, and as there aren't many around, I often unconsciously manufacture my own.[18]

Because her own qualities were applied to the achievement of high ambitions, meanwhile, she had developed her consciousness to the full from the start. She also recognized the limitations of Cartesianism:

if you have no past or future which, after all, is all the present is made of, why then you may as well dispose of the empty shell of present and commit suicide. But the cold mass of gray entrail in my cranium which parrots, 'I think, therefore I am,' whispers that there is always the turning, the upgrade, the new slant...[19]

Like Sartre, in other words, she was finding such centre as she had in endless restlessness. Even the substantiality provided by her American upbringing largely dissolved when she moved to an English environment. Hughes, by contrast, measured to her specification more than she expected, possessing a strong identity and linked firmly to a time and place from which he could effortlessly draw nourishment. He and she could thus be said to exemplify, respectively, the difference between a strong consciousness of Being and a mercurial being of consciousness. During the positive phase of their marriage the two modes of existence were complementary, he benefiting from the stimulation of her intelligence while she could allow her mental energies to swarm on the stable centre he provided. The nature of the divergence was, however, such that given unpropitious circumstances it might change from fruitful dialectic to serious rift. Hughes himself was to recall how, at the beginning, though captivated by her, 'slim and lithe and smooth as a fish', he had been aware of an uncanny warning voice saying 'stay clear'.[20] In spite of this her attraction was such that it proved all too simple to let himself be caught into the relationship and so offer the stable point of support she needed.

She soon relied inordinately on his presence, anxious to be with him at all times, drawing on him for reliable resource. Lucas Myers recalled that on one occasion when they were working close to one another in their London flat, Ted mentioned that he had counted the number of times she had called out to him that morning while he was trying to write: 104, he said. Myers also recorded the kind of effect that could be produced by her anxiety, describing how when he and Ted had stayed overlong (forty minutes, to be precise) at the local public house they returned to find her enraged and cold towards them.[21] In his later poem on a similar incident Hughes interpreted such behaviour in terms of her family background.[22] There could also be extreme jealousy when he showed attention to other women. An incident in which a friendly middle-aged BBC producer was regarded as an unseen rival, so that time devoted to her produced a hysterical reaction, is recounted in Anne Stevenson's biography.[23] She herself had come to see her reliance as dangerous, noting in America during the autumn of 1959 that she had no life apart from his and was thus likely to become an accessory; feeling that this destroyed an ability to project herself properly into characters and situations, she had determined to lead a separate life as soon as she returned to England.[24]

Many attempts to account for her personality fail through an assumption that it had a core of consistency, to be discovered by investigation with enough patience and perseverance. Yet anyone who has read the *Journals* will have noted the bewildering speed with which her viewpoints could change. In her student days she was capable of idealizing for herself a chaste, nun-like existence one moment, and a rip-roaring marriage of bed, babies and parties the next.[25] Her accounts of people, notably relatives, could change dramatically according to whether she was looking at them with affection or with the eye of 'that photographic mind which paradoxically tells the truth, but the worthless truth, about the world', as she once put it.[26]

On the view presented here a sympathetic and intuitive approach, without excessive attempts find consistency, is more appropriate. Her personality may then be seen rather in terms of an attempted organization of energies which would always be incomplete but which would find viable modes of patterning for a time in relation to the stable point of reference provided by Hughes. Not a simple, consistent patterning – rather a congeries of personal forces that could focus and refocus around various nuclei. A marked feature of her behaviour in this connection was the existence of two varying modes, described vividly in her *Journals*:

> It is as if my life were magically run by two electric currents: joyous positive and despairing negative – which ever is running at the moment dominates my life, floods it.[27]

The existence of such an alternating flow of energy in her unconscious self helps to explain some of her most puzzling contradictions, together with the enigma she often presented to her husband. Ted Hughes's father had survived the First World War, one of the few members of a group who had participated in the Gallipoli campaign, while his own adolescent consciousness had been dominated by the Second. Eventually, he spent some years of post-war National Service as a ground wireless mechanic on an isolated small radio station in east Yorkshire – where he had 'nothing to do but read and reread Shakespeare and watch the grass grow'.[28] Steadfastness had been, as previously, the keynote of those years. Even when he visited Paris his main thoughts were of figures in the French Resistance who had been fighting there only a few years before, leaving the walls holed and pock-marked, and now commemorated by street-memorials. (Sylvia Plath's feelings about that city were, by contrast, more traditionally 'American', romantically evoking the artistic spirit of the place.)

The bleakness that still surrounded the effects of the recent war, and its predecessor, in continental Europe was equally evident in England for Hughes; it haunted not only his own family but the whole area in which they lived and its past:

> Everything in West Yorkshire is slightly unpleasant. Nothing ever quite escapes into happiness.... A disaster seems to hang around in the air there for a long time. I can never escape the impression that the whole region is in mourning for the first world war.[29]

Hughes also found himself essentially isolated from the culture in which he grew up. He could not identify himself with the world of Yorkshire dissenting chapels, with their joyless Puritanism: what heart there had been in those had been torn out by the war that had claimed the service of his father. he would never wear a poppy for Remembrance Day.[30] Still less could he feel at home with the 'Establishment' world of southern England. From an early period of his life, his strong identity engaged him in a long struggle to discover a context for it that would make sense.

For him, 'Being' by no means excluded reasoning consciousness, of course, but was identified primarily with physical life. Much of his poetry can be read in the light of his central idea that nature is to be understood by looking at animals and trying to establish where their true identity lies – a fine example being the well-known poem 'The Bull Moses'. The identity that was seeking a true context for himself had first been forged during boyhood shooting expeditions, in the course of which he learned the feeling for wild creatures which was to be the hallmark of his writing. In an interview for an American angling magazine[31] he described how between the ages of two or three and eight or nine he lived completely under the spell of his older brother, with whom he learned to hunt, carrying on after his brother had left for the war. When he was 11 he was killing wagtails, robins, wrens, grass snakes, 'everything that moved'. Later he trapped mice, stoats, weasels and water rats. While he went through the normal academic education for someone of his particular time and place, then, he came to the sense, like the young Wordsworth before him, that he was most himself when out on the moors on the track of a wild animal. The early passion of shooting was later replaced by fishing, until he went to university and became more preoccupied by the intellectual life.

This was the craggy, opinionated, independent-minded Yorkshireman whom Sylvia Plath encountered and married. Although in terms of some of the factors discussed earlier it would be hard to imagine a greater contrast, in one respect at least they had a similarity of background, both having enjoyed unusual rapture in their childhoods: Sylvia Plath grew up by the sea, delighting in such things as the objects found on the shore, as related below,[32] until the family moved inland – 'Whereon those nine first years of my life sealed themselves off like a ship in a bottle – beautiful, inaccessible, obsolete, a fine, white flying myth.'[33] Ted Hughes's Yorkshire childhood was spent in Mytholmroyd on the moors, hunting wild things, until his parents moved away to Mexborough when he was eight, which 'really sealed off my first seven years ... [and which] became a sort of brain – another subsidiary brain for me'.[34]

In each case the vision 'sealed off' in childhood had a decisive part to play in establishing the being of the later artist, but Hughes, the hunter, had the stronger sense of who he was and where he was trying to go. Given his background and nature, the most obvious mould to fit him would be that of Heathcliff, and the evidence of a poem such as her 'Wuthering Heights' is that Sylvia Plath at the very least glimpsed a connection which others must have made more strongly. The poles of male characterization between which the mind of a literary-minded woman is likely to swing in such a situation are those provided by Jane Austen and Emily Brontë; and Emma Tennant's evidently moved in that orbit: 'Mr D'Arcy he is not,' she wrote of him in her diary; her preoccupation with his self-referring character and his interest in violence suggesting an identification of him instead with Brontë's Yorkshire hero.[35]

After Sylvia Plath's suicide it was perhaps inevitable that the descriptions of violence in his poetry should have provoked some to conclude that that element in his personality had been in some way dominant. Others denied the existence of such a connection. 'He was the most considerate intellect in our circle and never did anything violent that I saw,' wrote his friend Lucas Myers. 'He never even made a violent gesture. There was violence in his poetry – it expressed the violence of the universe.'[36] There is little evidence to show that others came across any difference; the few instances that might suggest otherwise seeming more like rare experiments, testings of a limit he was careful not to cross.[37]* Hughes himself was evidently bemused by descriptions of his writing as 'the poetry of violence' and wrote a whole essay on the subject, arguing, at what might seem unnecessary length – though understandably in view of the accusations against him – that there could be such a thing as 'admirable violence'. At the same time he appreciated that a reader, faced with his comparison of the thrush's efficiency in carrying out its instinctive slaughter to the work of a composing Mozart, might feel that a wanton act of 'violence' had been carried out, 'perhaps with the express, Dadaesque intent of violating the reader's sensibilities'.[38]

So far from his behaving violently towards Sylvia, the evidence is most commonly of an anxiety to understand and placate her sensitivities. An important turning point in his attitude to animals came, for example, when, walking on the Yorkshire moors with her and coming across a red grouse, clearly sick or wounded, he followed his usual practice with living things in such a state and killed it. The grouse, it turned out, had been part of her personal mythology, so that she saw the killing as something other than a simple act of mercy:

> As she went berserk, I felt it go through me like an electric shock. A total transference to me of her feeling. I realised that I didn't want to kill any bird or animal, ever again. And I didn't. I stopped shooting. But I went on fishing.[39]*

This lasted until after her death. One day, however, a friend invited him to join him in a day's shooting:

> The moment I got hold of that gun, suddenly I could see everything again, all my senses had been restored to me – by the gun. I came awake in some weird way. I had a wonderful day, as though I hadn't been away from a gun. But at the end of the day, I gave him the gun back, told him how wonderful it had been and relapsed into my desire to shoot no more. So I'd been given a day's glimpse back into this paradise that I used to live in... that I'd completely lost.

Hughes then describes how fishing nevertheless survived for him as the activity on which he still relied to preserve his sense of connectedness with the natural world, the interview evolving into a series of meditations on this need for connection between one's body and the 'system of interaction that created us'. It was a notion of Being that Lawrence would have fully endorsed.

When it came to literary interests he, unlike Sylvia, showed little sign of being drawn to Woolf, but (as might be inferred from the remark just quoted) was even more fascinated by Lawrence, whose work he 'read entire in my teens ... except for all but a few of the poems', and which, he said, coloured a whole period of his life.[40] (*The Rainbow* he read when he was about eighteen.[41]) The enthusiasm assisted his sense of belonging with people of a primitive nature and searching within the records of anthropology for lifestyles akin to his own instinctiveness. His fascination with the primitive inhabitants of the Calder Valley was akin to Lawrence's sympathy with the midland colliers who, he claimed, led a wild existence, close to the earth they mined, until the passing of the 1870 Education Act led to their being subdued by the Board Schools.[42*]

Alvarez noted this propensity in Hughes, remarking that he gave a sense of his being in touch with some primitive area, some dark side of the self which had nothing to do with the young literary man. This, after all, was what his poems were about: an immediate, physical apprehension of the violence both of animal life and of the self – of the animality of the self. It was for this reason, Alvarez believed, that he showed an obsessive interest in things such as astrology, primitive religion and black magic. 'It was almost as though, despite all the reading and polish and craftsmanship he had never properly been civilized – or had, at least, never properly believed in his civilization.'[43] The most extreme example of an equivalent genius was, he thought, Blake.

That affinity was close in another respect. Like Blake, Hughes tried to express his unusual sense of Being by producing a general mythology of the human condition, alternative to the Christian, against which individual events could be interpreted. He universalized his sense of the wild into something of a private mythology, but unlike Blake needed to develop that mythology further to give it a social aspect. This entailed detachment from the general cultural consensus in England, and particularly the metropolitan culture of London. He attended the lectures of F.R. Leavis in Cambridge, where scorn for the contemporary literary scene would probably not have struck him as out of the way; nor would the rearguard action in which Leavis believed himself to be engaged have seemed to reflect more than the contemporary need for radical action. His own course took the form of firmly rejecting elements in the previous poetic tradition that many readers would regard as indispensable, such as lyrical, musical verse. His verse often seems governed, in fact, by a refusal to follow the benign courses on offer. He himself put it another way, remarking on the difficulty of singing one's own tune 'against the choir of the past': 'It is easier to speak a language that raises no ghosts.'[44]

In his desire to become a good poet, he sought to trace roots further back, adopting an interpretation of the growth of the English differing from the generally accepted account. Not finding an easy existence with any groups in his contemporary culture, he was forced to look instead for companionship with individual friends, while forging a poetic style in line with what he took to be the genius of the English language as developed by writers such as Shakespeare and Hopkins, and including a reliance on the vigour of old English, with firm use of consonants – as persisting in his native Yorkshire. Turning against the chapel culture and uniform Sundays of his Yorkshire upbringing, and contrasting what he found in Shakespeare – his central guide – he built up his own picture of an England that had lost its way in the early seventeenth century when it finally severed its links to the pagan goddesses whose cult had hitherto been nurtured covertly and committed itself to puritan, restrictive forms – forms which according to him had been strangling its life ever since.

The result of his work on Shakespeare amounted to a reading not just of the poetry and plays but of all English history, with a contention that the traditional Catholic religion had kept England – via the cult of Mary, presumably – in touch with the older cult of the Great Goddess, the Goddess of Complete Being, which the rise of Puritanism opposed and violated, and which it was Shakespeare's genius to have fostered. He grafted his conviction on to a view that good poetry was essentially twofold, appealing to the ordinary reader at a popular level while, at a deeper, ritualistic level, addressing itself to an educated few who can respond. In *As You Like It*, for instance,

> two different dramas are being performed simultaneously. One for the public who wants to be entertained, and one for Shakespeare himself – and, it may be, a small circle of initiates. The first audience enjoys a romantic comedy and accepts the confusing details (the fact that there are two characters called Jaques, for instance) as part of the rich complexity of general effect. The second audience watches an active ritual in which a shattered individual is put back together again on the realistic plane, and is simultaneously, on the mythic plane, committed to the spiritual quest.[45]*

Hughes was not alone in noting Shakespeare's likely contact with English Catholicism, but to suggest that he saw its mariolatry as keeping alive the myth of the great Goddess (when it can be argued that its concern was rather to propitiate her worshippers even while it suppressed them) would require evidence of a kind that he did not offer. Instead, he simply developed his theory at enormous length, maintaining that the initial key to Shakespeare's entire development was to be found in his early poems *Venus and Adonis* and *The Rape of Lucrece*. In the first case Venus, great goddess, wooed the puritan Adonis and on being rejected by him turned, in her persona as Queen of Hell, into the bull who slew him; in the second the rapist Tarquin violated the figure of chastity (the virginal element in Catholicism) and in so doing destroyed his own soul. This dual, slightly confused myth then became for Shakespeare the 'Tragic Equation' behind all his plays.

It is highly doubtful whether any audience has ever seen, or ever will see the plays in such terms; nor can one easily imagine a production that would facilitate such a viewing. It was unlikely also that a book which paid so little attention to other interpretations of Shakespeare would be favourably received: even points which had little to do specifically with the mythology would have benefited from a less cavalier attitude.[46*] Behind all, however, lay the concept of the Goddess of Complete Being, which in European terms was thought by him to lie at the heart of the struggle between Puritanism and Catholicism and to reconcile them.

Hughes's attempt to discover a unified mythology led him to other poets who had looked for such a general interpretation of human affairs, notably to Coleridge, prompting similar sweeping judgements. (In this case he had the justification that Coleridge, particularly during his earlier career, had been engaged on a similar enterprise.[47]) He might also have devoted more time to Blake, whom he and Plath both admired,[48*] where he might have been forced to acknowledge that a similar attempt to discover a universal myth had also produced eccentric results. Blake himself acknowledged this paradox when he put in the mouth of his hero the words 'I must create a System or be enslav'd by another Man's'.[49] Hughes's reluctance to attend to other interpretations bore the stamp of an individuality as firm as Blake's, though he was concessive in one respect where his predecessor had not been:

what I have to say here may be of use only to me. The only value of these remarks to some other reader may be – to prompt them to fill the vessel up themselves, from their own sources. Like the variety of potential readers the variety of potential interpretation is infinite.[50]

There is no need to regard his interpretation of Shakespeare's poems as offering universal validity; indeed, the contradictions set up when it was turned into a detailed programme were laid bare when *Shakespeare and the Goddess of Complete Being* was published and came under review.[51*] It is rather the case that Hughes was visiting his own existential predicament and his resulting interpretation of English social history on Shakespeare's poetry, turning that into a joint work partly his own. The 'mythological' basis of his views, formed through reading Shakespeare, Hopkins and much anthropological matter, may be historically shaky, but it was strong enough in its general plausibility to provide a nucleus around which to shape an interpretation that had a poetry of its own.

That a confidence in his own rightness did not totally survive in his later life is shown by the conviction he developed in his last days that spending so long on writing a prose book had been responsible for the destruction of his immune system, facilitating the development of the fatal cancer.[52*] Elsewhere he had made a statement that seemed to run counter to the idea of a mythology which might be objectified and presented in this way as an organized system (which would mean that poets wrote according to a code of mythology delivered before they were born, for which they could do no more than find new expressions) in his assertion that poets had each his or her own 'fountain', which they needed to discover if it was to release what they had to give.[53] It was an idea which he took partly from an essay in Yeats's *Ideas of Good and Evil* where he stated 'I have often had the fancy that there is some one myth for every man, which if we but knew it, would make us understand all he did and thought.'[54*] The idea, which was linked perhaps to his devotion to writing by children and the belief in it as a 'thing apart'[55] might have been a better one with which to understand Sylvia Plath, whose 'myth', as with Shakespeare, he devoted much time and effort to eliciting. Given his larger view it was not surprising that Hughes should have praised Judith Kroll's attempt, in her book *Chapters in a Mythology*, to read all Plath's work in mythical terms: he was happy, it seems, to be offered a unifying pattern in her writing which might interpret the events of her life, particularly since it suggested that there had been in her later behaviour an element of inevitability, ascribable to the fact that she was pursuing the implications of her own myth – which Kroll believed she had reconstructed in detail. In what appeared to be an endorsement of her main thesis Hughes wrote of Plath,

> She faced a task in herself, and her poetry is the record of her progress in the task. The poems are chapters in a mythology, where the plot, seen as a whole and in retrospect, is clear – even if the origins of it and the dramatis personae, are at bottom enigmatic.[56]

Despite the fact that he actually uses the words of Kroll's title, it is by no means clear that a considered view would have led him to corroborate her whole position. Having investigated the mythic element in the poetry to an extent unrivalled by any other researcher, however, Kroll herself was in no doubt:

> If her poetry is understood as constituting a system of symbols that expresses a unified mythic vision her images may be seen to be emblems of that myth...
>
> To deal with the structure of Plath's poetry is primarily to deal with the voices, landscape, characters, images, emblems, and motifs which articulate a mythic drama having something of the eternal necessity of Greek tragedy.[57]

To look for such a 'unified' mythic vision in Plath's poetry, however, and to give it such 'necessity' was to fix an aspect of her Being, ignoring two further crucial factors: a personality which was, as stated earlier, constantly changing and not to be tied into the forms of a single unified mythology, and her extraordinarily enhanced and developed consciousness. The latter impressed other intelligent observers, such as Alvarez, who placed her particularly with T.S. Eliot, Zbigniew Herbert, John Donne and John Keats, poets whose particular gift was 'to clarify and intensify the received world':

> Her intensity was of the nerves, something urban and near screaming-point. It was also, in its way, more intellectual than Ted's. It was part of the fierceness with which she had worked as a student, passing exam after exam brilliantly, effortlessly, hungrily.

Given this preoccupation with the 'received world' she was more at home when an immediate connection could be made between an element in mythology and some immediate physical reality, drawn on for that purpose alone. In her later poetry, certainly, she was often concerned to universalize particular experiences in a manner that equates with myth-making, but the enterprise had limits of its own. If she refers to a well-known legend, classical or otherwise, it is tempting to import other parts of that story to aid interpretation, but such an approach ignores the basic fragmentation of her vision.

Sylvia Plath had her own way of treating fragments 'mythologically', which could produce something more like a kaleidoscope of shifting images or symbols. An early formulation of this element in her is to be found in the essay 'Ocean 1212-W', mentioned earlier. There she describes her lost childhood by the sea, with its clean vision of things – including the moment of her brother's birth when, in a lapse from her habitual vision of her own unity with the universe, she suddenly appreciated for the first time the fact of her separateness. The unity of things turned into separatenesses, now to become beautiful again in their isolate details – the sea-washed shells, pebbles, even the items of detritus.[58]

This delight in isolated things played an essential part in her poetic method. Hughes himself commented on the strong tendency she showed to start her writing with things precisely realized in isolation:

> She wrote her early poems very slowly, Thesaurus open on her knee, in her large, strange handwriting, like a mosaic, where every letter stands separate within the work, a hieroglyph to itself.

Yet there was also, he claimed, a strong impulse from the organic:

> Every poem grew complete from its own root, in that laborious inching way, as if she were working out a mathematical problem, chewing her lips, putting a thick dark ring of ink around each word that stirred for her on the page of the Thesaurus.[59]

In spite of Hughes's feeling for her poems, this particular assessment again suggests a misapprehension, springing from a determination to cast them in the same pattern as his own. One searches vainly in most, if not all, her poems for such an organic core. What is being described in Hughes's account is essentially a fragmented creation, in which the energies of the words she lights upon are to be allowed to work together until a satisfactory pattern emerges – a process similar to that which she evokes when describing how the sound of early morning is 'suddenly, by mental magic, transmuted into something infinitely rich and ineffably strange ... the dismembered sound fragments integrate suddenly into a unity of music'.[60] If the results in her poetry are equally magical, they rely upon a reader who will not be in search of an organic centre, but appreciate, even enter into, something of the heuristic process by which they were made. The best account of the needed mode is given by Clarissa Roche:

> Most of us who knew Sylvia knew a different Sylvia Plath. This is partly because she was secretive and devious and selective, but I think, too, it was because aspects of her character were dispersed. In

a curious way she seemed uncompleted. Like fragments of mercury racing and quivering toward a center to settle in a self-contained mass, the myriad ramifications of her personality sought a focal point. At various stages Sylvia had tried to center her existence on school, on love, on children, even on market gardening, but always her creative genius was the core which drew everything to it but could not muster control. It seemed as if every thought, passion, regret, delight, terror, experience, vision, bruise, contempt, anything and everything – darted straight to a sort of honeycomb (bypassing tangibles), where it was trapped, zealously hoarded by her greedy genius, which forbade her simple, uncomplicated reactions or feelings, and where it cruelly barred her from ordinary living. The only way to govern this confusion of incarcerated emotion was to regiment it in magnificent, tidy lines of metaphor, meter, meaning, and beauty on shiny, virginal bits of paper.[61]

Sometimes the poetic process would reflect very directly such a feeling for energy. An early example is the poem 'Night Shift', which Alvarez, to her great pleasure, singled out for praise in his early review.[62] The fascination could also be an asset when there *was* an organicism, but in the subject – as in one of the most accomplished of her poems, 'Snakecharmer'. The Charmer has two powers,

'moon-eye, mouth-pipe'.

The whole poem relies on the interplay between the two as he produces a snake-play so powerful that the scene, and the verse describing it, are one in their intricate interweaving of sinuosities.

And now nothing but snakes
Is visible. The snake-scales have become
Leaf, become eyelid; snake-bodies, bough, breast
Of tree and human. And he within this snakedom
Rules the writhings which make manifest
His snakehood and his might with pliant tunes
From his thin pipe.

As he tires, what has been created subsides into its constituent elements: the interweaving snake forms become straightforward warp and weft, which in turn is seen as a cloth, dissolving then into green waters, until only the charmer himself is left, silent and unseeing.

The fit of energies and poetry is superb throughout: no further meaning need intrude beyond the story of the charmer's enterprise and his eventual tiring, which precipitates the relapse of the snakes and the closing of his moony eye. Technically, she has touched perfection. And the tight intricacy of the threefold pattern, music, interplaying energies and moonlight reveals itself as one of the most important paradigms in her visionary identity.

Another key to the play of energies in her writing can be found in the strong nostalgic feeling for stability which sometimes emerges unexpectedly, as if in compensation for her own inherent volatility. This comes out in her self-identification (endorsed by Hughes) with Shakespeare's Ariel,[63*] and in the poem of that name, which by contrast opens at an opposite extreme from energy:

> Stasis in darkness.
> Then the substanceless blue
> Pour of tor and distances.

By the close of the poem she has figured herself as the contrary power to such stasis by herself becoming the very essence of movement, flying into the fount of energy itself, the sun:

> And I
> Am the arrow,
> The dew that flies
> Suicidal, at one with the drive
> Into the red
> Eye, the cauldron of morning.

From the first, Plath's nature found its best expression in such plays between stability and energy, diffusions which when operating fully made even questions of poetic form irrelevant., Stephen Spender saw something of this when reviewing *Ariel*:

Considered simply as art, these poems have line to line power and rhythm which, though repetitive, is too dynamic to be monotonous. Beyond this, they don't have 'form'. From poem to poem they have little principle of beginning or ending, but seem fragments, not so much of one long poem, as of an outpouring which could not stop with the lapsing of the poet's hysteria.[64]

Spender, whom she met in March 1956, 'blue-eyed and white-haired and long since become a statue',[65] had evidently become for her too static, too much the poet of a form-obsessed consciousness to enjoy the dialectic between consciousness and Being that drove her. At the opposite extreme from her projective identification with movement and dynamism may be set the alternating lapses into stillness and light which could on occasion produce striking achievements of form and come closer to justifying Hughes's analysis. The most obvious example would be her self-identification with the moon, sometimes coupled with a fascination by the myth of Isis. At the mythical end of the inter-pretative spectrum, the Isis interest links with her absorption in Lawrence's tale 'The Man Who Died', encountered during her supervi-sions with Dorothea Krook at Cambridge. In Egyptian mythology the career of Isis followed that of the moon: she was seen as continually endeavouring to recreate the usurped lost sun Osiris; but every month as she repeatedly failed to find the *membrum virile*, the vision of whole-ness would disintegrate again until the new cycle began.[66] Lawrence had taken over these elements of the myth to the degree that in his story 'The Man who Died' he created a priestess who was a figure searching, her quest being connected with male virility. Plath responded intensely in her reading, mentioning in her journal her 'shiver of gooseflesh' on reading of 'the temple of Isis bereaved, Isis in search'.[67] Two days later, she repeated the phrase, dreaming of herself in Paris, in search of Richard Sassoon, 'Isis bereaved, Isis in search, walking a dark barren street'.[68] The sexual element in the search for Osiris's virile member may well have chimed with the intensity of her other obsession at the time, peaking in her first encounters with Ted Hughes. Later, as she lived in London with him, a recess in their sitting-room was filled with a large reproduced engraving of the 'great mother of the gods': Isis, as described by Apuleius.[69]

The use of the moon-symbol itself was, by contrast, naturalistic and immediate, concentrating mainly on its cold, deathly qualities in a way that chimed with the extreme purity of her vision, particularly in austere moods. This was in direct contrast to the volatility of her face, its expression rendering a changing personality that could never settle into finality of form, which could, as various observers pointed out, vary in the most extraordinary manner from one impression to the next until, looking from one photograph to another in a collection, one might find it difficult to believe that they were of the same person. Ted Hughes dwelt on this lack of fixed Being – evident even at one of their earliest encounters – as 'A device for elastic extremes / A spirit mask transfigured every moment / In its own séance, its own ether.' More than that,

> It was like the sea's face – a stage
> For weathers and currents, the sun's play and the moon's.
> Never a face until that final morning...[70]

Yet Hughes was assured that in contrast to that volatility, a new voice had been emerging during the last months of her life – a conviction which may be set beside Alvarez's belief in her liberation into her 'real self' from 1960, after the birth of her first child,[71] and the account of his visit in June 1961 when she struck him as no longer 'a housewifely appendage to a powerful husband' but 'solid and complete, her own woman again'.[72] Such a picture should still, however, be placed within the context of her own account that she herself embodied alternating currents. Her life in Devonshire may have given her a temporary sense of establishment as a rooted country Being, but her developed consciousness yearned for the stimulus of her metropolitan friends. Clarissa Roche, who visited her a few months after Alvarez, was impressed both by her vitality and by her evident loneliness, bordering on desolation, in such a non-literary community. Being and ranging consciousness were certainly not at one; and in such circumstances Sylvia Plath's consciousness was more likely to win, opening the way to a suicide which would in one sense be a supremely conscious act.

In the same way, Hughes's sense of Being would come to the fore when he was overcome by passion for a woman who showed more signs of a firm identity – the Assia Gutman whom he encountered in the summer of 1962, and with whom he found himself communicating directly at an instinctual level:

> A German
> Russian Israeli with the gaze of a demon
> Between curtains of black Mongolian hair.

After she had told her previous night's dream, of a pike with a human foetus in its golden eye, he says,

> I refused to interpret. I saw
> The dreamer in her had fallen in love
> With the dreamer in me and she did not know it.

> That moment the dreamer in me
> Fell in love with her, and I knew it.[73]

He refused to interpret, because he did not need to. It was a moment of subterranean commerce between their daemonic selves, their Beings, which, if allowed its course, would sweep aside anything standing in their way.

Given Hughes's nature, the sequel was predictable. A more responsible married man might simply have left his demon to howl (to adopt Lawrence's term), but it was hardly in the realm of possibility that so insistent a follower of Lawrence could have let the occasion pass by. It became for him instead a decisive moment of *kairos*. The electric thrill of sympathy that had passed through him from Sylvia's conscious reaction to the death of the grouse, the closest approach to a supreme experience in his upper consciousness, would count for nothing in the face of this new, deeper passion.

It has been natural for some to see his turning away from Sylvia Plath in favour of Assia Gutman simply as a heartless act, the behaviour of a callous, insensitive husband. Cruel the effects certainly were, to a degree that he may not even have glimpsed at the time. But Sylvia Plath was no passive creature such as Tennyson's Maud or Dickens's Rosa Bud; she was an independent woman in her own right who had in her early days asserted her freedom to love where she chose. Whether she fully appreciated the problems created by trying to conjoin such an over-developed consciousness as hers to an instinctive Being such as Hughes's is another matter. It is evident that the obsessive behaviour described earlier, coupled now with the demands of domestication created by a growing family, had made it increasingly difficult for him to sustain the relationship in conjunction with his career as an exploratory artist. Some of his friends (including Assia herself) maintained that if Plath had been content to give him a little more freedom the problem would in due course have been resolved, but this may be over-optimistic given the deep existential level at which the encounter had taken place, differing qualitatively from his relationship with Plath. This is the interpretation suggested by his remark to Assia's sister after her death: 'Assia was my true wife and the best friend I ever had'[74] – an astonishing statement, given the posthumous expressions of love addressed to Sylvia in which the poem just quoted is embedded, and one to be explained if at all only by an assumption that he regarded the two loves as having involved different levels of his personality. In these terms Hughes had found himself caught up in a further version of the dilemma that had been coming to the fore during the previous century. Hardy's Jude had been caught between the intensely cerebral religious morality of Sue Bridehead and the earthy, animal Arabella; in the next generation Lawrence had produced a similar tension for his Paul Morel between Miriam Leivers ('With Miriam he was always on the high plane of abstraction'[75]) and Clara Dawes ('Often, as he talked to [her] came that thickening and quickening of his blood, that peculiar concentration in the breast, as if something were alive there, a new self or a new centre of consciousness.'[76]) It is not surprising if Hughes was bemused by this new and still more sophisticated version. If his love at the instinctual level for Assia was more deeply satisfying, it was inevitably in later days to be disturbed by the continuing memory of a woman whose strong sexual energy had been dominated by a development of conscious intelligence hardly available to women in the previous century – and providing in turn a powerful stimulus to the more conscious element in his own poetic creativity. Caught as he was between the two needs, neither woman could offer satisfaction: the result of this incompleteness was predictably tragic. In the end Assia, finding herself lonely and demonized by literary London as the villain of the affair, and perceiving also that Ted was now taking refuge from the demands of the double pressure created for him by embarking on a further relationship, emulated Sylvia's act of self-destruction. The difference between the two women – Sylvia's intensified consciousness as against Assia's fury of Being, one might say – crystallized in the fact that whereas Sylvia's final act was one of affectionate tenderness, guarding her children from the encroachment of the poisonous gas and leaving them sustenance for survival, the consuming, even demonic power raised by Assia's plight drove her to think only of taking her child with her into the final immolation.

Hughes's own view was expressed in terms of a comprehensive struggle for ownership. In one of his poems to Assia, 'The Other', he addresses her as one who had nothing and who therefore felt justified in taking some of her rival's plenitude, and went on taking until, with her death, she realized she had taken too much – at which point the dead woman, with a smile, took some, 'just a little'.[77] This, however, ignores the matter of social identity. In a larger, social respect Assia Gutman *did* possess a plenitude: in her Jewishness she had direct access to traditions that were at once powerful and rooted. In London, on the other hand, she had no extension into a discursive social context that might have offered her satisfaction. Sylvia Plath, by contrast, lacked such deep roots from the start. The contrast showed in their respective attitudes to Jewishness itself. As the daughter of a Russian, German-speaking Jew married to a German Protestant, whose family had fled to Tel Aviv in the 1930s, Assia's had a consciousness penetrated by the tensions of Europe, her nationality playing an essential part in the drama. Sylvia, by contrast, reading the sufferings of the Jews as a means of interpreting her own individual plight, could take them readily as metaphor ('I think I may be a Jew'). Her immigrant parents being a Prussian and a second-generation Austrian, she exemplified the kind of American citizen who needed to draw their sense of identity from conformity to a social setting that was increasingly insubstantial, created rather by its own impetus. Her wealth of consciousness always swirled around this central deficiency, which in unpropitious moments threatened to become an abyss. If the incompleteness of Assia's Being lay in her lack of social recognition, that of Sylvia lay at the very core of the unconscious element in the intelligence by which she wrote. It was predictable, therefore, that the result of discovering her husband's change of love should be devastating. Her words to Elizabeth Sigmund, 'When you give someone your whole heart and he doesn't want it, you cannot take it back. It's gone forever',[78] are eloquent of her existential loss.

She faced the situation resolutely, nevertheless, determining to make a new life for herself and her children in isolation and finding that her work as a poet was unexpectedly energized. Repeatedly in letters of the time she wrote of her new life in positive terms:

> Now that my domestic life, until I get a permanent live-in girl, is chaos, I am living like a Spartan, writing through huge fevers and producing free stuff I had locked in me for years.[79]

It was in this ecstatic state that she freed her voice into the incandescent fury of poems such as 'Daddy' and 'Lady Lazarus', which she read with delight to her friends. One effect of her loss, in fact, was to make her consciousness even more active, an increase of intensity which enhanced Hughes's later sense that she was living out a preordained mythology of which suicide was the necessary conclusion. Her controlling myth, he thought, was that of Phaeton. Its high and low points were to be traced in the soaring energy of the poem 'Ariel',[80*] followed by the one begun five weeks later, 'Sheep in Fog', where the drafts contained a blackening 'dead man', whom he read as the fallen charioteer, with the completed poem revolving around a still horse – countering the earlier drive into the sun, he believed, by indicating a dead stasis, reduplicated endlessly. He interpreted her personal myth, in other words, as a supreme myth of motion followed inevitably by the figure of death. The idea presumably consoled him by turning the conclusion of her career into a poetic act, and introducing an element of fatalism which made it possible to see her death as part of a symbolic pattern, 'complicated and inevitable',[81] palliating the pain induced by remembrance of the part he himself had played. That he felt some guilt in the matter appears from the saying reported by Elizabeth Compton when she went to see him after Sylvia's death. As he gave her a copy of *The Bell Jar* she was impressed by the powerful working of his emotions; 'And then he said – I know he didn't mean it – "It doesn't fall to many men to murder a genius."'[82] Although Janet Malcolm comments 'Memory is notoriously unreliable' and invites the reader to discount the remark, it is not of a kind that is easily distorted or likely to be unmeant. Although he was clearly not speaking literally, he must have felt that at another level what he was saying corresponded to the truth. Indeed, it is hard to resist the sense that he turned over the events of Plath's last days again and again in his mind, now reproaching himself, now asking himself how he could have acted otherwise, finally seeking comfort in an assurance of inevitability.

His belief in the myth-fulfilling necessity of her death is also at odds with a detail recorded by more than one person. Lucas Myers states that Hughes felt the most tragic feature of the ending to be that she was about to return to him: another two weeks and they would have been together again, he believed.[83] According to Jillian Becker, similarly, he had told Sylvia that in six months' time they would be living together again in Devon.[84]

To put the matter so simply would be, one might think, to ignore all the writings that she had been producing in the previous few months, Yet it is not to be supposed that they had marked a total revolution. They had come from another area of her being, still ravaged by loss. If she was now touched by his pleas for her to let him return, the tension set up between this newly won independence and her surviving longing for the happiness she had achieved when they were together must have been overwhelming. Something of this is to be traced in his poem 'The Inscription' where in a late conversation they find themselves hopelessly entangled in a lack of understanding as she (unexpectedly) begs for assurance that *he* has faith in *her*, and he asks what he can do – whether she wants him to leave the country, as she had said, or to travel north with her together. The activity of the self that is begging for reassurance, clearly different from the new self she has recently been celebrating, betrays her psychic wounds. The dialogue of mutual incomprehension is then interrupted by her noticing the Shakespeare volume, which she had destroyed in a rage at discovery of his infidelity, now replaced by a volume newly inscribed – presumably by Assia. Then she begins again,

> Begging for that reassurance and he gave it
> Over and over and over and over he gave
> What she did not want or did
> Want and could no longer accept or open...

The passage is strongly reminiscent of R.D. Laing's *Knots*. Rarely have the contortions and intricacies of an impossible situation in a human relationship, with the protagonists helplessly united in the strife that binds them, been more teasingly rendered; it was the irresolubility of that conflict, surely, and not the working out of a dominating mythology, that brought about the final overwhelming impulse to self-destruction.[85*] As with Myers's Annie Marshall, who found herself in an intolerable marital situation, yet with children she loved dearly whom she found herself forced to abandon as she ended her life,[86*] one has the sense of a woman in a place where she can go neither forward nor back. Her poetic creativity might take the myth-making step of projecting herself as protagonist of such a poem such as 'Edge'; the existential physical woman was meanwhile being destroyed by the actual contradictions of the situation. Alvarez, one of the people who knew her best during this period, believed that she had not intended to take her own life, pointing to the fact that she left a note asking for her doctor to be rung and giving his number.[87] He thinks that the suicide bid had rather been a reckless gamble on her part. As with Edmund Gurney, the evidence is so ambiguous as to make the puzzle impossible of resolution. In both cases there was a chance, at least, that they might have been revived if found in time, but the overriding hazard is of minds in such extremity that their acts were undertaken when they no longer really cared whether they survived or not.[88*]

Ted Hughes's fatalistic belief that her suicide was an inevitable act within the logic of her private mythology may also be linked with an interest in the occult that complemented his firmness of identity. He was, from an early stage, taken with the significance of the subliminal and its potential importance for poetic creation. His mother had occasional powers of second sight, if his short story 'The Deadfall'[89] is a guide, and he was interested in every phenomenon that involved such possibilities, constantly encouraging Sylvia Plath to cultivate her poetic potentialities by means of hypnotism and psychic exercises. They experimented together, for example, with various versions of the Ouija board.[90*] Alvarez notes Plath's corresponding interest in the paranormal: 'And because her natural talents were very great, she discovered she had "psychic gifts".' To describe such gifts in terms of 'talents', however, is to mistake their nature. If she did indeed have them (and *some* element of the paranormal is suggested, as was seen earlier[91]) they would not thus have fallen within the sphere of her conscious intellectual self-cultivation, belonging rather to the subliminal level of Being – which in her was constantly in motion.

Hughes's encouragement of her subliminal exploration was a by-product of his growing sense of responsibility towards her, coexisting with his determination to pursue his own independence. (It is natural to compare him with Wordsworth, whose attitude to his sister showed a similar blend of responsible tenderness and personal independence.) Subsequent commentators have argued about the extent to which this was distinguishable from possessiveness: Jacqueline Rose draws attention to his statement at the time of the controversy concerning the desecration of her grave: 'I hope each of us owns the facts of her or his own life.'[92] As she points out, the statement includes two words the meaning of which is taken for granted without examination: 'facts' and 'owns'. One may disagree with her reserve about the first (which seems to conceal a post-structuralist assumption that there is nothing outside the text), but the second certainly suggests that after the death of his wife he felt himself vested with even more authority over her career.

Rose also writes how Hughes's sense of her extreme, elusive volatility went along with an insistence that her central problem was to find her true voice:

What starts to become clear is that his concept of an emergent true self carries a very specific psychic weight. It is for him the end of contradiction and simultaneously the creation of pure unadulterated speech. 'A real self, as we know, is a rare thing. The direct speech of a real self is rarer still .... Most of us are never more than bundles of contradictory and complementary selves.'[93]

Variations on this interpretation recur in his reminiscences: 'an old shattered self, reduced by violence to its essential core, has been repaired and renovated and born again, and – most significant of all – speaks with a new voice'.[94] 'Her real creation was that inner gestation and eventual birth of a new self-conquering self...'[95] This assertion that the true story of her career was that of a steadily emerging 'true self' can sometimes be put quite blatantly, as when he states that though he spent every day with her for six years, and was rarely separated from her for more than two or three hours at a time he never saw her show her real self to anybody – except perhaps in the last three months of her life. By this he must mean that she did not show it to anyone except himself, since he goes on,

> Her real self had shown itself in her writing, just for a moment, three years earlier, and when I heard it – the self I had married, after all, and lived with and knew well – in that brief moment, three lines recited as she went out through a doorway, I knew that what I had always felt must happen had now begun to happen, that her real self, being the real poet, would now speak for itself, and would throw off all those lesser and artificial selves that had monopolized the words up to that point, it was as if a dumb person suddenly spoke.[96]

As he does not record what the lines in question were, his meaning is even more obscure, except as asserting the existence of a self that he knew but which she never showed anyone else and which, it seems, never normally spoke – being able to speak only, perhaps, in her poetry. Taken literally, the underlying supposition seems to be that each human being has a true self, which needs to be cultivated if it is ever to show itself to any except the most intimate relatives. As a statement of fact this might be challenged. Wendy Campbell affirms the contrary: 'she was wholly remarkable for being wholly authentic. By which I mean that she was true to herself, or truly herself, something which is extremely rare.'[97] This, of course, is by no means the same thing as to assert the existence of a 'true self'. Hughes's statement certainly strikes one as dangerously simplified, ignoring her description of the alternating currents of her unconscious and, still more, the interplay we have tried to trace between the intense activity of her consciousness and the essential volatility of her Being. The working of a 'real' self, supposing it to be available for contemplation, should at the very least be acknowledged as embodying the possibility of interaction between both elements.

This is relevant to other criticism which, like Hughes's, is posited on the existence of a 'real' and a 'false' self – to which the writer claims privileged access. Marjorie Perloff, for instance, in an article focused on Sylvia Plath's 'Sivvy' poems,[98] has set up a firm distinction between the 'false' self which was always aiming to please her mother and a 'real' one which had emerged into bitter realization of the truth. Although there is undoubtedly some truth in such a characterization, which can be supported from her own writings, given the relationship and her understandable desire to support her mother in return for all that had been done for her in the past, a disinterested reader could be forgiven for finding many of the loving letters and poems written with her mother in mind just as sincere and 'real' in their own way as the bitter invective in the later work. If so, Hughes's attempt to read Sylvia's personality in terms of a 'real' self endeavouring to emerge, and his whole-hearted attempts to devote himself to its furtherance – largely at the expense of her cultivated consciousness – looks more like a tragic misunderstanding.

Not only does the existence of alternating currents in her personality help to negate the assumption that there were 'real' and 'false' selves but it also dispel the assumption that she was firmly committed to the end that overtook her. The belief that all her writing was really about death, the whole an acting out of a long-standing death-wish, owes much to Robert Lowell, who gave it momentum in the foreword he contributed to the 1966 American edition of *Ariel*. It seems rather, however, that views of life and death jostled one another for precedence in the mobility of her being. Several writers dwell on her fondness at times of treating the idea of death as a plaything – even an aphrodisiac. On such occasions it was almost as if she could not take it quite seriously. Nor, in terms of such alternations, is there any need to think of her as wraithlike. On the contrary, her sharper critics commented that her intensity of behaviour did not inhibit her from relishing large meals, and she herself, as mentioned earlier, recognized this trait. Her friends were struck equally by her substance and her animation. Wendy Campbell wrote that when she heard the news of her death she was simply unable to believe it: 'Suicide often seems to be a very reasonable means of leaving a disastrous life but it was very difficult to connect Sylvia with self-slaughter ... for me Sylvia's quality, her personal style of being, her vitality are summed up in an image of the Winged Victory as I have seen it flood-lit in the Louvre.'[99] Elizabeth Sigmund, who received a last letter from her in February, full of plans to resume her life in Devon, also found the news unbelievable: 'I remember walking in the dark country lanes, and saying over and over to myself, "Where is she?"'[100] Clarissa Roche was so stupefied that she was sure a mistake had been made: 'A dead Sylvia didn't make sense. There was something almost powerful about her physical presence. Dead! With that great lusty laugh and original flair for life? ... she was skilful, creative, alive. There was nothing ethereal about Sylvia.'[101] Alvarez wrote incredulously, 'There was too much life in her long, flat, strongly boned body, and her longish face with its fine brown eyes, shrewd and full of feeling.... I sometimes catch myself childishly thinking I'll run into her walking on Primrose Hill or on the Heath, and we'll pick up the conversation where we left off.'[102]

None of the accounts suggests solidity of Being; instead they stress the mobile version that has been proposed throughout this chapter: a vividly present consciousness giving a firm but multivalent *impression* of Being. That mobility also helped her constantly to overcome the insidious death-wish with which it interplayed, involving a diffuseness of controlling consciousness that came close to disintegration, taking her in some respects beyond Virginia Woolf. Although Woolf's career had been affected by a dispersal of personal identity, her context and inheritance as a writer had been strong enough to empower the making of a continued pattern from the fragments. Only in her last days, when external factors combined overwhelmingly with tensions already present in her work, had lapse into permanent unconsciousness finally seemed the better option. For Sylvia Plath, by contrast, the attraction to despair which was already displayed in her adolescent suicide attempt (partly inspired, she said, by Woolf's) coexisted with a life-consciousness more powerful than hers. Reading the *Diary* later she enjoyed learning how Woolf had worked off a publisher's rejection by cleaning out the kitchen and cooking haddock and sausage:

> But her suicide, I felt I was reduplicating in that black summer of 1953. Only I couldn't drown. I suppose I'll always be overvulnerable, slightly paranoid. But I'm also so damn healthy & resilient. And apple-pie happy.[103]

By comparison with the common experience of those suicides who turn out to prefigure their future fate by a consistently depressive view of existence, she gave many such signs of her underlying vitality and richness of personality. A further key to the enigma of her personality may be looked for in a small incident in *The Bell Jar* which Teresa de Lauretis has lighted on as crucial. Esther Greenwood breaks the nurse's thermometers in a fit of mischief and is moved to another room – but not before she has scooped up a ball of mercury:

I opened my fingers a crack, like a child with a secret, and smiled at the silver globe cupped in my palm. If I dropped it, it would break into a million little replicas of itself, and if I pushed them near each other, they would fuse, without a crack, into one whole again. I smiled and smiled at the silver ball.[104]

De Lauretis suggests that this locates a crucial element of her personality, which could accurately be described as 'mercurial', and which had just this property of joining, disjoining and rejoining incessantly. The intelligence of mercury, all too readily descending into a poisonous strain of self, yet capable of being transformed into the winged Hermes who is Mercury's sublime form, had been for Blake, I have elsewhere contended, an apt symbol of basic being. For Plath, it may be argued, the other potentiality of mercury's material substance, its twofold capability of being at once single and multifarious, was equally significant. The perception can be read as ultimately self-revelatory on Plath's part, prompting the speculation that if her suicide attempt had not after all succeeded she would within a short time have re-emerged into yet another positive incarnation of herself, every bit as vital as those that preceded her plunge into the gulf of despair.

This capability of self-division, with the ability to make each projection utterly convincing for the moment, should also be borne in mind when considering the quality and nature of some of the later poetry. Those who think that in 'Daddy' the 'real' Sylvia Plath emerged should ponder the words of Miriam Levine in a review of the *Journals*, where she writes of 'her fall from grace, her incomplete self':

Like Virginia Woolf Plath did not have a secure sense of who she was apart from either the praise or criticism of other people. Rage is not an identity, nor is the poem – no matter how good – an equivalent of identity.[105]

The other notable feature of such poems, moreover, is that their verbal achievements could proliferate into extraordinary ambiguities, leaving scope for varying interpretation.[106]* There is something particularly appropriate in the imagery which came most naturally to her now. Her father had made his name in the study of biology through his work on bumblebees; trying to make a way of life for herself in

Devon she projected herself in the persona of the Beekeeper's Daughter. There could hardly be a better imagery of energies seeking to relate to a central form of being than that of bees, needing to find a point of swarming; in her case the relationship to a father whose premature death had provoked her early crisis of identity made it a quite uncannily apt contribution to her 'mythology of the actual'.[107*]

At this point it is appropriate to return to Wordsworth and Coleridge, for it can be suggested that the two versions of Being that have been traced here between Hughes and Plath reflected with some accuracy those between the two earlier poets. It is natural to relate Hughes to Wordsworth, his fellow North Countryman, and to discuss the degree to which his own relationship with the rangingly intelligent and volatile Sylvia Plath mirrored that between his egotistical predecessor and the equally mercurial Coleridge – who remarked of him in turn that it was 'good for him to be alone'[108] while himself exhibiting all the largesse of an outgoing sympathetic imagination. Plath's very invocation of bees, energies in quest of a stable centre, is reminiscent of Coleridge's similar imagery of vitalism.[109] Of him, as of her, it might have been said that he had a 'very weak ego'[110] – coupled, as in her case, with extraordinary powers of projection, convincing self-dramatization – and even, on occasion, confabulation.[111*] Wordsworth once remarked that Coleridge was 'a subject which no Biographer ought to touch beyond what he himself was eye witness of';[112] one catches something of the same weary, wary implication in Hughes's attitude towards the many biographers who attempted to produce over-simple interpretations of Plath's life and conduct. Indeed, the labyrinthine complexities involved may help to explain his cruel-sounding comment when Linda Wagner-Martin succeeded in publishing hers.[113*]

In their own fashion the two writers corresponded, in fact, to the two forms of genius as distinguished by Coleridge himself:

While the former darts himself forth, and passes into all the forms of human character and passion, the one Proteus of the fire and flood; the other attracts all forms and things to himself, into the unity of his own IDEAL.[114]

This qualitative distinction between two kinds of creative mind, the one dispersive, the other centripetal, is in my view crucial to an understanding of their differing versions of Being and more important than any considerations based on politics or gender. The same imbalance that could be traced in the relationship between Coleridge and Wordsworth respectively, between a dispersed range of energies in a highly intelligent psyche and a range of verbal facilities in a well-organized centripetal system, operates equally convincingly, I would argue, for Hughes and Plath.

It is also an essential element in the argument as it has been developed here that in certain respects their two versions of Being were inseparably linked. It was indeed a function of their mutual attraction that the their lack of complete understanding of one another should not have prevented, rather may have fuelled, a fascination that would not be broken by death. For corroboration one need only turn to Hughes's *Birthday Letters*.

In terms of the dialectic between Being and consciousness that has emerged in the course of these studies this provides, in other words, an example more extreme than any that have preceded it. It is natural to think first of this volatile Sylvia Plath as an exponent of consciousness, with the firmly identified Ted Hughes as an embodiment of Being. Yet if one turns to think of volatility as itself a version of Being, or takes account of Hughes's' need to express himself into conscious language, the terms begin to change places, until Hughes and Plath can be regarded as offering the best instance of the bewildering interchange-ability of these categories in the post-Romantic era, calling for quite unusual mental agility if one is to follow the twists and turns between the two kinds of apprehension involved. Hughes's initial impression of her, 'you were slim and lithe and smooth as a fish',[115] is eloquent of her motion and elusiveness as he later appreciated it, his sense of a consciousness that was always slipping from his hands, while Plath, even more than Coleridge a century or more earlier, had at one extreme of her personality a desperate urge to anchor herself against someone who could offer the stability of a firm point of reference.

Hughes himself may have grasped something of this parallel. He certainly developed a fascination for Coleridge in his later years, going so far as to project for him an underlying mythology which he believed to lie under all his work and proceeding to read off his work against it.[116*] Further inquiry might have led him more profitably to Coleridge's conception of 'the one Life', an interest in the relationship with nature and man that would have been closer to Hughes's more lasting interests and which could also be thought of as a 'mythology of the actual' (not altogether unlike Sylvia's complementary mode). He would have been enabled to compare Coleridge's concept of Being with his own and to see the extent to which it illuminated his gradually enlarging sympathies. It is a view that can be supported by reference to a few occasions when his mythical thinking rose to a dimension no longer bound by the limitations of space and time, belonging rather with experiences such as Ursula's illumination in *The Rainbow* when she looked at a cell in the laboratory and perceived that it could not be limited by any measuring of the space in which it existed: 'It was a consummation, a being infinite.... To be oneself was a supreme, gleaming triumph of infinity.'[117] It was the sense that visited Lawrence again, as on the occasion, years later, when he delighted in the sight of flying-fish out at sea. Before him Coleridge, enjoying the sunset described in 'This Lime-Tree Bower...' had found himself empathizing with a rook that he last saw flying into the figured crucible of the sun's orb.

In his poem 'That Morning', describing an experience in Alaska when he and their son were pursuing the son's work in the fisheries there and saw an overwhelming number of salmon moving together in a stream, in accordance with the laws of their nature, Hughes's vision of Being reaches a similar rare moment of clarification. The closest parallel to that experience had been a sight of Lancaster bombers once seen moving majestically in formation over Yorkshire (and presumably usurping the sense of the sky with their mechanical menace, as the salmon now over-whelmed his sense of the whole landscape with their life).

> There the body
> Separated, golden and imperishable,
> From its doubting thought – a spirit-beacon
> Lit by the power of the salmon
> That came on, and came on, and kept on coming
> As if we flew slowly, their formations
> Lifting us toward some dazzle of blessing
> One wrong thought might darken.

In one of Shakespeare's darkest moments 'Light thickens | And the crow Makes wing to the rooky wood.' The comment suggests the manner in which even the more questionable beings in nature still have need of companionship (just as Macbeth was to be distressed in time by the absence of 'troops of friends'). For Hughes his vision of the salmon was evidently an experience akin to Coleridge's view of the sunset in North Somerset, gazing 'till all doth seem | Less gross than bodily...' and blessing the homeward flying rook, with the comment that 'no sound is dissonant that tells of life' – a reflection prefiguring, in turn, the moment of unconscious blessing by the Ancient Mariner:

an existential action from deep within his being and a simple affirmation directed towards the luminous energies of the water-snakes as they 'coil'd and swam' to be recreated, as we have seen, in Coleridge's later vision of the luminous activity in the shadow of the boat at sea as 'Spirals, coiling, uncoiling, *being*'.[118] It was a version of Being that he could hold in parallel with his Christianity, a vision of the relation between human beings and Nature that had little to do with human guilt yet which could, at least in his 1798 poem, be regarded as in some sense redemptive.

In the same way Hughes, lifted towards a 'dazzle of blessing' by the crowding, shining, directed life of the salmon about him, found it entirely fitting that this should be the end of a journey. In this rare moment the senses of *aion* and *kairos* for once combined. It was as if he had come close to reconciling the visionary quality which he could appreciate yet never quite comprehend in Sylvia Plath with his own insistence on living by his own instincts, and recognize something of the degree to which, together, they complemented rational conscious-ness by providing a twofold version of Being that might serve towards the furnishing of a human completeness. There was much in space and time that had called, and would continue to call, for his penance, but here, at least, however temporarily, he could enjoy the consciousness that his history as a human being and his relationship to the Being of Nature were both in motion, and both at one.

Notes

(Place of publication is London unless otherwise stated. Notes marked by an asterisk in the text give information or comment in addition to, or instead of, bibliographical references.)

Chapter 1

1. Antonio R. Damasio, *Descartes' Error* (1996) p. 248.
2. Irish Murdoch, 'Hegel in Modern Dress', *Existentialists and Mystics* (1997) p. 148.
3. Karl Miller, *Doubles: Studies in Literary History* (Oxford, 1985); Jeremy Hawthorn, *Multiple Personality and the Disintegration of Literary Character: From Oliver Goldsmith to Sylvia Plath* (1983).
4. Morton Prince, *The Dissociation of a Personality: A Biographical Study in Abnormal Psychology* (1906).
5. C.H. Thigpen and H. Cleckley, *The Three Faces of Eve* (1957); cf. their paper 'A Case of Multiple Personality', *Journal of Abnormal and Social Psychology*, XLIX (1957).
6. Hawthorn, *Multiple Personality and the Disintegration of Literary Character*, p. 135.
7. A.S. Luria, *Cognitive Development* (Cambridge, Mass., 1976).
8. Ibid., 136.
9. T.S. Eliot, 'The Metaphysical Poets' (1921), in *Selected Essays* (2nd edn., 1934) p. 288.
10. T.S. Eliot, 'Milton II' (1947), in *On Poetry and Poets* (1957) pp. 152–3.
11. T.S. Eliot, 'John Dryden' (1922), in *Selected Essays*, 314.
12. John Beer, *Wordsworth in Time* (1979) p. 31.
13. Book i, 452–60 (1805 edn.), *The Prelude 1799, 1805, 1850*, ed. Wordsworth, Abrams and Gill (New York, 1979) p. 53.

Chapter 2

1. See my *Romantic Consciousness*, especially Chapter 5.
2. John Forster, *Life* (1872–4) *iii*, 425–6.
3. *DOED*, 17, 159.
4. See Edgar Rosenberg, 'Dating *Edwin Drood*', *The Dickensian*, 76 (1980) 42–3.
5. In a longer version of the present argument, published in the *Dickens Studies Annual*, 13, I considered in some detail the possibility that Dickens for a long time planned this as the story of a disappearance and rediscovery, and that his change of plan might subsequently have led to difficulties.
6. J.F. Daly, *The Life of Augustin Daly* (New York, 1917) pp. 107–8 (*DOED*, 239).

7. Letter by Luke Fildes, *TLS*, 3 November 1905 (reprinted *DCED*, 227–8).
8. Charles Dickens Junior, Introduction to 1923 edition of *Edwin Drood*, p. xv (*DOED*, xxvi–xxvii).
9. This may date from Sir Jasper in Fielding's *The Mock Doctor* (1733), though that Jasper was not evil. Susan Shatto has drawn attention to Southey's ballad 'Jaspar' (1799), a tale of a murderer whose guilt is discovered in a supernatural-seeming flash of blinding light. Dickens introduced into Mrs. Jarley's waxworks in chapter 28 of *The Old Curiosity Shop* 'Jasper Packlemorton of atrocious memory' (who had murdered fourteen wives). His friend Edward Stirling (who adapted several of his novels for the stage) acted in a play entitled *Sir Jasper's Tenant* in 1865.
10. Something of the same sort may be said about the echoes of previous stories in the novel. Rosa Bud, we recognize as a successor to Little Nell, while Jasper's projected confession in the condemned cell had been strongly foreshadowed by a short story, which appeared in 'Master Humphrey's Clock' under the title 'A Confession found in a prison in the time of Charles the Second'. In this story, the narrator tells how he murdered the infant nephew who had been entrusted to his charge because he reminded him of his deceased sister, and pretended that he had been drowned, the body eventually being discovered buried in his garden. Richard Baker, who noticed this in *The Drood Murder Case* (Berkeley and Los Angeles, 1957) pp. 91–5, is clearly right to connect the story with *Drood*, and it is hard to see why Dickens should have wished simply to repeat a previous story in so many details.
11. Revelation IV. 3; XXI. 11 and 18.
12. Ezekiel XXVIII. 12–15.
13. Ezekiel XVIII. 27.
14. One may detect traces of a similar irony in the name of Rosa Bud, this time pointing in a different direction. As a 'giddy, wilful, winning little creature', she has the chance to blossom 'later into the fullness of the mature rose, but if she had remained Jack's 'Pussy', she might have turned into something thorny and less pleasantly feline. Compare, in turn, the behaviour of the opium-woman, who keeps Jasper talking by laying her hand on his chest and moving him slightly to and fro 'as a cat might stimulate a half-slain mouse', and who is then described as 'unwinking, cat-like and intent' (23, 208–9).
15. *DOED*, 19, 167–73; Felix Aylmer, *The Drood Case* (1964) pp. 127–36.
16. *DOED*, 2, 7; quoted ibid., pp. 6–12.
17. Durdles was based on a figure familiar in its streets, Sapsea upon an auctioneer who had become mayor. See, e.g., *DOED*, 23, 215; cf. 2, 4. Other characters also had original prototypes of one kind or another. For an eloquent panegyric, see Edgar Johnson, *Charles Dickens: His Tragedy and Triumph*, (2 vols., 1953) ii, 1115–16.
18. Kate Perugini, '*Edwin Drood* and the Last Days of Charles Dickens', *Pall Mall Magazine*, 37 (June 1906), 648; Henry Fielding Dickens, 'A Chat about Charles Dickens', *Harper's Magazine*, 192 (July 1914) 191.
19. Pencilled marginal comment in John Forster's *Life of Dickens* (3 vols., 1874), quoted by Charles Forsyte, *The Decoding of Edwin Drood* (1980) p. 50. Collins is not likely, however, to have been in the best of humours

while reading Forster's *Life*, which played down his role in relation to Dickens: see R.P. Ashley, 'Wilkie Collins and the Dickensians', *The Dickensian*, 49 (1952–53) 59–65. For more restrained assertions of weakness in *Drood*, see K.J. Fielding, *Charles Dickens: A Critical Introduction* (2nd edn., 1965) pp. 242, 250; A.O.J. Cockshut, 'Edwin Drood and Late Dickens Reconciled', in *Dickens and the Twentieth Century*, ed. J. Gross and G. Pearson (1962) pp. 229–30.

20. *DLN*, iii, 124–5.
21. The syntax here is ambiguous, but the parentheses would seem to be governed by the 'not' of the previous clause.
22. *The Invisible Woman: The Story of Ellen Ternan and Charles Dickens* (1990) p. 126.
23. She abandoned her acting career, and for several years, from 1867 to 1865, vanished altogether. (The guess that she was in France is plausible.) Even when she did surface again it was as a woman living a hidden life in Slough. And her condition was in one sense merely intensified after Dickens's death, since she continued to be invisible – at least as Dickens's former lover. She lowered her age considerably and reinvented herself as the wife of a schoolmaster in Kent, so that her former life remained permanently unrevealed – perhaps even to her husband. Certainly, the facts of the matter, when discovered by her son after her death, shocked him so profoundly that he never really accepted them. Some of Dickens's admirers have found it equally impossible to believe their hero could have departed so blatantly from Victorian conventional morality. See Tomalin, *The Invisible Woman*, pp. 125, 264.
24. Quoted ibid., 231.
25. For a full account of the accident and Dickens's recurrent states of shock afterwards, see Johnson, *Tragedy and Triumph*, ii, 1018–21. Forsyte (*Decoding*, 83) comments on the resemblance between one of these fits and one of Jasper's.
26. *DOED*, 3, 15.
27. *The Moonstone*, third narrative, ch. x. It should be observed, however, that the reference to the actual phenomenon occurs in a book by Dickens's friend Dr. Elliotson (*Human Physiology* [1840] p. 646) and that Dickens might therefore originally have given Collins the idea. The resemblance between *The Moonstone* and *Edwin Drood* in this respect was drawn upon by 'Orpheus C. Kerr' in one of the earliest continuations (*DOED*, 214 and n.).
28. Edmund Wilson, *The Wound and the Bow* (1941, revised edn., 1961) pp. 75–93.
29. Aubrey Boyd, 'A New Angle on the Drood Mystery', in *Humanistic Series: Social Studies*, 9 (1921) pp. 35–85. Howard Duffield, 'John Jasper: Strangler', *American Bookman* (February 1930).
30. Wilson, *Wound and Bow*, 92.
31. *Old Curiosity Shop*, ch. 9.
32. *DOED*, 12.
33. For a lengthy comment on the parallels with *Macbeth* in this novel, see Philip Collins, *Dickens and Crime* (1962) pp. 299–300. Cf. also Forsyte, *Decoding*, 89–90, 98–9.

34. Forsyte, *Decoding*, 50–82, etc.
35. *DOED*, 14, 125.
36. For typical accusations see, e.g., Fred Kaplan, *Dickens and Mesmerism: The Hidden Springs of Fiction* (Princeton, NJ, 1975) pp. 189–90nn.
37. Ibid., 74–112, etc.
38. *DLN*, iii, 752–3.
39. Kaplan, *Dickens and Mesmerism*, 72–80, *et passim*.
40. Ibid., 119, 129–30, 145–6, 152–3, 164, etc.
41. Ibid., 103.
42. Notably the parts to be played by Neville and Helena Landless.
43. *DLN*, iii, 776.
44. Introduction to his edition of *Edwin Drood* (1974) p. 20.
45. *DOED*, 23, 212.
46. Introduction to *Edwin Drood* (1975) p. 20.
47. *DOED*, 23, 204–5.
48 See *Romantic Consciousness*, pp. 100, 104.
49. *DOED*, 3, 15–16; 11, 92–3. These are only two of the many 'doubles' that Forsyte finds in the novel: see *Decoding*, 84–92. For an absorbing reading of this element of the novel, specifically in terms of human identity, see Charles Mitchell, '*The Mystery of Edwin Drood*: The Interior and Exterior of Self', *ELH*, 33 (1966) 228–46.
50. *Hard Times,* Chapter 5.
51. George Dolby, *Dickens as I Knew Him* (1885) p. 426. See *DOED*, xvii–xviii, which also quotes an earlier reference by Dickens to church-music: 'the drawling voice, without a heart, that drearily pursues the dull routine' (*Household Words*, 28 September 1850).
52. *DOED*, 1, 3; 23, 203.
53. *DOED*, 2, 11. K.J. Fielding notes that in the last chapter the opium-woman is compared to one of these carvings (Fielding, *Dickens Introduction*, p. 250). She is demonic in appearance, though not necessarily in intent.
54. *Pickwick Papers*, ch. 5; *David Copperfield*, ch. 13; *Great Expectations*, ch. 49; Dyson, *Inimitable Dickens*, 270. (Dyson is wrong to say that David had his encounter with the Goroo man here, however; that was at Chatham.)
55. *DOED*, xxiii, 215.
56. *DOED*, 6, 40; *DOED*, 2, 7.
57. Forsyte, *Decoding*, 93–9, discussing *DOED*, x, 79–80.
58. Another image of benevolence is that of Handel, whose picture presides above 'with a knowing air of being up to the contents of the closet, and a musical air of intending to combine all its harmonies in one delicious fugue'; Handel's presence is a benevolent one elsewhere in Dickens: it is his name that is given to Pip by Herbert Pocket in *Great Expectations* (ch. 22). Cf. *DLO*, ii, 34n; iii, 483 and n. The words 'saccharine transfiguration' which conclude the passage as a whole have since been compromised by association with a substance that was not invented until a few years after *Edwin Drood*. In Dickens's time the use of the word 'saccharine', though sometimes satirical, was mainly sportive.
59. *DOED*, 6, 44.
60. *DOED*, 7, 50.

61. *DOED*, 10, 84–5.
62. Dickens's will (Forster, *Life*, iii, 517); Storey, *Dickens and Daughter*, 140.
63. *DLN*, iii, 735.
64. Ibid., 731.
65. Ibid., 733.
66. *All the Year Round*, N.S., ii (21 August 1869) p. 288.
67. Edgar Johnson's biography contains repeated references to it and to his 'wretchedness': see, e.g., pp. 752, 820, 878 and 882. One way of seeking relief was to go off on short expeditions with companions such as Wilkie Collins.
68. *Mr and Mrs Charles Dickens. His Letters to Her*, ed. Walter Dexter (1935) pp. 225–9.
69. For a full account and text see R.L. Brannan, *Under the Management of Mr. Charles Dickens* (Ithaca, NY, 1966).
70. Johnson, *Tragedy and Triumph*, ii, 879–82.
71. Brannan, *Management*. 84, quoting *DCN*, ii, 859 (cf. 824–5).
72. Ibid., 72 (from *The Dickensian*, 38 [1942] 189–91).
73. *Romantic Consciousness*, pp. 100–4.
74. See ibid., p. 103.
75. See above at note 72.
76. Johnson, *Tragedy and Triumph*, ii, 1102.
77. Ibid., 1103.
78. Storey, *Dickens and Daughter*, 92.
79. Dolby, *Dickens as I Knew Him*, 388, quoted in Wilson, *Wound and Bow*, p. 87.
80. *DOED*, 16, 146.
81. *DOED*, 3, 23.
82. *DOED*, 9, 63–4.
83. *DOED*, 14, 128.
84. *DLN*, iii. 773.
85. See above, pp. 55–8.
86. The Ternans may have had some quality of wildness in Dickens's perception of them that provided a further natural connection with the Landlesses. The clearest link, however, is between Helena's integrity and the 'pride and self-reliance' of Ellen 'which (mingled with the gentlest nature) has borne her, alone, through so much', to quote Dickens's praise (Letter to Mrs. Frances Elliot, *DLN*, iii, 476). Claire Tomalin points out that the only woman character in Dickens who bears any real resemblance in personal appearance to Ellen is Lucie in *A Tale of Two Cities* – the 'maddening' fact being that she is otherwise 'almost a blank' (*The Invisible Woman*, pp. 125, 264). That 1859 portrayal belongs of course to the earlier part of their relationship, the later perhaps leading to the more interesting features found in characters such as Estella in *Great Expectations*.
87. This suggestion seems to have been made first by Aubrey Boyd (see Wilson, *Wound and Bow*, 83).
88. *DLO*, i, 597: 'I have just turned lazy and passed into Christabel and thence to Wallenstein.'
89. See my discussion in *Coleridge the Visionary* (1959) ch. vi.
90. Coleridge is relevant to the novel in a further respect, for the kind of endeavour, with its attendant problems, that is to be traced in 'Christabel'

is also visible in his influence on later nineteenth-century religious thought, and on Anglicanism in particular. A general survey of the Victorian Church would show many examples of the bland 'cool heads and warm hearts' policy advocated by the dean of Cloisterham. For something more energetic we look to men such as Charles Kingsley, Thomas Hughes and Frederick Denison Maurice, all of whom had in common a devotion to the religious teachings of Coleridge, and all of whom impressed their hearers by the very intensity of their ardour. (see, e.g., Owen Chadwick, *The Victorian Church* (1960) i, 545–50). Such men succeeded through a commitment to the emphatic of which John Jasper exhibits the dark opposite. It is not accidental, I think, that Dickens's Crisparkle has been seen as of their company: see Angus Wilson, Introduction to *Edwin Drood* (1975) p. 26.

91. See above, p. 12.
92. A.A. Adrian, 'A Note on the Dickens–Collins Friendship', *Huntington Library Quarterly*, 16 (1953) 211–13.
93. Johnson, *Tragedy and Triumph*, ii, 1143–8.
94. See letter of 3 March 1929 from Mary Angela Dickens (daughter of Charles Junior) enclosed with one from Bessie Hatton in the Driffield collection (Oxf. 253).
95. *DOED*, 20, 175.
96. See above, p. 29.
97. Letter of 20 May 1861, *DLN*, iii, 221.
98. See above, note 8.
99. See above, note 9.
100. *Eustace Conway, Anthony Munday and Other Essays* (New York, privately printed, 1927), p. 95; Perugini, '*Edwin Drood* and the Last Days of Charles Dickens', 654 (*DOED*, xxvii).
101. Rudolph Lehmann, *An Artist's Reminiscences* (1894) pp. 231–2 (*DOED*, xxvii).
102. Coleridge, *Table Talk*, 1 [6] July 1833 (*CC*, i, 409–10).
103. Compare Lamb's apprehension, 'Never tell thy dreams, and I am almost afraid that Kubla Khan is an owl that wont bear day light': to Wordsworth, 26 April 1816: *Letters* (ed. Marrs) II, 214.
104. Dyson, *Inimitable Dickens*, 272.
105. Pansy Pakenham, 'The Memorandum Book, Forster and *Edwin Drood*', *The Dickensian*, 61 (1955) 120.
106. Perugini, '*Edwin Drood* and the Last Days of Charles Dickens', p. 646.
107. Letter to Forster, 16 February 1874. Quoted Johnson, *Tragedy and Triumph*, ii, 1155.

Chapter 3

1. This was perceived even by those who did not know him well. On one occasion De Quincey was invited to meet Thackeray at a dinner in Edinburgh, but to Thackeray's disappointment pleaded an indisposition. A second party was arranged, only to produce further excuses; when Hogg persisted, he finally came out with the true reason: 'No; much as it troubles me to see

people, if it had been Dickens, now, I might have gone – I should have gone; but not Thackeray. There is a benignity in everything that Dickens has done' (James Hogg, *De Quincey and his Friends* (1895) p. 194).

2. He was particularly drawn to the sect by meeting William Ellery Channing during a visit to Boston. See Edgar Johnson, *Charles Dickens: His Tragedy and Triumph* (1953) I, 378 (cf. 464, 573–4, II, 1133). Channing's links with the Lake Poets are explored in my essay in *Providence and Love* (1998) pp. 98–115.

3. What he actually said was, 'I believe it will be absolutely necessary that you should prevail on our future masters to learn their letters.' See *Oxford Dictionary of Quotations* (2nd edn., 1953).

4. He names B.F. Westcott, J.E.B. Mayer, J.B. Lightfoot, E.W. Benson and F.J.A. Hort among the first group and Henry Sidgwick, Henry Jackson, the Balfour brothers, Walter Leaf, Edmund Gurney, A.W. Verrall, F.W. Maitland, Henry Butcher and George Prothero among the second: *Godliness and Good Learning* (1961) pp. 27, 229, cited in Alan Gauld *The Founders of Psychical Research* (1968) p. 64.

5. See my *Providence and Love* (1998) pp. 119–32.

6. Letter to Sidgwick 11 March 1871: TCL MS Myers 12[100].

7. *Fragments of Prose and Poetry*, ed. E. Myers (1904) p. 6.

8. See *Providence and Love*, 133–4.

9. 'George Eliot', *The Century Magazine*, XXIII (November 1881) 62–3; *Providence and Love*, 134–5.

10. Obituary of Sidgwick: *Proceedings of the Society for Psychical Research*, XV (1901) p. 454. The exact date of this walk is uncertain. Alan Gauld points out (*Founders*, 103) that it is here given as 3 December 1869, but in *Fragments of Inner Life* the interest is dated from 13 November 1871. Both dates were evidently significant in some sense: in Myers's Journal the entry for the first date is marked 'On Ghosts?', that for the second 'H.S. on ghosts'.

11. Letter to Myers, April 1872: *Sidgwick Memoir*, 259.

12. Stephen, *George Eliot* (1902) p. 191.

13. Letter to his wife, 16 December 1882: Ralph Barton Perry, *The Thought and Character of William James* (Cambridge, Mass., 1948) p. 155; James, *The Will to Believe and Other Essays in Popular Philosophy* (1897) p. 308.

14. See his 'Autobiography' in Charlotte Leaf, *Walter Leaf* (1932) p. 95.

15. Peter Gunn, *Vernon Lee* (1964) pp. 84–5.

16. See below, p. 55.

17. Perry, *William James*, 155.

18. F.W.H. Myers, 'The Work of Edmund Gurney in Experimental Psychology', *Proceedings of the Society for Psychical Research*, V (1888–9) 360 (Trevor Hall, *The Strange Case of Edmund Gurney* (2nd edn.,1980) p. 35).

19. Ibid., V, 360.

20. See his attempt to adjudicate between the advocates of vivisection and their opponents in his discussions in 'A Chapter in the Ethics of Pain' and 'An Epilogue on Vivisection': Gurney, *Tertium Quid* (1887) I, 204–26.

21. See the arguments in his 'Chapter in the Ethics of Pain', ibid., I, 151–203.

22. See his essay, 'A Permanent Band for the East-End': ibid., II, 96–118.

23. The main initiating events were the strange happenings at Hydesville, in New York State, when otherwise inexplicable rappings and noises led to the discovery of coded messages and the recounting of a crime that had been committed there a few years before. Partly as a result of the sensation caused by this story, interest in spiritualism spread like wildfire across the United States; E. Hardinge Britten (*Modern American Spiritualism* (New York, 1870) p. 546), estimated that by then eleven million believers existed there. A highly sceptical account of these events is given by Ruth Brandon, *The Spiritualists* (1983) esp. pp. 1–41: she points to a number of pieces of evidence, including public confessions, which strongly suggest that all the phenomena were created by the young women themselves. A more sympathetic account provides the opening for Alan Gauld, *The Founders of Psychical Research* (1968). (Although my own study of the manuscripts was carried out independently, his study has provided much further material for the present chapter.)

24. For accounts of some of the investigations see Gauld, *Founders*, 104–14.

25. See Gauld, *Founders*, 37–47.

26. For a good account, see Janet Oppenheimer, *The Other World* (Cambridge, 1985), pp. 212–13.

27. Lodge, *Past Years* (1931) p. 280. (With his own absorption in physics, he may not, of course, have appreciated the extent to which certain aspects of scientific method employed by classical scholars for their researches required equal stringency.)

28. Unfortunately, the circumstances of this previous acquaintance are not known.

29. 'Frederic Myers's Service to Psychology', *William James on Psychical Research*, ed. G. Murphy and R.O. Ballou (New York, 1960) p. 214.

30. Letter to William James of 8 April 1887, Houghton bMS 1092.9 (205).

31. Worrying about the rules of evidence that ought to be adopted, they corresponded with lawyers and others – though it is not clear that the question of what is acceptable in a court of law would be properly relevant in this field.

32. Myers, *Fragments of Inner Life* (1961) pp. 40–1.

33. Report in the *Brighton and Hove Herald:* see Hall, *Strange Case*, 17. The verdict brought in was that he had been 'accidentally suffocated by an overdose of chloroform taken probably for the relief of pain'.

34. Contemporary report in *Brighton and Hove Herald*, quoted ibid., 15.

35. *DNB* article, cited ibid. As mentioned above, Robertson, who knew Gurney well, here repeated the inquest verdict without question, giving the cause of death as 'an overdose of narcotic, taken to procure sleep'.

36. Since we cannot know whether his Brighton visit came on the crest of a manic wave of intellectual excitement following recent work or in the trough of a subsequent depression caused by reviving doubts about its worth, the mood in which he went to the hotel room cannot be gauged, though it is reasonable to suppose that he was in extremity of some kind. Trevor Hall's theory that in Brighton he had discovered evidence of comprehensive deception on the part of his associate G.A. Smith has some plausibility but is ultimately a matter of speculation. Even accepted, it is still hard to be sure whether the emotion produced by such a discovery

would have been one of devastation at such betrayal, prompting suicide, or a massive and complex desire to discover what could now be rescued, leading to a nervous state in which resort to a narcotic might have seemed called for.

37. Myers. 'Work of Gurney', 361, cited in Hall, *Strange Case*, 29.
38. Ibid., 25 and n. Gurney's undergraduate career had been lengthened to five years on account of 'broken residence, caused by a depression of mind and spirit that was apt with him to follow upon moods of high enthusiasm and consuming activity' (*DNB*).
39. TCL MS Myers $4^{12(1)}$.
40. Letter of 2 August 1877. *The George Eliot Letters*, ed. Gordon Haight (New Haven, Conn., 1954–78) VI, 398; 380, 387, 396.
41. Gunn, *Vernon Lee*, 84–5. George Eliot's mention of the father having lost his property suggests that the account below from Alice James, describing her as the daughter of a solicitor, is to be trusted more than that from Vernon Lee, who was not averse to embroidering her accounts.
42. His work for the Society, wrote Lady Battersea, meant that 'his wife had to encounter many dark days, also hours of unavoidable loneliness, in spite of which her devotion to her husband never flagged'. Lady Constance Battersea, *Reminiscences* (1922) p. 206, cited Hall, *Strange Case*, 25.
43. Letter from Alice James to her aunt, Catharine Walsh, 31 July 1888. Houghton bMS Am 1094 (1536).
44. Letter of 21 August 1888 to her brother William and his wife: Houghton bMS Am 1094 (1482), printed (var) *The Death and Letters of Alice James*, ed. Ruth Bernard Yeazell (Berkeley, Ca, 1981) pp. 146–7. On 24 April 1887, she had written (ms. cited 1479): *Death and Letters*, 127) that she had sent Henry James Senior's book to Kate Gurney, 'having heard from Mrs Edmund that she hankered after it greatly & I was glad to find that it had not gone amiss.' (She may have enclosed a copy of Emilia Russell Gurney's gushing tribute to the book, which Gurney sent independently to William.) Reporting that some papers sent for Kate had gone astray, she continued, 'I have only seen her once this winter she has been in Brighton. If it was a joke she lost nothing, her gift lies not in that direction.'
45. Letter of 11 March 1877: TCMS 2 [81]. Myers's diary for this time includes several favourable references to Kate, suggesting that he himself took more than a passing interest in her.
46. In this context Oliver Lodge's comment on his first visit to them – 'I was introduced to his wife, but didn't see much of her' (Lodge, *Past Years*, 270) – is resonant.
47. See his essay 'A Permanent Band for the East-End', in *Tertium Quid*, II (1887) 96–118.
48. *Death and Letters* 145–6, corrected from Houghton bMS Am 1094 (1482).
49. MS Letter to James of 18 April 1886.
50. Kate herself was not always in the best of health, as Gurney told William James in a letter of July 1885, quoted Gordon Epperson, *The Mind of Edmund Gurney* (1997) p.145, according to which she had been suffering from a 'very long low feverish attack' for the previous four months.
51. *Death and Letters of Alice James*, 145.

52. Undated letter to William James, Houghton bMS Am 1092 (323). Quoted Epperson, *Mind of Gurney*, 146–7.
53. In the year following her husband's death she married Archibald Grove, editor of the *New Review*. Henry James, who met the couple then in Paris, commented dryly, 'how the drama of life rushes on and how out of it all poor chloroformed Edmund Gurney seemed'. *The Diary of Alice James*, ed. Leon Edel (1965) p. 65.
54. Letter of 11 July 1888, *Correspondence of William James*, ed. J.J. McDermott *et al*. (Charlottesville, Va.1992–) II, 88–9.
55. 'A single inauspicious day has robbed all.' Lucretius *De Rerum Natura*, iii, 398–9. I owe this reference to Professor E.J. Kenney, who points out that the language echoes that of funerary inscriptions.
56. Letter of 22 August 1888, Houghton bMS Am 1092.9 (3548), ibid., VI, 429–30 (cf. 449).
57. Houghton MS bMS Am 1092.9 (524), ibid., 434–5.
58. *Proceedings SPR*, VIII, 450.
59. *Proceedings SPR*, VII, 307.
60. *Proceedings SPR*, VIII, 472.
61. Ibid., 349.
62. Ibid., 443.
63. *Proceedings SPR*, VII, 329.
64. Ibid., 329.
65. See Podmore's comment on his wonderful belief in 'the goodness and honour of others, of all whom he knew', quoted Hall, *Strange Case*, 26.
66. See *Tertium Quid*, I, 242.
67. See Hall, *Strange Case*, especially chapters 8–10.
68. The mention of him by Alice James (quoted above) as having behaved as 'more of an idiot even than usual' receives backing only from Caroline Jebb, who described him as a 'goose' at the time when he was looking anxiously for someone to marry (Mary Anne Bobbitt, *With Dearest Love to All: the Life and Letters of Lady Jebb* (1960) p. 141). Both descriptions are rendered suspect by the writers' distaste for psychical research. Jane Harrison, the Newnham anthropologist, wrote more level-headedly of her encounters with members of the society:

> Frederick Myers rang, perhaps, the most sonorously of all, but to me he always rang a little false. Edmund Gurney was, I think, the most lovable and beautiful human being I ever met. This was the Psychical research circle; their quest scientific proof of immortality. To put it thus seems almost grotesque now; then it was inspiring. (*Reminiscences of a Student's Life* (1925) p. 55)

Other comments on Myers from his contemporaries suggest a nasal voice, with perhaps a touch of the sanctimonious, and something about him which, at least on a casual acquaintance, did not make him readily comprehensible. As a young man, particularly, he seems to have enjoyed taking controversial positions. After a visit from him Henry Taylor wrote, 'Fred Myers was exceedingly agreeable, but there is a fiery vehemence half apparent in him which made one feel that he might not be so to all men and in all moods' (Una Taylor, *Guests and Memories: Annals of a Seaside Villa* (Oxford, 1924) p. 249). This was written in the autumn of 1868; at the following Christmas, when Taylor was writing on the question of criminal reform, Myers sent him his current views: 'I cannot agree in your wish to assimilate [the criminal's] condition to the condition of a lunatic in a well managed asylum. On the contrary, I think that of all classes whose treatment the nation is in any way called to determine, the lunatic ought to receive the best treatment and the confirmed criminal the worst.' He went on to maintain that once it had been established that a criminal was irretrievably set in his ways it would be better for everyone if he were put to death. In later years, however, he modified his views, on the ground that if human beings were immortal, as he now more firmly believed, a 'death' penalty might not after all be the most appropriate.

69. *Proceedings SPR*, VII, 355.
70. *Proceedings SPR*, VIII, 404.
71. *William James on Psychical Research*, 319–20. His comment on Myers's early nature may be compared with Henry Taylor's detecting (note 67 above) of a latent vehemence, contrasting with the more calm and stately demeanour noted by later observers. It helps to account for the undercurrent of excitement that can sometimes be sensed in his later writings beneath the calm waters of the experimental accounts, as when, having shown himself well content to give accounts of crystal gazing that dwell on the power possessed by some of the subjects to see imagery in the crystal which is more vivid than would be evoked in other circumstances, yet gives no hint of the supernatural, he goes on with apparently equal calmness to present evidence from some cases suggesting that the images seen are produced by telepathic powers.
72. Letter of 29 October 1885, TCL Add Ms 97$^{25(107)}$.
73. Letter of December 1887, TCL Myers 2^{82}, quoted Gauld, *Founders*, 176–7.
74. This relationship is described at greater length in my *Providence and Love*, chapter 4.
75. Unlike his friend and senior Henry Sidgwick (who might have been expected to press his case) Myers was never a member. His brother Arthur, by contrast, *was* elected. It is supposed that Myers's links as an undergraduate with some of the 'fast' members of his own college was responsible for this; and it may well be that the attempted scandal over the award of the Camden medal (see my *Providence and Love*, 120–30) also lingered in some members' minds as a stumbling block. Nevertheless, hints of the Apostles' ethos must have filtered through to Myers through his constant communications with Sidgwick and his own brother. More surprising is the failure of either Myers or Gurney to become members of the Metaphysical Society (founded in 1869 and eventually dissolved in 1880), which was in some senses a continuation of the Apostles in London and which would have brought them into direct contact with Tennyson. Reflecting the acute intellectual disquiet of the 1870s, its aims and topics for discussion were so relevant to their own concerns that one would have expected them to find them enthusiastic participants alongside figures such as Henry Sidgwick. Leslie Stephen, T.H. Huxley and John Ruskin

Myers later joined its attempted successor, the Synthetic Society, but that was not founded until 1896, a few years before his death.

76. See *Providence and Love*, 247–301.
77. *Hortus Inclusus* (Orpington, 1887) p.18, reprinted in Ruskin's *Works* (ed. E.T. Cook and A. Wedderburn) XXXVII, 117.
78. 'There is grandeur in this view of life, with its eternal powers, having been originally breathed by the Creator into a few forms or into one; and that, whilst this planet has gone cycling on according to the fixed law of gravity, from so simple a beginning endless forms most beautiful and most wonderful have been, and are being evolved.' *The Origin of Species* (1859) Conclusion.
79. The *Saturday Review* was still more caustic: 'If this is the spirit-world, it is much better to be a respectable pig and accept annihilation, than to be cursed with such an immortality.' Both are quoted in *William James on Psychical Research*, 22.
80. *Life and Letters* (1900) I, 420.
81. *Proceedings SPR*, VIII, 528.
82. 'The Human Ideal', *Tertium Quid*, I, 33.
83. 'The Controversy of Life', ibid., I, 133.
84. Myers, *Fragments of Inner Life* (London, Society for Psychical Research, 1961) p. 41.
85. Hardy, *Collected Poems* (1976) p. 430.
86. *William James on Psychical Research*, 26.
87. His very interesting record is transcribed in Gauld, *Founders*, 130–2.
88. Letter of 4 August 1877: TCMS Myers 12^{145}.
89. See, e.g., *Providence and Love*, 150–4.
90. Myers, *Science and a Future Life* (1893) pp. 171–92.
91. Ibid., 195.
92. See, e.g., his *Wordsworth* (1880) p. 121.
93. Lines 346–54, *TP*, 536–8.
94. Myers, *Science and a Future Life*, 134.
95. See Wilfrid Ward's essay 'Tennyson', in *Problems and Persons* (1903) pp. 217–25 for an account of Tennyson's detailed exposition of the latter poem.
96. Maisie Ward, *The Wilfrid Wards*, p.363.
97. 'De Profundis' lines 53–6, *TP*, 1283.
98. See, e.g., the opening to 'The Destiny of Nations', especially lines 4 to 6: *CPW* (Beer) 126.
99. *Selected Essays* (2nd edn., 1934) p. 288; see also above, p. 6.
100. Hallam Tennyson, *Memoir*, II, 481.
101. See *Romantic Consciousness*, p. 123. If Myers knew the passage it was probably directly from Hallam Tennyson himself, since his *Memoir*, in which it was published, did not appear until 1897, a few years after *Science and a Future Life*.
102. Lines 229–38, *TP*, 1356.
103. *Romantic Consciousness*, p.130.
104. Reported *Memoir*, II, 343.
105. Hall, *Strange Case*, 198–9.
106. Ibid., 41. See below, chapter 4, note 8.

107. Myers, *Science and a Future Life*, 113.
108. Myers, *Collected Poems* (1921) pp. 369–70.

Chapter 4

1. For their earlier correspondence see, e.g., the letters of 17 October 1888, Houghton bMS Am 1092.9 (409), and of 3 January 1894, Houghton bMS Am 1092.9 (417). One of them accompanied the best-known photograph of Gurney.
2. William James, *The Varieties of Religious Experience* (1903) p. 511.
3. Myers, quoted ibid., 512.
4. Ibid., Index, s.v. Subconscious.
5. Letter of 12 January 1891: typewritten version Houghton bMS Am 1092.9 (413).
6. Letter of 30 January 1891, L I 305–6: *William James on Psychical Research*, 68.
7. Quoted Gauld, *Founders*, 277, from *Proceedings SPR*, XVIII (1903) 30.
8. Myers's account did not go into further detail, however. A problem was apparently created by the fact that Hodgson thought the message to be that of a recent suicide, a belief which Gurney's friends did not wish to see in print: see Gauld, *Founders*, 178–9 and nn.
9. Letter of 3 February 1897, TCMS Myers 11[155], p. 3. Gauld, who examines the case of her mediumship critically, finds most accounts heavily biased against her: *Founders*, 361–3.
10. Alice James, *Journal*, ed. Leon Edel (1965) p. 231.
11. R.W.B. Lewis, *The Jameses: A Family Narrative* (New York, 1991) p. 495. Henry James, who had declared himself 'alien' to the whole spiritualist business, was later deeply impressed when a message was passed on to him from Mrs Piper about a matter which was, he acknowledged, known to no one in the world but himself. Ibid., 497.
12. Letter of 3 January 1894, Houghton bMS Am 1092.9 (417), quoting *Aeneid*, iv, 530: 'Receive the night into your eyes and heart.' 'Phinuit' was the name of Mrs Piper's control.
13. Letter of 1891 (see note 3).
14. Letter of 3 February 1897, Houghton bMS Am 1092.9 (420).
15. Letter of 24 October 1899, Houghton bMS Am 1092.9 (422).
16. Letter of 4 December 1899, Houghton bMS Am 1092.9 (424).
17. Axel Munthe, who as a doctor was partly responsible for looking after him there, records that his last words were 'I am very tired and very happy' (*The Story of San Michele* (1929) p. 372.) He afterwards sent a letter appreciative of Myers to Eveleena, also in Rome: TCMS Myers 19[111], post-marked 20 January 1901. William James sent an account to his brother. He too was much impressed by Myers's composure, and his appetite for reading even 'with the death rattle almost begun and drugged with morphia': 'All this intellectual vitality and general moral superiority in Myers is in the grand style and something decidedly exceptional' Letter of 17 January 1901, James, *Correspondence*, III, 156.
18. Houghton bMS Am 1092.9 (3318). Hodgson's devotion to Mrs Piper he found, by contrast, 'a real monstrosity of patience. From the neuro-

pathological point of view I should say that he was now in the stage of complete systematization of his delusion concerning Phinuit George & Co. It is now a scaffolding of interlinked hypotheses, and speaking seriously, there is no doubt but on his ordinary friends he makes this impression. In strict science I imagine the work now being done is the most important that yet has been done by him. But it is fearfully tedious to a mere hearer, and I am much afraid will get few readers careful enough to do justice to all the points it covers.' Ibid.

19. *William James on Psychical Research,* ed. G. Murphy and R.O. Ballou (New York, 1960) 216.

20. Ibid., 41.

21. *William James on Psychical Research,* 311. James names 'the eminent psychiatrist Morselli' and 'the eminent physiologist Botazzi', citing as well a hostile researcher from the Society. According to Lodge (*Past Years,* 309), Myers was deeply shocked at the Cambridge exposure, yet on seeing her again when he visited Richet in Paris, found the phenomena she then displayed inexplicable and his confidence restored. He made no public statement, nevertheless, before his death, which occurred shortly afterwards.

22. *William James on Psychical Research,* 61.

23. See above chapter 3, note 70.

24. Ibid., 310, from an article in *The American Magazine,* October 1909.

25. See above, p. 64.

26. Letter of 18 May 1909: Houghton bMS Am 1092.9 (225).

27. See his *Past Years* (1931) pp. 287–8.

28. See especially Lionel Trilling's essay on that poem, reprinted in *The Liberal Imagination* (1951) pp. 129–59.

29. I have unfortunately mislaid the reference for this quotation.

30. A. Koestler, 'The Three Domains of Creativity', in *The Concept of Creativity in Science and Art,* ed. Denis Button and Michael Krausz (The Hague, 1981) p. 14.

31. Notable examples are Little Father Time in *Jude the Obscure* (1895), the decadent Eloi in H.G. Wells's *The Time Machine* (1895) and Hanno in Thomas Mann's *Buddenbrooks* (1901).

32. *Der Feldweg* (3 vols., Frankfurt 1962) III, 89. Quoted M.E. Zimmermann, *Eclipse of the Self* (Athens and London, 1981) p. 3.

33. Ibid.

34. *Basic Problems of Phenomenology* (Bloomington, 1982) p.160.

35. Thomas Sheehan, 'Reading a Life: Heidegger and Hard Times', in *The Cambridge Companion to Heidegger,* ed. C.B. Guignon (1993) p. 71.

36. 'German Men and Women!', *Freiburger Studentzeitung,* 10 November 1933; quoted Jeff Collins, *Introducing Heidegger* (Duxford, Cambs, 1999) p. 96.

37. 'National Socialist Education', in *Der Alemann: Kampfblatt der Nationalsocialisten Oberbadens,* 1 February 1934; quoted ibid.

38. According to Heidegger's report, the colleague 'very actively frequented the Jew Fränkel'. Sheehan, *Cambridge Companion to Heidegger,* 86.

39. Ibid., 87.

40. See his *The Question concerning Technology,* trans. William Lovitt (New York, 1977) p.137, quoted in Hubert L. Dreyfus, 'Nihilism, Art, Technology, and Politics', *Cambridge Companion to Heidegger,* 312.

41. Ibid., 377.
42. H.W. Petzet, *Auf einen Sternen zugehen* ... (Frankfurt-am-Main, 1983) p. 81, quoted Ott, *Heidegger*, 81.
43. See, for instance, Herbert Marcuse's account of his explanation in an interview of his earlier activities: 'He refused (and I think I find this rather sympathetic), he refused any attempt to deny it or declare it an aberration... because he did not want to be in the same category, as he said, with all those of his colleagues who suddenly didn't remember any more that they taught under the Nazis, that they ever supported the Nazis, and declared that actually they had always been non-Nazi.' This is rather breathtaking: not necessarily arrogance, but certainly approaching the egotistical sublime.
44. Ott, *Heidegger*, 370–1.
45. Richard Rorty, 'Heidegger, Contingency, and Pragmatism', *Cambridge Companion to Heidegger* (1993) 214–16.
46. Toril Moi, *Simone de Beauvoir: the Making of an Intellectual Woman* (Oxford, 1994) p. 80.
47. Ibid., 31, quoting Annie Cohen-Solal, *Sartre 1905–1980* (Paris, 1985) p. 116.
48. Heidegger 'WHD, 94/142', quoted in M.E. Zimmermann, *Eclipse of the Self* (Athens and London, 1981) p. v.
49. *L'Âge de Raison* (1945): 1947 English translation by Eric Sutton (Harmondsworth, 1961), pp. 168–9.
50. *Les Mots*, translated by Irene Claphane as *Words* (1964) pp. 62–3.
51. Letter of June 1822: *SL*, II, 435.
52. Ibid., 158.
53. Ibid., 168–9.
54. Ibid., 161–2.
55. Ibid., 164.
56. Iris Murdoch, *Sartre* (1967 edn.) p. 60, quoting *variatim* from *Middlemarch*, chapter xxi.
57. Ibid. 58.
58. 'Modern Fiction': *The Common Reader* (1925) p.189.
59. *Words*, 129–30.
60. Ronald Hayman, *Writing Against* (1986) p. 420.
61. See the Introduction to *Letters to Olga*, 17–19.
62. Ibid., 147–8.
63. Printed in the *New York Review of Books*, 27 September 1990, p. 19.
64. CN II 2398; Annotation to Leighton, *Expository Works* (1748) I, 219 (*CM* (*CC*) III, 512).
65. *The Friend*, 1809–10 (*CC*) II, 348.
66. The speech was reprinted in the London *Independent* on 9 December 1989.
67. *Letters to Olga*, 191.
68. See *CAR*, 19 and refs.
69. See *CAR*, 389–90 and nn.
70. *Speak, Memory* (New York, 1966) p. 25; quoted by P.J. Eakin, *Fictions in Autobiography* (Princeton, NJ, 1985).
71. *Letters to Olga*, 272.
72. 'The Eolian Harp', *CPW* (Beer) 53.
73. *CL*, II, 810.
74. *E.M. Forster: A Life* (1977–8) II, 297.

Chapter 5

1. 'Notes on D. H. Lawrence', in *The Moment, and other Essays* (1947) p. 81.
2. 'The Leaning Tower' (1940), in ibid., pp.105–25.
3. Ibid., 109–10. Wordsworth's account is, of course, the one in his 1800 preface to *Lyrical Ballads*: *WPrW* , I, 148.
4. Wordsworth's 'spots of time' are characterized in *Prel* (1805) xi, 257–78 (= 1850, xii, 208–25).
5. See her account, transcribed in *Virginia Woolf: Moments of Being. Unpublished Autobiographical Writings of Virginia Woolf,* ed. J. Schulkind (1976) esp. pp. 70–9.
6. Ibid., 66.
7. Ibid., 71.
8. Ibid.
9. Ibid.
10. Ibid., 72.
11. Ibid., 70.
12. Ibid., 72.
13. Ibid., 122.
14. (1925) p. 9.
15. *Selected Essays* (1932) p. 27.
16. *East Coker*, section iii.
17. Ibid., v.
18. *The Waves*, ed. G. Beer (Oxford 1992) pp. 240–1.
19. *Diary*, 22 June 1940: *VWD*, V, 8.
20. *Between the Acts*, ed. G. Beer (1991) Introduction, p. xiv.
21. 'The Leaning Tower', p.123: see above, note 2.
22. *Between the Acts*, ed. G. Beer (1991) pp. 112–13.
23. *The Waves*, ed. G. Beer (Oxford, 1992) p.186.
24. F.R. Leavis, *D. H. Lawrence: Novelist* (1955) pp. 306–8.
25. The fullest account is that by S.P. Rosenbaum, 'Keynes, Lawrence, and Cambridge Revisited', *Cambridge Quarterly*, XI, 252–64.
26. See W.T. Andrews, 'Laurentian Indifference', *Notes and Queries*, CCXIV (1969) 260–1.
27. Representative accounts may be found in, e.g., Knut Merrild, *A Poet and Two Painters* (1983) *passim*.
28. *LL*, I, 251.
29. Ibid., 147.
30. *L Record* (1935) 112.
31. Immanuel Kant, Conclusion to *Critique of Practical Reason* (1788).
32. Ernst Haeckel, *The Riddle of the Universe* (1900) p. 344 and *passim*.
33. From J.W. von Goethe, 'Das Göttliche', lines 31–6: *Werke* (Frankfurt, 1981) I, 114.
34. *L Record*, 113. *Pragmatism* and *The Varieties of Religious Experience* are mentioned especially.
35. William James, *A Pluralist Universe* (1909) p. 322.
36. Ibid.
37. D.H. Lawrence, *The Rainbow* (1915) chapter xv (Cambridge edn., 1989) pp. 408–9.

38. Ibid., 438–9.
39. Ibid., chapter i (p. 40).
40. Heidegger's phrase is quoted by Thomas McFarland in *Romanticism and the Forms of Ruin* (Princeton, NJ, 1981) p. 382.
41. *CL*, II, 864.
42. Coleridge, 'The Eolian Harp', ll. 47–8: *CPW* (Beer) 53.
43. D.H. Lawrence, *Kangaroo* (1923) chapter viii (Cambridge 1994) p. 155.
44. Wordsworth, 'Tintern Abbey', ll. 41–9.
45. D.H. Lawrence, *Sons and Lovers*, chapter vii (Cambridge 1992) p.195.
46. Ibid., end, p. 464.
47. Ibid., chapter vii, p. 190.
48. Lawrence, *Kangaroo*, chapter viii, p.156. See above, note 40.
49. *W Prel*, 623–4.
50. See my *Wordsworth in Time* (1979) chapter ix.
51. Lawrence, *The Rainbow*, end, p. 459.
52. George Neville, *A Memoir of D.H. Lawrence (The Betrayal)* (1981) pp. 42–3, 188–9, quoting 'Early Days', ms 1.
53. *L Record*, 136.
54. Ford Madox Ford, *Mightier than the Sword* (1938) pp. 109–10, 106–7, 112.
55. *LL* I, 159–60 ('Siegmund' was the first version of *The Trespasser*).
56. Ibid., 214.
57. Ibid., 231.
58. Ibid., 240.
59. Ibid., 285.
60. See Lawrence, *The White Peacock* (1911) ch. iii (Cambridge 1983) p. 28, and my discussion in '"The Last Englishman": Lawrence's Appreciation of Forster', *E.M Forster: a Human Exploration*, ed. G.K. Das and J. Beer (1979) p. 247.
61. *LL*, I, 217.
62. Ibid., 361n.
63. Ibid., 366.
64. Ibid., 359.
65. D.H. Lawrence, *Collected Poems*, ed. V. de S. Pinto and W. Roberts (1964) II, pp. 849–50.
66. *LL*, II, 470.
67. Bertrand Russell, *Portraits from Memory and other Essays* (1956) p. 107.
68. *LL*, II, 503.
69. *L Phoenix*, 541.
70. *BE*, 707; *BK*, 878.
71. 'Democracy', *L Phoenix*, 715.
72. *L Record*, 115.
73. Unpublished foreword to the collection of 1928: *Collected Poems*, II, 851.
74. Ibid., I, 349. The serpent-imagery of 'Christabel', also, has thematic links with the 'serpent of secret shame' that Lawrence is concerned to sublimate: see his essay 'The Reality of Peace (II)', *English Review*, xxiv (1917) p. 518 (*L Phoenix*, 677) and my discussion in *Coleridge the Visionary* (1959) p. 196.
75. *L Record*, 184.
76. See Lawrence, *The Trespasser* (1912), ed. E. Mansfield (Cambridge, 1981) chapter iv, p. 64. The allusion is to Rachel Annand Taylor's poem 'The

Epilogue of the Dreaming Women', in *The Hours of Fiametta* (1910): see Mansfield's edition, pp. 236, 18.
77. Letter to Forster of 23 July 1924, *LL*, V, 77. See also *E.M. Forster*, ed. Das and Beer, 256.
78. Introduction to his American edition of *New Poems: L Phoenix*, 219.
79. See, e.g., his 'Introduction to these Paintings': *L Phoenix*, 567.
80. *Collected Poems*, II, p. 697 (cf. 955).
81. David Ellis, *D.H. Lawrence: Dying Game 1922–30* (Cambridge, 1998) pp. 238, 432.
82. *L Phoenix*, 793, 794–5.
83. *L Phoenix*, 795.
84. *L Record*, 76.
85. See *Romantic Consciousness*, p. 96.

Chapter 6

1. For a pained, honest account, see George Steiner's piece 'The Last 'Philosopher?', reviewing Bernard-Henri Lévy, *Le Siècle de Sartre*, *Times Literary Supplement*, 19 May 2000, p. 3.
2. See Ronald Hayman, *Writing Against: A Biography of Sartre* (1986) p. 6.
3. Dorothea Krook, 'Recollections of Sylvia Plath', in *Sylvia Plath: The Woman and her Work*, ed. Edward Butscher (1979) p. 49.
4. Jane Baltzell Kopp 'Gone, Very Gone Youth: Sylvia Plath at Cambridge, 1955–1957', in ibid., 71–2.
5. See Anne Stevenson, *Bitter Fame, A Life of Sylvia Plath* (1989) pp. 185–6, 203–4, 318–19, 327–31.
6. Janet Wagner, recorded in Paul Alexander, *Rough Magic* (New York, 1991) p. 113.
7. See below, p. 150.
8. *PJ*, autumn 1950, 9, 22, 24.
9. Ibid., 29 January 1953, 168.
10. Ibid., 1950–1, 29.
11. Ibid., 1950–1, 31.
12. 'And I sit here without identity: faceless.' Ibid., 26. Cf. the title of Richard Howard's article, 'Sylvia Plath: 'And I Have No Face, I Have Wanted to Efface Myself...' in *The Art of Sylvia Plath, A Symposium*, ed. C. Newman (1970) pp. 77–88 and the remarks about the photograph of her which is reproduced in her *Journal* for 10 January 1953: *PJ*, 155. For Rhoda, see above, p. 120.
13. *PJ*, 21 February 1958, 337–8.
14. Ibid., 17 July 1957, 286.
15. Ibid., 2 March 1958, 342.
16. Unpublished comment by Aurelia Plath, quoted Alexander, *Rough Magic*, 333.
17. Ibid., 12 February 1953, 173.
18. Ibid., 5 May 1953, 182.
19. Ibid., 1950–1, 30.
20. *HBL*, 24.

21. Stevenson, *Bitter Fame*, 318–19.
22. 'The Minotaur', *HBL*, 120.
23. Stevenson, *Bitter Fame*, 206.
24. It was some years before she did, of course. *PJ*, 7 November 1959, 524–5.
25. Ibid., 6–7 March 1956, 221.
26. Ibid., 25 February 1956, 210.
27. Ibid., 20 June 1958, 395.
28. *The Art of Ted Hughes*, ed. K. Sagar (Manchester, 1983) p. 8.
29. 'The Rock', quoted in *The Achievement of Ted Hughes*, ed. K. Sagar (Cambridge, 1993) p.10.
30. See Dennis Walder's tribute in *Literature Matters* no. 25 (1999) p. 1.
31. Extracted and summarized in *The Guardian*, 9 January 1999, Review section, pp. 1–2.
32. See p. 156.
33. *PJP*, 124.
34. Sagar, *Achievement of Hughes*, 4.
35. See her piece in the *Sunday Times*, September 1999.
36. Letter to Anne Stevenson, quoted in her *Bitter Fame*, 76–7.
37. A possible such example would be her reference in April 1956 to 'Something very terrifying' which had started two months before, which 'needed not to have happened' (in a passage of her Journal addressed to Sassoon, *PJ*, 236) and which remains unexplained. Another would be the frightening moment in Spain when, according to Paul Alexander, he tightened his hands around her throat, so that she thought he was about to strangle her, only to relax them again immediately afterwards. (See Alexander, *Rough Magic*, 194.) The evidence for his statement is obscure: according to his note it came from 'interviews with a confidential source' and was reported when the marriage was 'under enormous stress'.) Both, if founded on fact, were incidents early in the relationship. Years later, the report of him 'slavering' over a dead hare was related to Janet Malcolm: *The Silent Woman* (1994) p. 170.
38. *HWP*, 254–8.
39. Plath's inability to hurt members of the kingdom of living things, equally, did not inhibit her from some kinds of fishing, as in the incident described in 'Flounders', when they took bait with them on a trip without success until as they returned 'Something I Suggested easy plenty' and

> ... out of about six feet of water
> Six or seven feet from land, we pulled up flounders
> Big as big plates, till all our bait had gone.(*HBL* 65–6)

40. Interview with Egbert Fass, *London Magazine*, January 1971, X, 10, p. 12.
41. Sagar, *Art of Hughes*, 232.
42. Lawrence, who had begun his own schooling about 1890, believed himself to be among the first generation to have gone under: see his essays 'Enslaved by Civilization', *Phoenix*, II, 580–1 and, e.g., ibid., 586 and 'Nottingham and the Mining Countryside', *Phoenix*, 137.
43. A.Alvarez, *The Savage God* (1971) p. 24.
44. Fass interview, *London Magazine*, 20.
45. *HSGCB*, 109. It is quite possible that, arriving in Cambridge in 1951 after years of National Service when he spent much time reading Shakespeare,

Hughes attended some of the lectures of the late A.P. Rossiter, himself a somewhat Heathcliffian figure, who was fond of making a not dissimilar point about Shakespeare's dual audience.

46. Some of the most interesting passages were those where he devoted himself to Shakespeare's language, arguing that it contained what he termed something like a Shakespearean signature – his habit of using double phrases, coupling a rather esoteric word with a very simple one, and thus appealing both to the highly educated element in his audience and the groundlings. The point is made partly to support his view that among the highly educated there would have been devotees of esoteric knowledge, but of course as a device it is not confined to Shakespeare. It was common to use such pairings in his time, often linking a Latinate form to an Anglo-Saxon one, to ensure that while some hearers would be duly impressed by the grandeur of the one others would be equally responsive to the honest directness of the other. The language of the Prayer Book continually provides telling examples of what could be achieved in this mode.

47. For this interest, particularly in his earlier days, see my *Coleridge the Visionary* (1959).

48. In Plath's story 'The Wishing Box', the first mention of the protagonist's power of vivid dreaming comes when to his wife's envy he speaks of discussing manuscripts with William Blake (*PJP*, 48); Plath herself spoke of him as an influence on her poem 'The Pursuit' (Interview in *The Poet Speaks*, ed. Orr (1966) p. 170) and as someone she 'looked to' for inspiration (Interview with Ekbert Faas, *London Magazine* (January 1971) X, 12. Hughes remarked that he connected Blake inwardly to Beethoven, and that if he could dig to the bottom of his strata their names and works might be the deepest traces (Fass interview, note 40 above, p. 12). His feeling for Blake probably reflected an intuition that Blake's basic sense of Being had taken him, too, well beyond the refinements of traditional English culture.

49. *Jerusalem* 10:20. *BK*, 629; *BE*, 151.

50. *HWP*, 394.

51. John Carey demonstrated how the general opposition set up in the book between the fertile creative female principle and the sterile rational male one, with its 'repetitive tested routines' was undermined by Hughes's adopting of just such dreary repetitive routines in his own critical writing, while his constant imagery of violence, nuclear physics and explosions exposed the dominance of a notably masculine ego. Hughes was predictably furious, branding Carey as having 'the mental freedom of one of those blinded donkeys that spend their days plodding in a small circle turning a millstone' – a Blakean riposte (*BE*, 1–2; *BK*, 97) to which Carey replied with similar invective. It seems likely, however, that Hughes felt, more than he was prepared to acknowledge, the force of the charge that he had abandoned his true poetic vocation by turning to this kind of critical endeavour; that it was he, rather than his critics, who was in danger of being blinded at the mill with slaves. In his last days, he sent Carey a 'magnanimous and affectionate' letter, enclosing the well-known ambiguous 'duck/rabbit' design – a rueful acknowledgment, presumably, that both of them had truth on their side. See John Cornwell, 'Bard of Prey', *Sunday Times Magazine*, 3 October 1999.

52. Ibid., 37. So far as the latter theory is concerned, it seems more likely, as Elizabeth Sigmund has pointed out, that the real cause was the time Hughes spent sheep-dipping in Devon: 'Very toxic chemicals could have contributed to some of his more extreme health problems. Organophosphates are the cause of most of the untimely deaths among farmers down here.' It has been suggested that Sylvia Plath, likewise, died because her medication set in motion a depression too extreme to be corrected, in time to save her, by the expected upswing. The ironic possibility arises, therefore, that both Ted and Sylvia, each of them critical of over-developed technology, died prematurely as a result of mistaken chemical methods.

53. Cf. *HWP*, 374n.

54. From 'At Stratford-on Avon', in *Essays and Introductions* (1961) p. 107, quoted by Hughes as his epigraph to *HSGCB*, xv. Interestingly, Yeats had his own version of Shakespeare's controlling myth, which was quite unlike Hughes's: light is thrown on it, perhaps, by the 'wise man' mentioned there, who 'was blind from very wisdom', and the 'empty man who thrust him from his place, and saw all that could be seen from very emptiness'.

55. *HWP*, 30–1.

56. Hughes, 'Notes on the Chronological Order...', reprinted Newman, *Art of Plath*, p. 187; but see K. Moses, *Wintering* (2003) for another view.

57. Judith Kroll, *Chapters in a Mythology: the Poetry of Sylvia Plath* (New York, 1978) pp. 4, 6.

58. *PJP*, 120: see also above, p. 149.

59. Hughes, 'Notes on... Plath's Poems', 188.

60. *PJ*, 18 January 1953, 158.

61. In Butscher, *Plath and her Work*, 89–90.

62. See his account of their first meeting in Alvarez, *Savage God*, 8–9.

63. Judith Kroll's attempt (*Chapters in a Mythology*, 181) to identify the 'primary' significance of 'Ariel' from its appearance in the Bible as 'the city where David dwelt' (Isaiah 29.1), i.e. Jerusalem, is unconvincing; I have not seen any evidence that she even knew this reference – which in its original setting is in any case tangential.

64. Stephen Spender, 'Warnings from the Grave', *The New Republic*, 18 June 1966, XXIII, 25–6, reprinted, Newman, *Art of Plath* (1970) p. 202.

65. *PJ*, 1 March 1956, 216. Spender had described how he found India depressing.

66. For Hughes's interest in this myth, see, e.g., *HSGCB*, 5.

67. *PJ*, 8 March 1956, 229.

68. Ibid., 10 March 1956, 234.

69. See Anne Stevenson, *Bitter Fame*, 107n and illustration facing p. 223.

70. *HBL*, 23.

71. Newman, *Art of Plath*, 58.

72. 'Sylvia Plath: a Memoir', in *Ariel Ascending*, ed. P. Alexander, p. 192.

73. *HBL*, 158.

74. Eliat Negev, 'Haunted by the ghosts of love', Review Section, *The Guardian*, 10 April 1999, p. 1.

75. *Sons and Lovers*, chapter vii (Cambridge edn., 1992) 209–10.

76. Ibid., 294.

77. *HNP*, 305.

78. Elizabeth Sigmund, 'Sylvia in Devon: 1962' in Butscher, *Plath and her Work*, 104.
79. Ibid., 268.
80. *HSGB*, 41–2. It should be noted that, according to Elizabeth Sigmund, the horse 'Ariel' who figures in this poem was actually old and rather reluctant to move fast, though extremely safe to ride (Butscher, *Plath and her Work*, 105), On another occasion, in Cambridge (Stevenson, *Bitter Fame*, 66), Plath had the different experience of being on a supposedly safe horse that bolted with her, as described in her poem 'Whiteness I remember', *PP*, 102, and in Hughes's 'Sam', *HBL*, 10–11.
81. Negev, 'Haunted by the ghosts of love', 3.
82. Malcolm, *Silent Woman*, 133
83. Stevenson, *Bitter Fame*, 320.
84. Hayman, *Sylvia Plath*, 14.
85. The ultimate blow may well have been her realization that Assia, dismissed by her as one of the 'barren women', was pregnant. See Alexander, *Rough Magic*, 328 and Elizabeth Sigmund's article, Review Section, *The Guardian*, 23 April 1999, p. 4. The pregnancy was aborted about 1 March.
86. See above, p. 65 and my *Providence and Love*, (1999) pp. 163–7, etc. Her language to Trevor Thomas, calling Assia Gutman a 'Jezebel' and insisting on paying for the stamps he gave her, 'or I won't be right with my conscience before God, will I?'(Alexander, *Rough Magic*, 329) suggest that she might in her extremity, like Annie, have undergone a reversion to earlier religious beliefs – even that she might have seen her suicide as sacrificial for her husband's happiness.
87. Alvarez, *Savage God*, 39.
88. It is a disposition of the human mind to believe that what actually happened is more likely than any alternative. Had Sylvia Plath survived her suicide bid and gone on to find happiness and fulfilment, later readers of her work including the *Journals* and letters, would have been able to find countless pieces of evidence there suggesting that she was a born survivor.
89. The first in the collection *Difficulties of a Bridegroom* (1995). See also Elaine Feinstein, *Ted Hughes, The Life of a Poet* (2001) p. 8.
90. Here the wantonness that has been noted above as an apparent characteristic of such phenomena proved a drawback. When they used the board to predict the results of football matches in the hope of supporting themselves by winning the pools it duly obliged, the only problem being that each correct prediction proved to be one out in the sequence – as if the powers were at one and the same time confirming their existence and mischievously refusing to be turned to trivial use. See Stevenson, *Bitter Fame*, 112n.
91. See above, pp. 142–3.
92. Ted Hughes, 'Sylvia Plath: the facts of her life and the desecration of her grave', *The Independent*, 20 April 1989.
93. Jacqueline Rose, *The Haunting of Sylvia Plath* (1991) pp. 102–3, quoting Hughes's Foreword to Sylvia Plath's *Journals* (1982 edn.) p. xii.
94. *HWP*, 183.
95. Ibid., 189.
96. Ted Hughes, Foreword to Sylvia Plath's *Journals*, p. xii.
97. In Newman, *Art of Plath*, 186.

98. 'Sylvia Plath's "Sivvy" Poems: a Portrait of the Poet as Daughter', *Sylvia Plath: New Views on the Poetry*, ed. Gary Lane (Baltimore, 1979) pp. 155–78.
99. Newman, *Art of Plath*, 186.
100. Butscher, *Plath and her Work*, 107.
101. Ibid., 90.
102. Alvarez, *Savage God*, 34.
103. *PJ*, February 1957, 269.
104. *PBJ* (Faber edn.) 194.
105. Review in the *American Book Review*, republished in *Sylvia Plath: The Critical Heritage*, ed. L. W. Wagner (1988) p. 311.
106. Jacqueline Rose has noted one of the most striking, in 'Daddy': the well-known line, 'Daddy, daddy, you bastard, I'm through'. 'Through' in the sense of a final rejection, or in the sense of finally making a successful telephone contact? ('Communication as ending, or dialogue *without end?*') (Rose, *Haunting*, 234). While in one sense the occasion of the poem seems to be driving towards a single interpretation that has partly lost touch with the whole truth it is as if the verbal facility is showing a life of its own which can create a richness out of what might otherwise be a dearth.
107. To explore Plath's 'mythology of the actual' fully falls outside the scope of the present study, which is concerned primarily with Being as a subjective issue. Her mastery of Being in objective terms is, however, manifested not only by the formal achievements in her poetry, but by her skill as a visual artist, examples of which are reprodiced in Anne Stevenson's biography.
108. From Allsop's recollections of his Table Talk: *CTT*, II, 391.
109. See *Romantic Consciousness*, p. 169.
110. See above, p. 145.
111. Clarissa Roche tells of a scheme they evolved together to acquire a rich Polish lover for Sylvia, which involved the false conviction that her own father had been a Pole (Butscher, *Plath and her Work*, 88), while Dido Merwin gives a list of the 'fictions' to be found in a letter of December 1962: Stevenson, *Bitter Fame*, 345n.
112. *WL* (1821–53) III, 590.
113. Writing to Andrew Motion in 1986 he said, 'She is too naïve for the subject. She's so insensitive that she's evidently escaped the usual effects of undertaking this particular job – i.e. mental breakdown neurotic collapse domestic catastrophe – which in the past has saved us from several Travesties, of this kind, being completed.' This part of the letter is reproduced in John Cornwell's 'Bard of Prey'.
114. *CBL*, II, 27–8. Coleridge was writing about Shakespeare and Milton, of course, but the distinction can be generalised to other artists without disturbing the implications of his original point.
115. *HBL*, p. 24. Cf. above, p. 146.
116. I have explored this matter further in my article 'Coleridge and Ted Hughes: Mythology and Identity', contributed to the forthcoming collection *The Monstrous Debt: Modalities of Romantic Influence in Twentieth-Century Literature*, edited by Damian Walford Davies and Richard Maggrath Turley (Wayne State University Press).
117. See above, p. 125.
118. *CN*, II, 2070: see above, p. 95.

Index

aeon, aeonic, 32
agnostic, agnosticism, 45, 53
aion, 8, 9, 174
albatross, 138
Alcinous, 63
Alexander, Paul, 193
Alvarez, A., 151, 155, 157, 160, 165, 166, 169
Anglican, Anglicanism, 3, 44, 116, 180
Anglican Church, 27,
animal magnetism, x, 4, 18, 84
anti-Romantic, 1
anti-Semitism, 89
apart, apartness, 40, 41
Apostles, Cambridge, 10, 22, 28, 46, 54, 55, 56, 57, 65, 185
Apuleius, 159
Ariel, sailing boat, 95
Aristotle, 88
Arnold, Matthew, 46
atheism, 3
Austen, Jane, 113, 149
Aylmer, Felix, 13, 36, 38

Bacon, Francis, 61
Baker, Richard, 176
Balfour brothers, 181
Ball, Sir Alexander, 102
Barrett, Professor W.F., 51
Battersea, Lady Constance, 54, 183
Becker, Jillian, 164
Beer, Gillian, 118
bees, 27, 171
Beethoven, Ludwig van, 113, 194
Beever, Susan, 66
being, x, 1, 8
benevolence, 34
Bennett, Arnold, 121
Benson, E.W., 181
biblical criticism, 44
Birrell, Augustine, 55
Bismarck, Otto von, 89

Blake, William, 3, 40, 117, 137, 151, 153, 170, 194
Blavatsky, Madame, 53, 78
Blochmann, Elisabeth, 90
blood consciousness, 136
Bodichon, Barbara, 54
Bolshevik Revolution, 88
Botazzi, Professor, 188
Boucicault, Dion, 41
Bourbons, 103
'box of toys' (Woolf), 110
Brandon, Ruth, 182
Brighton, 53, 54, 74, 76, 182
    poem, 73
Brontë, Charlotte, 4
Brontë, Emily, 37, 149
Bud, Rosa, 12, 14, 15, 18, 19, 35, 37, 40, 42
Buddha, 105
Burrows, Louie, 123, 132, 133, 134
Butcher, Henry, 181
Byron, George, 9, 15

Cambridge, 50; *see* Apostles
Campbell, Wendy, 168
Carey, John, 194
Carlyle, Thomas, 42
Cartesian, Cartesianism, 87, 92, 93, 145
Catholic, Catholicism, 89, 90, 123, 152, 153
Chambers, Jessie, 130, 133, 135 ('Miriam'), 138
Channing, W.E., 181
character, 96
Chaucer, Geoffrey, 112
Chenevix, Richard, 20
clairvoyance, 61
Coleridge, Samuel Taylor, x, xi, 3, 4, 22, 24, 25, 39, 42, 71, 84, 86, 87, 92, 100, 101, 102, 105, 106, 107, 108, 127, 137, 140, 171, 172
Ancient Mariner, The, 137, 138, 173